SIX OF THE BEST

'No, you agreed to do it of your own free will, so now you have to do *whatever* I say. And I say, first of all, that you have to kiss him again.'

'No.'

'Do it.'

He stiffened with anticipation. The lips brushed his cockhead again, petal-soft, and withdrew.

'Have you done it?'

'Yes.'

'Properly?'

'Yes. Of course.'

'OK, then carry on doing it. Kiss his head all over. And kiss it hard.'

'But he doesn't like it! I know he doesn't! He's only saying he does because he doesn't want to hurt our feelings.'

'Bollocks. You're only saying that because you don't like doing it.'

'I do. I like it. It's nice. I like kissing his head. It feels nice and warm.'

'Then stop causing trouble and *kiss*. Kiss his head all over. Hard.'

'OK, I will.'

SIX OF THE BEST

Wendy Swanscombe

Nexus

This book is a work of fiction.
In real life, make sure you practise safe sex.

First published in 2003 by
Nexus
Thames Wharf Studios
Rainville Road
London W6 9HA

www.nexus-books.co.uk

Typeset by TW Typesetting, Plymouth, Devon

Printed and bound by Clays Ltd, St Ives PLC

ISBN 0 352 33796 6

Contents

1 Stroke I: A Cock-and-Balls Story – 1   3
2 Stroke II: A Cock-and-Balls Story – 2   17
3 Stroke III: Semper Sputamus   115
4 Stroke IV: Dungeons & Dicksuckers   148
5 Stroke V: One Hand Clapping   183
6 Stroke VI: School Yards   217

As Tamara later told the story, the Cheka came for Tadeusz in the middle of the night, their customary calling time. He and Tamara were making love, and they failed to hear the men pounding on the door. The police didn't wait for an answer but just kicked it in. Tamara, nude, wrapped the sheets around herself as the soldiers ogled her. The contrast between their black leather coats and her nakedness stood out in her memory for ever.

Tamara de Lempicka: A Life of Deco and Decadence, Laura Claridge, Bloomsbury 1999

Mme de Saint-Ange: J'ai précisément votre affaire.

Dolmancé: Ne serait-ce point par hasard un jeune jardinier, d'une figure délicieuse, d'environ dix-huit ou vingt ans, que j'ai vu tout à l'heure travaillant à votre potager?

Mme de Saint-Ange: Augustin! Oui, précisément, Augustin, dont le membre a treize pouces de long sur huit et demi de circonférence!

Dolmancé: Ah! juste ciel! quel monstre! . . . et cela décharge? . . .

Mme de Saint-Ange: Oh! comme un torrent! . . . Je vais le chercher.

La Philosophie dans le boudoir,
Quatrième Dialogue, D.-A.-F. de Sade, 1795

When we are victorious on a world scale I think we shall use gold for the purpose of building public lavatories in the streets of some of the largest cities of the world.

'The Importance of Gold Now and After the Complete Victory of Socialism', Vladimir Ilyich Lenin, 1921

Stroke I

When she woke up she had a cock. She lay staring up
at the ceiling, trying to remember the night before;
then, as she turned over and looked across the room
to the window, something heavy and warm and loose
readjusted itself at her groin and a thick tube of flesh
slid and settled across her thigh.

She screamed and her hands threw up the sheet so
that she could stare down the arch of filtered light at
her body. It was still slim and still white and her
breasts were still there and her flat stomach and flared
hips and rounded thighs, but at the juncture of her
flat stomach and rounded thighs there was a mat of
thick black hair and rising from it something that
lolled, almost crouched, that lay luxuriating in continued sleep, ignorant of her alarm and the pulses
that thrummed in her throat and neck. It was an alien
cluster of meats. Meat and two veg. A cock and two
balls. A large cock and balls. A very large cock and
balls.

Vomit pistoned up in her throat, sharp and sour,
and she forced it down, choking a little. She tried to
be calm, almost scientific, staring down the arch of
the lifted sheet at the new flesh she had acquired in
the night. She rocked her hips a little, side to side, and
noted sickly that the cock rode with the motion. It

3

was there. It was part of her. Heavy white cock above thick black pubic hair. And she was blonde.

She dropped the sheet and stared back at the ceiling, swallowing. She took two deep breaths, then another and another. Then she cautiously lowered her hands beneath the sheets, crawling them down her body, across her stomach, through the mat of thick pubic hair, harsh on her soft female fingers, and started to probe the alien meat between her thighs. The cock. It was warm and the skin was smooth, almost silken, but somehow textured more coarsely. Alien skin on alien meat. Then she screamed again and flung her hands back. It had stirred. No, it was erecting; a derrick of thick meat filling with blood and rising, lifting the sheet that lay over it. For a moment she felt dizzy, as though the blood it was filling with had been drawn directly from her head, from the dense yolk of her brain, but then she realised that the difference in her head was not of quantity, but of quality. Not less blood, not dizziness. It was lust. Male lust. She had a hard-on. Because her female hands had touched her male cock.

She looked down the bed at it. At the shape rising beneath the sheet, lifting it in a white hillock. A hard-on. A hard-on in her bed. Her hard-on. Her hard-on in her bed. She looked back at the ceiling, then closed her eyes. Her hands went crawling back under the sheet, fingertips sliding through the thick pubic hair, like the pelt of an animal, to reach the warm round solidity of the hard-on. She tried to put her fingers of her right hand around it, to circle the blood-pumped tube, and her fingertips didn't meet. She swallowed and slid her hand up, up, and gripped the head, lifting her left hand to her breasts, and realised with surprise that her nipples were hard and aching, aching painfully, singing little songs that had gone unheard in the blood-thunder of her cock.

4

She took a deep breath and adjusted her right hand around the head of her cock, experimenting with the foreskin, teaching herself how it felt, how she wanted to do it as she scratched slowly at her left nipple with her left hand, tugging the nipple, teasing it, feeling her cock swell and harden even more, to full erection. Full-to-bursting erection. But not bursting. Not yet. So she started to wank. Slowly at first, right hand almost timid, almost frightened on the warm head of her huge cock, sliding the smooth curtain of the foreskin up and down over the cockcrown, riding the surge of pleasure with the sharper, brighter sensations of nipple-teasing. Up and down, up and down, her right hand growing more confident, more practised, tightening on the cockcrown, sliding the smooth flesh of the foreskin more expertly over it, her left hand squeezing and teasing her nipples faster, cycling between them, squeezing, scratching, tugging. Breasts and balls. She had breasts and balls.

She was panting now, breath coming harsher and faster over the soft rustle of the sheet over her wanking hand. And she was starting to groan. The wrist of her right arm was tiring and starting to ache with the effort of working at the cockhead. She was paying for her pleasure, forcing herself to keep the rhythm smooth and relentless, keeping her cock at a gallop, spurring it on with cruel fingernails at her nipples, scratching them, squeezing harder at them, trying to hang on to herself, to her femaleness, in the rising of her male orgasm. Sweating into the light sheet. Wanking and groaning and working at her stiff nipples with the practised fingers of her left hand as her unpractised right hand wanked at her greedy cockhead. Greedy for movement. For the smooth flesh of her foreskin sliding up and over and down her cockcrown. Greedy for it again and again and again, over and over. The whole bed was bouncing with the rhythm of her wanking, shuddering beneath her buttocks as she pressed them harder and harder into the mattress, trying to set solid foundations for orgasm.

She stiffened and her mouth came open, soundless for a moment, then filled with a low, gathering gasp that hardened to a groan. Ah. Ah. Ah. She was coming. Oh God, she was coming. Her balls had bunched, tightening themselves to the root of her cock, and she almost flung her hand at her cockhead in a final frenzy of strokes, squeezing hard at her left nipple, hard at her right, then she groaned again, almost choking with the sensation of it, the mountain of sensation that forced itself up into her as orgasm came and her cock began to spurt. She rode the spurts with her nipples, wanting them to continue for minutes, wanting them to soak the sheet completely, to cover her stomach and thighs with thick warm spunk, and for the first few – one, two, three, four – it seemed as though they would, as though her cock would continue to fire those heavy liquid shells, to pump out the contents of her heavy balls, but no – five, six, seven, eight – they were starting to slow, to shrink, and the pulses of pleasure that accompanied them were fading too. Nine, ten, eleven, twelve – she was tightening her buttocks, squeezing harder at her nipples, trying to wring out a thirteenth. It came, a final feeble spurt, and she smiled weakly, her right hand still clutching at the cockhead.

She let go, and felt spunk running all over her hand and forearm and thighs, dribbling from them to the mattress. She opened her eyes. She could feel that her cock had softened but when she looked down the bed it was still lifting the sheet in a spunk-darkened hillock. She wiped her spunk-soaked hand on her stomach, then cycled the sheet off with her feet and stared down at her cock, trying to remember what had happened the night before. She couldn't remember. There was nothing inside her head, not even who or where she was. All she knew was that she was a woman. That was what she had woken up with: the proprioception of femaleness, breasts and thighs and buttocks beneath a light sheet. She hadn't known she had a cock. Not till she moved.

'Cock,' she said aloud, almost as though she were speaking to it. 'Cock. Cock. Cock.'

It was only semi-erect now, starting to bend forwards, glistening with spunk, the huge red berry of the cockhead half hooded by the white foreskin.

'Cock,' she said again, affection creeping into her voice. She lifted her right hand and took hold of it again, shaking it a little. Droplets of spunk splattered the bed and she felt them land higher up her body, little shining discs of spunk on her breasts and flanks. The spunk on her stomach, where she'd wiped her hand, was starting to dry and she could feel the skin tightening under it. She dabbed at the fresh spots of spunk with her free hand and rubbed some into her right nipple, then her left, then lifted the hand to her mouth. She opened it, hesitating a moment, then cautiously licked. Her own spunk. Her own flavour. But it was a male flavour. Down her body, beneath her right hand, her cock stirred and began to re-erect.

She tightened her hand on it, then swung her body sideways, slipped off the bed, and stood up. She began to wank idly at her cock again as she walked across the room to the window. She couldn't remember this bedroom either, couldn't remember whether it was hers or someone else's. Grey carpet, white walls and ceiling, a long, high, window with no curtains.

She reached the window and looked out. She was in a flat, high up in a town she didn't recognise, anonymous under bright sunshine, offices and ware-houses and factories and there was a white football stadium in the middle distance. She looked down at the street below. She was on about the tenth or eleventh floor, looking down on a row of shops – a newsagent's, a florist's, a butcher's, a video rental, a bank – and a set of traffic lights and a pedestrian crossing striped black and yellow, like the flayed pelt of a giant wasp. But there were no cars, no pedes-trians, only two women. The stood in black uniforms at the poles of the pedestrian crossing, one on either side of the street. She was still wanking, still working at her new cock, but it hadn't stiffened fully again. Not until now, when she saw the women at the pedestrian crossing. Women on duty. Waiting for the day's work to begin.

She swallowed and with an effort of will stopped wanking and just clutched her cock instead. One of the women walked a little way from her pole, then walked back again. She was restless. Because she was waiting. Waiting for the day's work to begin. Her hand tightened harder on her cock and she almost started wanking again. She wanted to come against the bare glass of the window, splatter spunk up and across it so that she could watch the two women below through trickles of spunk. That would be so much fun. But not as much fun as going downstairs and joining them. She looked away from the window and saw the half-open bedroom door that led to the rest of the flat. What would she find there? Clues to who she was? To where she was? To how she had acquired this cock?

She walked to the door, pushed it fully open, and walked through to a larger room with two more doors and with black walls and ceiling and a white carpet that was warm and deep under the soles of her feet. She stooped for a moment and ran the fingers of her free hand through the pile. It was pure wool. Highly suitable for fucking on, but it would get dirty very quickly. It would already be dirty, if this room had been used, but it didn't seem to have been. Like everything in the bedroom, everything here seemed brand new: the white carpet, the red furniture – three armchairs and a sofa, the black walls and ceiling and discreet paintings in gilt frames and the three rows of books in a bookcase of dark wood. She walked over to one of the paintings, sat down on one of the armchairs and slid her arse left and right for a moment, letting go of her cock to tighten both hands on the armrests.

She got up from the chair, took hold of her cock again, and walked to the painting, still savouring the feel of the chair on her arse-skin. Red velvet. Would black velvet feel different? Yellow velvet? Would she be able to identify colour by the feel of it on her arse alone? She stood in front of the painting, released her cock again, and slipped her hands behind her to cup the cheeks of her arse. She joggled them as she looked at the painting and her cock, which had started to soften again, lifted upright, ticking gently to her heartbeat. She lifted one hand from her buttocks, took hold of it, and began to strum gently at the head. There was a little label underneath the painting. It read CRUJSVO INVETSEJ. She stopped wanking and turned away. She walked towards the bookcase, twice stopping to look at other paintings, strumming gently at her cockhead in front of each before turning away and walking on.

She reached the bookcase: three rows of paperbacks with shiny virgin spines. *Tsodum-û Hseriìk 120* by Marquis de Sade. *Vlorrg-î Bilitis* by Pierre Louÿs. *Hledohi tsani* by Wendy Swanscombe. She slipped

Hledohi tsani out of the bookcase and opened it. The pages were stiff, as though they'd never been opened before and, when she lifted the book to her face and sniffed, the book smelled brand new. Because it was brand new. Everything was brand new. She read a paragraph, wondering why her cock was getting harder and she wanted to start wanking again. Wanking seriously. Wanking to orgasm. She read the next paragraph. Yes. Something in her understood it and was excited by it. Emotion without intellect.

She closed the book and slipped it back into the bookcase. She imagined living in this room and reading the books one by one, not understanding them, only intuiting them, wanking her way through a pornographic library in a language she didn't understand. She turned and looked around the room. No television set or radio, but there were three doors. One, she knew, led back to the bedroom and the spunk-soaked bed. Where did the other two lead? She walked to the nearer one, opened it and looked through. A kitchen. Cooker, fridge, three cupboards, white tiled floor, window overlooking the same street. She walked in. The cool tiles kissed the soles of her feet as she opened one of the cupboards. FSÒZ it said on jars which contained something dark and viscous-looking. The label showed a bee-clouded hive sitting amid summer flowers. Honey? She took one of the jars out, unscrewed the lid and sniffed. Yes, honey. She dipped a finger into it and lifted the finger to her mouth. Honey. She put the lid back on the jar, re-screwed it, put it on the sideboard and opened the next cupboard.

Squat little bottles with a label saying GEUDR sat above a little heap of onions and gherkins. Vinegar? She took a bottle out, unscrewed the cap and sniffed, then jerked her head back to stop a sneeze. Her eyes were watering. Yes, vinegar. She screwed the top on the bottle, put it on the sideboard and opened the next cupboard. Brand-new packets with a label saying TSELE HRAÌ sat above a scattering of seeds and pods. Some kind of spice? She took a packet out and opened it. It was full of dark brown powder. She lifted it and sniffed. Curry powder? She dipped the honey finger, still moist with saliva, and lifted it to her mouth. She licked it cautiously. Yes, curry powder. She resealed the packet, put it on the sideboard and stooped to open the fridge. Cold air folded around her and she shivered as her nipples peaked. All there was inside it was a black bowl. Her cock lifted again as she reached inside the fridge and lifted the bowl out.

She pushed the fridge shut with her hip and squatted, resting the bowl on her thighs up against her jutting cock. It was heavy and felt smooth and cold on her skin, as though it were made of glass or crystal. It was filled with little transparent cubes. A bowl full of ice cubes. Ice cubes with little red spheres frozen inside them. She picked up one of the cubes, feeling the skin of her fingertips freeze instantly to it, and held it to the light to see what the little red sphere was. A cherry? She dropped her hand, rubbed the cube on the head of her cock, hissing a little with the sensation of it – the intense cold on hot skin – then rubbed it on her nipples. They peaked harder under the cold and smoothness of it as she rotated the cube slowly, lingeringly, pressing it hard to the nipple, closing her eyes to savour the sensation more fully. It felt good. Fucking good.

But that was enough. She dropped the cube back into the bowl with a *ching* and stood up, lifting the bowl off her thighs, then walked to the window of the kitchen and looked down. The two women were still at the pedestrian crossing, waiting in their black uniforms. She swung the catch on the window and pushed it open. The air outside was faintly cold but it tasted clean and uncontaminated and, when she listened, she couldn't hear anything. Just silence. She lifted the bowl and was about to tip it through the window when she heard a voice on the street, saying something she didn't understand. It was one of the guards, the one on the far side. The other guard started to reply and now she did tip the bowl through the window, listening for the sound of the cubes striking the street and pavement ten or so storeys below.

After a couple of seconds it came, a harsh irregular spatter of chimes, like a burst of giant hail and, when she looked down again, the cubes were scattered across the street, hard to see except where they caught the light and glittered. She had expected them to smash, scattering the street with cherries, but this somehow was better. Yes, much better. The silence was back and the heads of the two guards had swung, the peaks of their caps pointing towards the scattering of cubes, then swinging upwards, scanning the face of the flats. For a moment she listened hard, imagining she could almost hear their hearts beating faster in the firm breasts beneath the black cloth of the uniforms. She closed the window and turned away from it, put the bowl on the sideboard, picked up the jar of honey, the bottle of vinegar and the packet of curry powder, and went back into the main room, her hands full. One more door to try. She thought this one would lead her out of the flat to the lift and the street and the two young women waiting patiently to begin work at the pedestrian crossing.

She walked down the room towards the third door, the soles of her feet sinking into the warmth and softness of the carpet, and it was only now that she noticed the cupboard set in the wall beside the door. She stopped and put the jar, bottle and packet on the carpet, then walked forwards and opened the cupboard. A black suit was hanging inside. No, a black silk uniform, shirt, buttonless jacket and half-trousers on separate hangers, a peaked black cap and black gloves and shining black jackboots sitting beneath them on the floor of the cupboard, and a sleek black leather belt and giant black leather holster hanging from discreet silver hooks on left and right. There was lettering on the cap, embroidered in gold thread. She picked up the cap and twisted it one way, then the other. On the left she read NÎHHIRIWELQ and on the right QLEWIRIHHÎN, with a pair of crossed half-moons in between. Half-moons? No, bananas. She tried the cap on. It fitted her perfectly.

She began to put on the rest of the uniform. Shirt first, sliding on cool and smooth, buttoning up snugly over her bare breasts. She felt something hard and heavy in one of the pockets, pressing against her breast, and she opened the pocket and lifted it out. A whistle made, it seemed, of real silver. She slipped it back into the pocket, lifted the half-trousers down and put them on. She slid them up her legs, carefully fitted her half-erect cock into them, felt for the zip and pulled it up slowly, keeping her cock pressed into place. There. She looked down at the bulge of her cock and her white lower legs and feet, ready for the jackboots. She slipped her fingers under the elasticated waist of the trousers and tugged outwards. Plenty of give, but the trousers fitted her exactly. So why the belt? She turned back to the cupboard. Oh, yeah, it was to hang the holster on. She slipped the belt off its hook, slid it through the belt loops of the trousers and fastened it.

Now the jacket. She slipped it off its hanger, and realised it had buttons after they glinted in the light. Buttons of transparent crystal. She fingered one for a moment, wondering whether it was ice, then put the jacket on. The shoulders were padded. Wearing the jacket made her feel more powerful, more assertive, more dominant. More cruel. There was a bulge of something in one of the side pockets and she put her hand in to see what it was. Paper crinkled under her fingers and she drew out a loose bundle of banknotes. Brightly coloured, with ridiculously high denominations: 50,000, 100,000, 500,000, 1,000,000, 2,000,000, 5,000,000, even 10,000,000, and on every note a picture of a woman in black uniform, face pale and stern and beautiful beneath a peaked cap embroidered with gold thread. IMINÎHHELQ and QLEHHÎNIMI.

It was her. Her face on the banknotes. She paused, wondering for a moment, then pushed the notes back into the pocket and looked down at her bare shins and calves beneath the black trousers, her bare white feet hard to make out against the white carpet. She lifted the jackboots out and sat carefully on the carpet to pull them on, not wanting to crease her trousers. The boots were tight but slid on easily, almost greasily – right leg, left leg. She stood up and walked forwards and back, turned on the spot, turned back, tried a goose-step. Her cock stiffened in her trousers, straining at the zip.

'Wait,' she told it. Something on the heel of a boot caught her eye. She lifted her right leg backwards, caught the boot, and lifted it higher, balancing on her left leg to see what it was. Little eyelets. Something needed to be fastened there. What? She let the boot drop back to the carpet and turned back to the cupboard. Yes. There was a little black case she hadn't noticed before, sitting in one corner near the gloves. She took it out and opened it, frowning for a moment. What were these? Oh, yeah. Spurs. Spurs shaped like little silver bananas. She crouched and fitted them to the heels of her boots, stood up, walked forwards and back, turned on the spot, tried a goose-step, listening to the spurs jingle.

She turned back to the cupboard, smiling, and took down the holster. It had little straps to fasten it to the belt but she wanted to see what was inside. She unbuttoned it with a crisp *click*. There was a giant black pistol inside, vaguely Luger-esque. She lifted it out. No, not a black pistol. A black vibrator in the shape of a pistol, with a large bulbous muzzle. She gripped the handle, slipped her finger over the trigger, and held her arm up, aiming the pistol at the window. *Bang* she mouthed, and pulled the trigger. There was a thick, creamy buzz and her whole hand hummed with the vibration of it. The outline of the bulbous muzzle blurred. She released the trigger and the vibration stopped. *Bang* she mouthed again, and pulled the trigger. *Bang*. She slipped the pistol – no, the 'pildo' – back into its holster, buttoned it with another crisp *click* and strapped the holster to her belt. How did she look? No mirror in the room. She stood in front of the black-painted door next to the cupboard, trying to make out her reflection in it. No good. Well, time to begin the day's adventures. She buttoned up her jacket, adjusted her cap and cuffs, glanced down at her trousers, tugged at them a little, adjusting them, lifted each boot in turn and shook it, testing the spurs, gripped and shook the holster to make sure it was secure on the belt, then reached inside the cupboard for the last time and picked up the remaining item. The gloves. They were velvet. Black velvet gloves.

She drew them on slowly, luxuriating in the feel of the velvet, then stooped to pick up the jar of honey, the bottle of vinegar and the packet of curry powder from the floor. She held them in the crook of her left arm as she turned back to the door and took hold of the handle with her right hand. She turned it and pulled. The door swung open silently and she stepped through. *Clack. Clack.* Black boots on a black marble floor, almost mirror-like, and she peered down at herself for a moment, seeing herself hang upside down from the soles of her boots.

Stroke II

'It's this way, *Generalissima*,' someone said in a language she didn't understand and she almost dropped the honey, vinegar and curry powder with surprise. She looked right, then left. To the right the black marble floor ran a few metres between dark green walls to end in a wall and large window; to the left the black marble floor ran a few metres between dark green walls to a huge double mirror beside which a slim young woman in black uniform and jackboots was standing to attention, face pale under a peaked cap, the tip of a red tongue nervously moistening pink lips, then slipping back into her mouth. She strode down the corridor towards her, boots clacking menacingly beneath the jingle of her spurs, seeing herself get larger in the mirror. The red tongue-tip ran along the pink lips again and green eyes avoided hers, staring back down the corridor. There was a little wicker basket on the floor next to the woman's boots. The *guard*'s boots.

'Fill the basket,' she said in the same language, nipples hardening, cock swelling forwards at the note of command in her own voice. The guard stamped her heels together, jackboots crashing on the marble floor, and swung her right forearm across her stomach and forwards in salute, making a small fist, her forearm stiff and straight and pointing upwards at about fifteen degrees. Like an erect cock. It was a cock salute.

'Fill the basket,' she said. 'Now. Then you can suck me.'

The guard blinked, nodded, bent and picked up the basket, and came forward. What had she said? What had she *ordered*? The guard took the honey, vinegar and curry powder from her and put them into the basket, then put the basket on the floor and kneeled in front of her, and asked, 'Suck you, *Generalissima*?'

'Suck me,' she said. 'And swallow every drop.'

She watched in the huge mirror as the kneeling guard unzipped her trousers and reached inside them for her huge erection, gently took hold of it and manoeuvred it through the trouser-slit. Such soft, small, delicate hands. Her cockhead throbbed and her balls had rolled and started to ache.

'Every drop, *Generalissima*?'

Such a soft, delicate voice.

'Every drop,' she said, and in the mirror watched her mouth tighten and her nostrils flare as a warm moist mouth closed over the head of her cock. There was a line down the middle of the mirror, cutting her and the kneeling fellatrix in two. To the right of the mirror, set into the wall, there was a large button. The fellatrix mumbled, drawing her cock deeper into the warm mouth, and she saw her mouth come open in the mirror in a silent gasp. Her knees weakened for a moment. Only it wasn't just a mirror, she realised now. It was the door of a lift. She watched herself lift the fellatrix's cap off with her black-gloved hands and toss it to one side. It landed, spinning on the black marble floor and slid until it hit the wall. The fellatrix's hair was bright pre-Raphaelite red, knotted loosely above her neck. She slid her gloved fingers into it, unknotting it, allowing it to slip loose and flow over the gently rocking shoulders of the black uniform. She clutched at the back of the fellatrix's head, gloved fingers stirring in the soft red hair, forcing her cock to the back of the working mouth, towards the throat.

'Faster,' she said. She *ordered*.

The red head worked at her like a little engine, pumping on her cock.

'Good girl,' she said more gently. 'Very good girl.'

She watched herself release one hand from the head and unbutton the holster and slide the pildo out. She lifted it, aiming it at her own reflection, mouthing *bang* at herself. She pulled the trigger, and heard the soft buzz. The fellatrix's head jerked on her cock.

'Concentrate,' she told her, unbuttoning her jacket with her left hand, then her shirt, and lifting the pildo inside it with her right hand, pressing the bulbous muzzle to her stiff, aching left nipple, and dropped her left hand to clutch the fellatrix's head again. *Bang* she mouthed at herself. She pulled the trigger. She shivered and closed her eyes, hearing the creamy buzz of the pildo underplayed by the rustle of her shirt as it caught the vibrations in her hand and forearm. Cock and nipple. Male and female, in the same body. She released the trigger and opened her eyes. The red head was bobbing frantically on her cock, thrusting backwards again and again against her clutching left hand. She smiled at her own flushed face, then closed her eyes again and pulled the trigger.

Bzzz. Creamy buzz, silken rustle. Cock and nipple. Male and female. She opened her eyes, watching herself slide her legs apart, boots slanted at the marble floor, left hand pulling harder at the red head, forcing it further over her cock. She saw herself lift the pildo away from her nipple, out of her shirt, transfer it to her left hand, clutch at the red head with

19

her right hand as her left hand slipped the pildo back inside her shirt, the silk bulging as the hand adjusted the bulbous muzzle to her right nipple. *Bang* she mouthed at her reflection. She closed her eyes again and pulled the trigger. Bzzz. She released the trigger, pulled it again. Bzzz. Released it, pulled it. Bzzz. And that was enough.

She came, gloved right hand tightening convulsively on the delicate, red-haired skull, delighted cock firing into the warm moist mouth, down the slim throat, the guard choking and spluttering on the thick salt slime of her spunk. She opened her eyes, widening them on herself as she stood with vee'd legs, boots slanted to the marble floor. The final spurt came and she released a long sigh of satisfaction, right hand loosening on the skull, then beginning to stroke at the red hair.

'That was wonderful,' she said, stroking at the red hair that blazed in front of her groin. 'I'm very pleased with you.'

The small mouth came off her cock with a pop and she saw the head tilting backwards, lifting the pale face to hers. She looked down at it, and saw the coppery eyebrows raised in the milky skin above the green eyes.

'You're pleased with me, *Generalissima*?' the guard said.

'Very pleased,' she said. 'That was an excellent blow job. First fucking class.'

She stooped, feeling her boots slide further apart, as she lowered her own pale face to the pale face of the fellatrix, until their lips met, the fellatrix's warm and trembling under hers. She probed at them with her tongue and they opened, allowing her through to the warm, spittle-sugared mouth, and she probed for traces of her own spunk. She broke the kiss moistly, leaving the guard gasping, open-mouthed, and slid her legs back together, to stand straight again.

'First sucking class,' she said, slipping the pildo back into its holster, rebuttoning it. The guard twisted her head and she wiped her softening cock in the silky red hair, using it to rub her cockhead clean, sliding it around the gulley of the cockcrown.

'Now, whistle up that lift for me,' she said.

The guard slid away from her on her knees, got to her feet, stooped for her discarded cap and slipped it back on her disordered hair, as she ran to the large button set beside the mirrored doors of the lift. She pressed it and the line down the middle of the mirror gaped instantly as the two halves of the door slid apart. The lift had been ready and waiting for her. It was mirrored inside, too – walls, floor and ceiling – and was brightly lit by concealed lighting, and yes, there was another guard waiting: another slim woman in black uniform and jackboots, face pale and oval beneath a peaked cap. The outside guard ran to pick up the basket with the jar of honey, the bottle of vinegar and the packet of curry powder, and stood beside the open lift.

'It is ready for you, *Generalissima*,' the outside guard said, holding the basket out for her.

She nodded, fitting her cock back into her trousers, zipped them up again, then walked forwards, taking the basket with one hand, rebuttoning her shirt with the other, and walked into the lift, glancing to left and right, up and down, seeing five copies of herself and the inside guard, one in each of the three walls, one in the floor, one in the ceiling. She turned, to stand shoulder-to-shoulder with the inside guard, a head taller than her, and noticed that the guard had started to tremble. With excitement? With fright? No, with age. Christ. The inside guard was an old woman, pale oval face creased and worn, pale blue eyes in soft nests of wrinkles. She had been very beautiful once, was beautiful still, but old, very old. The pale eyes blinked.

'Close the doors,' she said.

The outside guard – the *young* guard – saluted again, stiff fisted forearm jutting at fifteen degrees, then trotted to one side of the open doors, and pressed the button in the wall. The doors began to slide shut, mirrored on the reverse too. The outside guard darted between them a second before the twin halves met with a soft click and the three of them were sealed into the mirrored lift. No, the eighteen of them: six of her and six of the young guard and six of the old guard: three of them in each of the three walls, three in the floor, three in the ceiling, three in the door. Next to the door was a vertical line of pearly buttons. Sixteen of them. The sixth from the top was lit, glowing rosily. That was the floor they were on. The tenth. On the other side of the door were two large buttons set side by side, one with an arrow pointing up, the other with an arrow pointing down. The two guards were standing to attention on either side of her, young and old.

'Ground floor,' she said.

The old guard stepped forwards, pressed the button for the ground floor, stepped back, standing to attention again, still trembling. Nothing seemed to happen. She began to open her mouth, then stopped. The glowing button for the tenth floor was dimming slowly. The lift was moving, but slowly. Slowly descending. She tried to smile at herself in the mirrored door, disgust curdling faintly in her stomach. She swallowed.

'You,' she said to the old guard, swinging her head up at her for a moment so that her chin pointed arrogantly at the wrinkled old face.

'*Generalissima?*'

The voice was husky, almost wheezing, with cracked harmonics of old age.

'Suck me.'

The old guard moved to her and she handed her the basket and watched her put it on the mirrored floor, then turn and kneel carefully in front of her, lowering herself cautiously. Something popped softly. A knee joint? Another pop. Yes, a knee joint. Now she was kneeling fully on the floor, reaching up for her trousers with small, soft, wrinkled hands. The disgust in her stomach swelled, rolling as the hands reached her zip and pulled. Her cock had shrivelled but a faint tremor of re-erection ran through it at the sound of the zip coming down. She unbuttoned her holster, ready to draw the pildo, staring at herself in the mirrored door as soft trembling hands lifted her limp cock through the trouser slit and warm breath folded over it. Her mouth twisted as the breath got warmer, moister, and the mouth closed over it and began to suck slowly, lovingly. Her cock was still limp and disgust rolled in her stomach again. But was there much difference? Was there *any* difference? All cats are grey in the dark. A mouth is a mouth is a mouth.

Another of the lift-buttons had begun to glow – the seventh from the top – brightening as the sixth from the top grew dull. There was plenty of time. She watched herself slip the black cap off the sucking head and spin it to the mirrored floor. The guard's hair was grey, knotted in a loose mass above the neck. She ran her fingers through it, unknotting it, encouraging it to flow down the black shoulders, stroking at it, encouraging the mouth on her cock.

'Faster,' she said. The head began to bob, working faster. Her cock was slowly rehardening, slowly swelling forwards into the moist working warmth. A mouth is a mouth is a mouth. Soothing mouth, reinvigorating mouth, simultaneously one and the other, but slowly less one as it became more the other. As her cock reawoke. The tenth button had gone out now and the ninth was fully alight, maybe starting to fade a little as the eighth button began to glow. Yes. Fading and beginning to glow. Like a series of erections. A series of cocks lifting and being inserted into a series of warm sucking mouths, spurting, softening. Or the same cock erecting, spurting, softening, then beginning all over again in a new mouth.

Her cock stiffened faster at the thought of it, sliding forwards deeper into the old woman's mouth. Her hands splayed on the back of the grey head, pushing it forwards harder on to her cock. Suddenly it was exciting again. Exciting to be sucked by an old woman. How many cocks had she sucked in seventy or eighty years? How many gallons of spunk had she swallowed or spat? She wanted to know. She wanted to fuck the ageing throat, thrape her, work her big cock to the very back of the ancient mouth and beyond. The thought of it made her cock stiffen the final inches, straighten the final degrees. Or was it the stiffening that made the thought? Were her excitement and the strength of her imagination leashed to the stiffness of her cock, so that the harder her cock grew the more filthily she thought? She didn't know. She didn't care. She was fully erect now, with nine inches of solid cock to fit into the warm moist mouth of an old woman in black uniform. It was time for action, not words.

'Are you ready to swallow?' she said.

The guard mumbled something huskily in reply. It felt good, a voice humming around her cock, so she said, 'Sing. Sing while you suck.'

The guard began to sing. Sucking her and singing, gasping for breath, gurgling, singing. The words were

24

impossible to make out, mumbled in a mouth stuffed with hard cock, but the tune was there, humming in the throat, humming in her cock. Bombastic, militaristic. Was it the National Anthem? 'O my country 'tis of thee'? Or praise of her? Praise of the *Generalissima*? Where had that come from? She stared at herself in the mirror, a tall young officer in black uniform being fellated by a kneeling veteran singing the national anthem. Officer in a black cap. Gold lettering on the cap. NISSIRIWELK on the left now. KLEWIRISSIN on the right. But what had it been before? She frowned a little, blinked. MISSIRIWINEG it said now. GENIWIRISSIME. Being deciphered by the pleasure of the mouth on her cock.

'Shut up,' she said. The singing stopped and the guard just sucked, just bobbed and sucked. She lifted the flap of her holster and slid her pildo out, unbuttoning her shirt again with her other hand. She lifted the pildo to her open shirt, pushed it inside, presented the muzzle to her stiff left nipple. *Bang*. Bzzz. She gasped silently. Mouthed *bang* at herself again. Pulled the trigger again. Bzzz. Now the gold lettering on her cap read GENERALISSIMA on the left, AMISSILARENEG on the right. Reversed in the mirror. The seventh button was fully aglow, maybe just starting to fade as the sixth started to glow too. Yes. Nearly halfway down.

'Squeeze my ballz,' she said.

More instructions. Was she telling the guard to start singing again? No. Not that. Soft wrinkled hands were reaching into her trousers, cupping her balls. Rubbing them. Squeezing them. Sliding them one over the other in the warm sack of her scrotum. Encouraging the juices to flow in heavy fruit. Thrape her, she told herself. Her velvet gloves closed on the grey head and pulled, clutching the delicate skull to her, the seventy or eighty years' worth of sexual experience, of fucking and sucking and spitting. But she wasn't going to spit this out. This was going down her throat. A mouth is a mouth is a cunt. And she was fucking it, fucking the cunt-mouth, the mouth-cunt, staring back into the eyes that stared at her from the mirror, black-gloved hands clasped and merciless on the grey head. Next to them the young guard shifted uneasily from foot to foot for a moment, trying to hide the disgust on her face.

Yes, it was disgusting, and that excited her more. The soft hands were still kneading at her balls, gentle but persistent, making them begin to ache, to feel as though they were slowly fissuring, would split apart unless she came soon, unless she spurted into the warm mouth and down the slender, airless throat. It must be a minute now since the sucking guard had last had a breath, but she accepted the cock without protest, veteran of a thousand such contests, of ten thousand, of twenty or thirty thousand. She knew that in the end the soft persistence of a mouth will conquer the hard arrogance of a cock, that the cock will spurt and splutter and soften and retreat.

The sixth lift-button was out, the fifth fully lit, the fourth just beginning to glow. Halfway down and well over halfway to orgasm. In the mirror her face was twisting, her lips starting to curl back as though in bitterness as her thrusts into the old woman's mouth became shorter, more urgent. What did they call them? The vinegar strokes. When the face twisted, the mouth gaped, belying the ecstasy of oncoming orgasm. But they were also known as the paradise strokes. Digging those last few inches into a moist cunt or arse or mouth, cock sheathed in warm flesh, balls tightening to the fork of the thighs, spunk compressing in them, ready to spurt. She closed her eyes, pressed the muzzle of the pildo hard to her left nipple, and pulled the trigger. Bzzz. Again. Bzzz. Again. Bzzz.

She came, panting, utterly shameless, pumping thick salty slime into the mouth of a woman three or four times her own age, forcing her to swallow every spurt, every drop, every thread of it. She opened her eyes again, blinking to clear her vision, feeling her wrist tremble with the weight of the pildo and her cock already beginning to soften in the old woman's mouth. The fourth button was fully alight, the third starting to glow. She tried to speak and couldn't and had to cough and clear her throat. She slid the pildo back into the holster and buttoned it, then licked her lips and said, 'Very good.'

The old woman's mouth came off her cock and she heard breath wheeze into the ageing lungs. She looked down, gripping the grey hair and trying to tilt the old woman's head back so that she could look into her face. The head resisted and she tugged harder.

'Look up at –' she started to say, then stopped, fright bursting in her stomach. The hair had slid under her hand, as though it were peeling off the skull. What had happened? She let go but the hair had definitely moved, sliding backwards on the skull, leaving a narrow crescent of clear white skin above the wrinkled, spotted forehead. Clear white skin? She frowned and took hold of the hair again. Tugged at it. It slid further, widening the crescent of clear white skin, revealing something beyond that. A golden fringe of hair, scraped back and pressed down beneath the wig. Because that was what it was. The grey hair was a wig.

Her hand clenched angrily and she tugged hard at the wig, feeling it slide further. Now the kneeling guard looked up at her, eyes narrowed mischievously, clear white skin showing above the wrinkled and spotted skin of her face, beneath the shining gold of the hair that had been hidden under the wig. You bitch, she thought. You fucking bitch. She wrenched again at the wig and it came off fully in her hand, a grey mass of hair. She threw it at the floor of the lift and gripped the head again, tilting the face further upwards, holding it horizontal as she gathered spittle in her mouth.

'Sneaky little bitch,' she said through it, her voice juicy with moisture. A smile lit the upturned face for a moment as she released a gobbet of spit. It landed with a small splat on the bridge of the nose and flattened, most of it sliding down the left side of the nose to the cheek. The guard had screwed her eyes shut as the spittle hit her face. She released another gobbet that landed with another small splat, then another, then, still holding the head in place with her left hand, lifted her right hand to her mouth and tugged at the fingers of the glove with her teeth. The glove slid loose and she shook it free, then dropped it to the floor.

'Keep your eyes closed,' she said. She started to rub at the spittle on the face, feeling a thick layer of make-up break and slide under her fingers. It was a young woman, not an old woman, who had sucked her, who had squeezed her balls and swallowed her spunk. As the make-up came off, dirtying her fingertips, the skin underneath was white and clear, the skin of an eighteen- or twenty-year-old. Bitch, she thought, then said it aloud. There was a smile beneath the patch of rubbed-clean skin in the middle of the face. Well, she'd wipe that off.

'Take that look off your face,' she said. 'Hand me the vinegar.'

She released the head and the guard, still kneeling in front of her, twisted her body sideways and reached for the basket sitting on the mirrored floor of the lift. The grey wig and black glove had landed near it, the wig flattened like a little pool of grey water, the glove flattened like the discarded skin of a huge black insect. The guard had to strain to reach the basket, fingers just scraping at it, nudging it nearer, managing to fasten on it, then sliding it across the floor so that she could reach inside and take out what the *Generalissima* had ordered her to take out. The bottle of vinegar.

'Give it to me,' she said.

The guard handed her the bottle of vinegar and kneeled back properly in front of her, lifting her face for punishment. She held the bottle for a moment in her bare right hand, loosening the glove on her left hand with her teeth, before shaking it loose to the floor. She unscrewed the cap of the bottle and dropped it to the floor too. It landed with a click.

'Close your eyes,' she said.

The guard closed her eyes, looking unhappy. Good. She lifted the bottle to her face and sniffed at it, her nose wrinkling at once. Good. She lowered the bottle about halfway to the waiting face and slowly tipped it. A thread of vinegar fell from it, splattered on the face, grew thicker, streaming down, splattering, soaking the face, splattering to the floor. It reeked acidicly and she had to wrinkle her nose again to hold back a sneeze. She stopped pouring.

'Open your mouth,' she said.

Reluctantly the mouth in the lifted face opened.

'Wider,' she said.

Hesitation for a moment, then the mouth opened wider, moist red tissues glistening inside. Her cock was still hanging outside her trousers, still thick with

29

subsided erection, and she felt it stir and jerk upright a little as she looked down into the waiting mouth. Not now, she thought. She swung the bottle above the gaping mouth, judging the drop, then tipped the bottle again. A thin stream of vinegar left the bottle and dropped exactly between the lips and teeth, filling the mouth with a sputter, spilling out of it, pouring left and right over the corners of the lips.

'Close your mouth,' she said.

The lips closed on the mouthful of vinegar.

'Swallow,' she said.

Nothing.

'Swallow it,' she said. 'Now.'

Nothing for a moment, then the slim throat noded slowly and smoothed. She'd swallowed it. First salt, then vinegar. She smiled and began to rub the vinegar-moistened face clean, feeling her cock get harder, beginning to stiffen towards the face as she rubbed at it, exposing more of the clear white skin. A thought struck her.

'Show me your hands,' she said, still rubbing at the face. The guard lifted her left hand and opened it, holding it flat, palm upwards, the skin there pink and smooth.

'The other one.'

The guard hesitated for a moment then lifted her right hand, but didn't open it.

'Open it.'

No movement for a moment, then the guard opened it, held it flat, palm upwards. Something small and made of plastic sat on the palm.

'Use it.'

The hand closed on the thing, fitting it between index and forefinger. Pop. Pop. It was the knee-popper. She snorted and slapped at the nearly wiped-clean face.

'Sneaky little bitch,' she said.

30

The smile broke on the guard's face again.

'Yes, *Generalissima*,' the guard said. The huskiness of old age was gone. It was a clear young voice. Her cock jerked fully upright. The guard twisted and reached for the basket again, lifted out the jar of honey and kneeled fully in front of her again, unscrewing the lid.

'Shall I honey you, *Generalissima*?'

Her cock twitched hungrily and she nodded, swallowing.

'Yes,' she said.

The guard slid two fingers into the honey, gouging it up in a thick curl, and began to anoint her softening cock, lifting it and sliding back the foreskin so that she could coat the head with it. She watched her at work, feeling her cock slowly starting to restiffen. She looked up. The third button from the bottom was fading, the second from the bottom glowing to full life. She felt the guard rubbing honey up the length of her cock and looked down.

'Suck me,' she said.

The guard put the jar of honey back into the basket and took hold of her cock. It was semi-erect now, lifting in a crescent, glistening with honey. The pale blue eyes glanced up at her as the mouth opened and the guard began to slide her cock home.

'Are you wearing contact lenses?' she said.

The guard nodded, mouth still open, her cock still presented to it.

'Then take them out first,' she said.

The guard released her cock, then put her honey-coated fingers into her mouth and sucked hard, cleaning them, first right hand, then left. Then she tilted her head back and slid the eyelid of her right eye open with the little finger of her right hand, probing cautiously at her eyeball with the index finger

31

of her left hand. The index finger lifted away, flicking something to the floor, and the eye blinked, bright blue. She had been right: the guard had been wearing contact lenses to make the blue of her eyes seem pale, faded. She was working at her left eye now, holding up the eyelid with the little finger of her left hand, probing at the eyeball with the index finger of her right. Then that eyelid blinked, bright blue.

'OK,' she said. 'Now suck me.'

The mouth closed over her cock, sucking hard at the coating of honey, slurping as the sweetness filled the warm mouth with spittle. She clasped the back of the delicate skull and began to work at the tightly wound hair, loosening it, wanting to see it flow down the black uniform in a bright golden fan, ears full of a noisy blow job, cock stiffening again, lifting her towards her fourth ejaculation of the day. But the lift shook gently for a moment and when she looked at the buttons the lowest one was glowing. They had reached the ground floor.

The door opened, cutting apart the image of the guard kneeling before her absorbed in fellatio, the first strands of loosened blonde hair raying down the black cloth of her uniform. There was a green-walled lobby outside, another black marble floor.

'Stop,' she said.

The blue eyes looked up, vinegar-cleaned eyebrows raised in enquiry, the mouth still busy sucking.

'Stop,' she said.

Reluctantly the guard slid her mouth off her cock.

'That's enough, *Generalissima*?'

'That's enough. For now. We're on the ground floor.'

The guard twisted her head, seeing the open door.

'Yes, *Generalissima*.'

'Hand me my gloves,' she said.

The guard went on her hands and knees, crawling to pick up her discarded velvet gloves and return them to her. She took them one by one, drawing them back on over vinegar-stained fingers.

'Good girl,' she said. 'Get the basket too.'

The guard picked up the basket and got back to her feet, then stooped to pick up her cap. She took the basket and handed it to the redheaded guard, then strode out of the lift, cock still unzipped and erect, jutting out ahead of her, glistening with the blonde guard's spittle. There was a small gasp to her right and she turned her head. Another guard stood in black uniform and peaked cap, dark eyes fixed on her cock in a pale, oval face. She looked back into the lift. The blonde guard had put her cap back on and was standing to attention beside the redheaded guard, staring straight ahead, the edges of her face smeared with make-up.

'Come here, you,' she said to the new guard, turning to stand directly in front of the open lift door, side-on. The new guard raised her right knee and stamped her jackboots together, forearm coming up and out in the cock salute.

'*Generalissima!*'

She understood the word now. It meant *Generalissima*. Meant her.

'Suck me. And swallow every drop.'

The new guard walked towards her, boots clacking on the floor, then kneeled in front of her, small hands reaching for her cock, eyes closing, mouth opening. She inhaled sharply through her nostrils as the mouth closed on her cockhead and set to work. This was the hottest, moistest mouth yet, with the silkiest, most skilful tongue. Out of the corner of her eye she watched the two guards in the lift, the redhead and the blonde, wondering what they were thinking. Were

33

they jealous? Jealous of the new guard sucking at her cock? She looked down at the kneeling fellatrix working skilfully at her fully re-erected cock, and lifted her cap off to see what colour her hair was. Black. Black hair, glistening like jet.

She tossed the cap to the floor and began to loosen the hair with her black-gloved fingers, allowing it to flow down the back, over the jerking shoulders.

'This is paradise,' she said. 'Your mouth is like fucking paradise.'

Praising her. Wanting the redhead and the blonde to be jealous. Wanting them to know that, as much as they had pleasured her, this guard was better. The guard gurgled happily, opening her eyes for a moment to look upwards, flashing thanks from warm amber irises, then closing them again, concentrating utterly on her task, on the servicing of the cock in her mouth.

'Squeeze my balls,' she said.

The guard lifted one hand and slipped it into her trousers, reaching for her balls. Only one hand? But that was enough. She was skilful at ball-pleasuring too, squeezing them, kneading them, juggling them, working at them one-handed while her mouth sucked and slid on the cock, welcoming it deep, half-expelling it, half-exiling it from paradise, welcoming it deep again, over and over. Even the sound of it was better than the previous two: the slurp and suck, the little murmurs of pleasure, the coos of excitement and admiration, the throaty chuckles timed just right to tremble in the head of her cock as it reached the back of the warm mouth, paused, and slid back. If this had been her first blow job of the day she would have come by now, unable to restrain herself, spurting torrentially, but it wasn't, it was her third blow job, or her third-and-a-half, counting the honey-suck the blonde had given her. Orgasm was on its way, but it was coming slowly, gathering slowly in her balls under the skilful ministration of that warm, soft, squeezing, kneading, juggling hand.

But even slowly was too fast. She opened her mouth to speak but the guard anticipated her, and withdrew her ball-teasing hand from her trousers, altering the rhythm of her lips and tongue, galloping her mouth more gently at her engorged cock. She wanted this to last. A blow job to end blow jobs. The mother of all blow jobs. Something falling inside the lift flashed in the corner of her eye, and she heard a tiny *splik*. She turned her head carefully. Another flash; another tiny *splik*. It was a falling drop of liquid. One of the guards was crying – the redhead who had given her a blowjob ten floors up. There was a shining trail down her right cheek and a tear was just beginning to trickle down her left. Another tear fell from her right cheek, flashed and landed with a tiny *splik*. She was starting to cry harder, faster. A tear fell from her left cheek.

The blonde guard who had given her a blow job in the descending lift was starting to cry too, a tear trickling down a face still dirty with make-up. What was wrong? Had she upset them so much with what she had said, praising the darkhaired guard for her skill, for her expertise on a cock? Yes. That must be it. They were jealous. Jealous of the darkhaired guard. She smiled cruelly, looking away from the lift, down at the bobbing black head, as light glistened on the thick, glossy hair. She stroked it, patted it, hearing tears fall inside the lift with a soft patter. Warm, salty rain.

'Good girl,' she said. 'Very, very good girl.'

Then, raising her voice, she said, 'You two. In the lift. Come here.'

The two guards came out of the lift, still crying, four eyes already beginning to redden and swell, blue and blue and green and green. She whipped at them contemptuously with her voice, wanting to see the tears fall faster.

'Get a fucking move on. I had to accept second-rate blow jobs from you. I'm not going to accept second-rate obedience.'

The tears fell faster and her stomach hollowed and glowed with excitement above the persistent pleasure of the sucking, slurping mouth on her cock. The redhead put the basket on the floor and stood to attention with the blonde, one of them on either side of the kneeling fellatrix, tears dripping from their cheeks, landing on the black marble floor, *splik, splik*. On the blonde's face the tear trails showed whiter, cutting through the vinegar and the remains of her make-up.

'Unbutton your shirts. I want to see your tits.'

The two of them began to unbutton their shirts with trembling fingers, looking down a little at what they were doing so that tears landed on the black cloth, leaving little wet marks.

'Open them,' she said.

They folded their shirts open, exposing tight black bras on small firm breasts.

'Bras off,' she said.

They reached inside their shirts and unclipped their bras with little snaps, lifted them forwards and away. Her cock throbbed convulsively with excitement in the sucking mouth and the closed eyes of the concentrating fellatrix opened for a moment, looked upwards in wonder, then closed again.

'Drop them.'

The two guards dropped their bras, letting them flutter to the floor. Her mouth had dried with excitement and she could feel a pulse throbbing painfully in her throat. Such beautiful breasts: small, firm, symmetrical. She looked from one pair to the other, trying to decide which she preferred, and could not. Such tender pink nipples, peaked with humiliation and excitement.

'Clasp your hands on the backs of your heads,' she said.

The guards clasped their hands behind their necks, elbows at either side of their faces, breasts lifting and firming.

'Come closer,' she said. 'Take my gloves off.'

She held out her gloved left hand to the redhead, her gloved right to the blonde, and small even teeth closed over a fingertip of each glove. She pulled back and the gloves slid off, held in the teeth.

'Drop them,' she said. The mouths opened and the gloves fluttered to the floor. She reached forwards for the tear-slick faces, rubbed her fingers across them, moistening her fingertips well, then lowered her hands to rub tears into the stiffened nipples. The blonde shivered with pleasure or humiliation. She moistened her fingertips again and rubbed tears into the nipples, squeezing them this time, scratching at them a little.

'Closer,' she said.

The two guards came forwards, pressing nearer to her, swinging their elbows awkwardly, and she bent her head and breathed in the warm air above the redhead's breasts, then lowered her mouth and slowly drew in a nipple, sucking, licking, savouring. Another nipple, sucking, licking, savouring. Warm, salty-sweet skin. She could read the trembling of the redhead's body with her lips. She sucked harder, then broke the contact with a pop and lifted and swung her head to sample the blonde's nipples and breasts. Her skin was warm too, salty with her tears, sweet with nipple-secretions, but lighter, almost flowery. The redhead's breasts were roses; the blonde's were lilies.

She broke the breast-sucking with a pop and lifted her head to kiss the blonde's face, sucking at her salty skin, then her warm, soft, swollen lips, and probed between them to meet and fence with the blonde's flickering tongue. Her cock throbbed in the warm mouth below and she knew orgasm was coming. She probed harder at the blonde's mouth, savouring her sweetness, then broke the kiss and turned her head for the redhead, licking her cheek for a moment to clear her tongue with saltiness. She wanted to compare their flavours, to see if the redhead's mouth tasted different. She kissed her and probed at the warm, soft, swollen lips.

They opened and her tongue slid through to the mouth that had engorged her cock ten storeys up. Yes, she tasted different, sweet, too, but darker, almost spicier. She broke the kiss almost reluctantly, said, 'Squeeze my balls again' to the kneeling fellatrix, and resumed the kiss, pressing her tongue deeper, wrestling with the snaking tongue that met hers. The fellatrix's mouth started to gallop on her cock and the soft hand crept into her trousers again, took hold of her balls and began to manipulate them expertly, almost painfully, hardening the ache that had begun to fill them, readying them to spurt.

She broke the kiss with the redhead again, gasping for air, her heart hammering, wanting to sample the blonde's spittle and tongue, too, but not wanting to leave the redhead's. Both were too sweet, too desirable. She kissed the redhead again, lifting her fingers to the exposed breasts and nipples and slowly began to torment them, squeezing, scratching, tweaking, twisting. The redhead moaned and she sucked at her mouth and lips as though she could draw pain out of her like nectar. She broke the kiss again and managed this time to turn her head for the blonde. She let go of the redhead's breasts, and put her hands on the blonde's, squeezing, scratching, tweaking, twisting as her mouth closed over the blonde's mouth and she inserted her tongue deep inside it.

Below, the fellating mouth was almost frenzied, working hard for spunk, and she could smell the fellatrix's spicy sweat. She raised one hand from the blonde's breasts and snaked it inside her open shirt, feeling for an armpit, sliding her fingertips into it. It was smooth and almost hairless, slick with a film of sweat. She brought the hand out, breaking the kiss, and licked at her fingertips, savouring the blonde's sweat. But it was time. She unbuttoned the holster and slid the pildo out. She didn't lift it inside her shirt this time, just pressed it to where her left nipple strained at the cloth of her shirt, and pulled the trigger. Bzzz. The moist flushed faces of the blonde and redhead, close to hers, pleaded for more kisses, for more nipple-torment, for more humiliation and pleasure, but she wanted orgasm. She shifted the pildo into her left hand and pressed it to her right nipple through the cloth of her shirt. *Bang* she mouthed, imagining that she could see herself in a mirror, and pulled the trigger. Bzzz.

She groaned, her free hand dropping to clutch the fellatrix's head hard over her cock for the final time, and began to come, spurting into the warm wonder-mouth, most skilful of the three, most energetic, most exciting, worthiest to receive and swallow the spurts of her thick, salty semen. Her hand relaxed on the soft hair and the fellatrix's head moved back a little, the warm mouth releasing an inch or two of her cock, but still sucking, still licking, trying to retain the erection, to begin to entice her cock back down the primrose path to orgasm. The rosy road. The lilaceous lane. She smiled and blinked, feeling very tired, then said, 'That's enough, you two. Put your bras back on.'

The blonde and redhead moved away from her, stooped to pick up and refit their bras over their licked and salted breasts, and buttoned up their shirts, their small white hands climbing up the black cloth like tiny albino crabs. But the fellatrix was still bobbing gently on her cock. The soft hand was still manipulating her balls inside her trousers.

'That's enough, soldier,' she said, sliding her pildo back into its holster.

The bobbing stopped and the closed eyes opened, looking up at her, dark eyebrows lifted.

'That's enough,' she said more softly.

Reluctantly the fellatrix released her cock, allowing it to slide out of her mouth, still stiff, glistening with moisture and heat. She held the cockhead for a moment longer, swirling her tongue over it, working her lips on it, then released that, too, with a sigh.

'Good girl,' she said.

The fellatrix slid back on her knees. She turned and crawled on her hands and knees to retrieve her cap, slipping it back on her head as she stood up.

'Line up,' she said.

The three guards stood shoulder to shoulder, redhead on the left, blonde on the right, darkhaired fellatrix in the middle, the redhead still working at a final button. Tears were dried on her face and the blonde's face was filthy with dried tears and vinegar and the remains of her make-up. Only the fellatrix looked clean and calm, face serene under her cap, red tongue still working at her swollen, faintly smiling lips. Her cock throbbed quietly at the sight of them, still sticking stiff and erect from her trousers, but she

40

took hold of it ruthlessly and pushed it back into her trousers, then zipped them up carefully, trapping the cock inside them. She fingered the bulge with her left hand, seeing that three pairs of eyes were fastened on it: green, blue, amber.

'Salute me,' she said.

Their forearms swung across their stomachs and out, small fists clenched, boots crashing together on the marble floor.

'Hail, *Generalissima*!'

She carelessly flicked up her own salute with her right arm, still fingering at her cock-bulge, then said, 'Pick up the basket, . . . Ginger.'

The redhead stepped away for a moment, bent to pick up the basket, then stepped back behind the fellatrix as the blonde stepped in front of her. The squad was ready, lined up and ready to march.

'March,' she said.

They began to march, boots loud on the marble floor, heading for the exit to the street. As they passed her she began to walk beside them, still fingering at her cock-bulge, gloating over the thought of the nine orifices that marched with her: three mouths, three arseholes, three cunts. The exit to the street was open. An arched glass doorway led to a short flight of vulgar white, gold-veined marble steps. She and the guards rattled down it, boots glistening in the sunshine, and reached the pavement. They turned up it for the walk to the pedestrian crossing and the two guards who waited there for them. For her.

Her fingers stopped working on her cock-bulge as outrage suddenly filled her. One of the guards had gone AWOL, the one on this side of the street. No, there she was. She was squatting next to her pole with her trousers half down, one jackbooted leg planted on the street, one on the pavement, head lowered as she watched a glistening arc of piss fall neatly into the gutter beneath the neat black triangle of her pubic hair.

'Stop!' she ordered the squad of guards marching with her.

They halted with a single, synchronised crash of their boots, and she continued alone, marching menacingly towards the crouching figure, whose head had swung up suddenly, eyes wide with surprise and fright, the falling stream of piss suddenly jerking and splattering.

'What the fuck are you doing?' she said, standing over her, her cock beginning to restiffen as she noted how the guard was trembling, the stream of piss dancing between her thighs, soiling her white skin.

A thin tongue of piss was flowing down the gutter, glistening in the sunshine, three or four metres long already. It was dark yellow, steaming faintly, and she could smell it. Warm and spicy. Now the piss-stream dribbled between the white thighs, spluttered, stopped.

'Well? What the fuck are you doing?' she repeated.

The guard's head swung up to meet her eyes. The guard nodded, swallowed, and said nervously, 'Pissing, *Generalissima.*'

'Pissing? *Pissing*?'

The guard got to her feet, trousers still around her knees, and stood ludicrously to attention. Where were her knickers? She didn't seem to wearing any. She looked down at the guard's bare thighs. They were splattered with piss, golden droplets on milky skin. She looked up. Across the street female shopkeepers were standing in the entrance to the florist's and butcher's and she thought she could glimpse faces in the window of the newsagent's and video rental. Watching. So she would have to make a stern example of the miscreant. She looked down the street where the ice cubes lay glittering in the sunshine, then turned her head towards the squad of three guards.

'You three,' she said. 'Snowy and Darky, get me those ice cubes Ginger, open the curry powder.'

The squad trotted towards her, boots loud in the silence. The crossing-guard who had pissed into the gutter was trembling again, blinking nervously as she waited to be punished. The redhead halted as the squad came level with them, but the blonde and darkhair carried on down the street till they reached the glittering field of ice cubes and squatted to begin picking them up. The redhead had put the basket on the pavement and lifted the packet of curry powder out of it. The stream of piss in the gutter was twice as long now, reaching down the street almost as far as the ice cubes and the squatting blonde and darkhair, right hands darting to and from the street and pavement, left hands held to their bodies, heaped higher and higher with ice cubes.

She sniffed and saw that the redhead had opened the packet of curry powder.

'Bend forwards and clasp your ankles,' she told the crossing-guard.

The crossing-guard obeyed. Her cap fell off and landed on the pavement with a dull slap. Her hair was black too, folded in a neat bun. She walked behind her, fingering at her cock-bulge again. The tails of the guard's shirt and jacket had ridden up over the backs of her thighs, exposing the lower halves of her buttocks. She folded the tails up with her left hand, exposing the buttocks fully, while her right hand flipped her holster open and slid out her pildo.

'Closer,' she told the redhead.

The redhead walked to stand next to the crossing-guard, holding the packet of curry power out and ready.

'Open your mouth,' she said, lifting the pildo.

The redhead opened her mouth and she put the pildo into it.

'Lick,' she said.

The redhead licked, moistening the bulbous muzzle. She withdrew the pildo and slipped the muzzle into the open packet, pressing into the curry powder, coating it thoroughly.

'Hold your arse-cheeks apart, Pissy,' she told the crossing-guard.

The guard hesitated for a moment, then reached behind herself for her buttocks, took hold of them, and levered them apart.

She squatted directly behind them, heart beating faster at the sight of the pink arsehole exposed between the milky globes of the buttocks. Exposed and vulnerable. She lifted the pildo and pressed the muzzle to the arsehole.

'Open your arsehole,' she said and pushed.

The guard resisted for a moment, then relaxed and the muzzle of the pildo slid inside, charged with curry powder, sliding deep between the milky globes of the buttocks, carrying curry powder deep between the velvet walls of her arsechamber. She pulled the trigger of the pildo, felt the vibration in her hand and saw it in the shudder of the guard's buttocks. She released the trigger and slid the pildo out, twisting it carefully left and right, and looked at the muzzle, noting with satisfaction that the curry powder was almost all gone – wiped off on the walls of the guard's arse. *It must be starting to burn inside her now*.

'Let go of your arse-cheeks,' she said.

As the crossing-guard relaxed her hold, she stood up and took hold of the arse-cheeks for a moment in her gloved hands, juddering them, enjoying their weight and rubbery solidity, then let go, gesturing the redhead to one side, and walked to stand in front of the crossing-guard. She stooped to inspect her face. Yes. It was twisted with discomfort and small white teeth were biting into the juicy pink lower lip. The curry powder was beginning to work, burning into the moist velvet walls of her arse. She looked back down the street. The blonde and darkhair were nearly finished, left hands clutching little pagodas of ice cubes to their bodies as they moved crabwise, still squatting, for the final cubes.

'That's enough,' she called to them. The blonde and darkhair looked up. 'Enough. Get back over here.'

They stood up carefully, securing the little pagodas of ice cubes with their right hands, and walked slowly back down the street. As they got closer she could see the cherries inside the ice cubes: tiny sugary hearts sealed in crystal. They reached her and stood waiting.

'Good girls,' she said.

She took an ice cube off the darkhair's pile, opened her mouth and slipped it inside. It was intensely cold, burning at her tongue, numbing it as she worked it to and fro, rattling it on her teeth, sucking it, trying to start it melting. She stopped suddenly.

'Leave it alone, Pissy,' she said, her words distorted by the ice cube in her mouth and by the numbness of her tongue.

The crossing-guard's hands were inching backwards on her arse, forefingers extended. How the curry powder must be burning. How she must be longing to slide her fingers into her arsehole and try to scratch it out, to soothe the stinging, the seething, the pain. She smiled cruelly and pulled one of her gloves off, tucked it into her belt, then spat the ice cube on to her bare palm.

'Open your mouth, Snowy,' she said to the blonde.

The small mouth opened and she popped the cube neatly into it.

'Close your mouth,' she said.

The mouth closed. She stepped behind the crossing-guard again, and put her bare hand up between the piss-splattered thighs, feeling for the cunt. It was glowing with heat, radiating it, so that she felt it on her hand even before she touched it. Then she touched. Ah. It was moist and oozing, split like an over-ripe fruit, the twin halves of the labia puffing and peeling away from each other to release a thick dribble of yelm. It was the curry powder in her arse, burning into her moist arse-walls, rich with nerves and blood vessels, starting a sympathetic reaction in her cunt.

And her breasts? She snaked the hand higher, up underneath the crossing-guard's shirt, up her smooth flat stomach, to her tit-cleft, up her left tit, and felt for the nipple. Yes. It was hardened and peaked, rolling under her fingertips like a berry. She felt for the right nipple. Hardened and peaked too. The pain of the curry powder had excited her, had started her cunt oozing, stiffened her nipples. Good. She lowered her hand, rummaged in the cunt again for a moment or two, feeling yelm coat her fingertips, then she twisted and looked back at the blonde.

'Has it melted?' she said.

The blonde shook her head.

'Let's see,' she said.

The blonde opened her mouth and poked out her tongue. The ice cube sat on it, only half-melted.

'Give me some cubes,' she said.

The blonde sucked her tongue back into her mouth and began to feed her ice cubes from the little pagoda balanced on her left hand against her body. Her palm must be freezing, poor thing. As she received each cube she slipped it between the crossing-guard's thighs and up into the cunt, and slid it deep between the warm, yelm-coated walls. One. Two. Three. Four. Five. Six. Seven. Then she stopped. She didn't want to give the insubordinate little bitch frostbite. Not yet. She stood up, asking the blonde, 'Has it melted yet?'

The blonde shook her head again. She looked across the street. The shopkeepers had gone back inside their shops, apparently satisfied at the punishment she had meted out to the crossing-guard for pissing in the street, for filling the gutter with that long tongue of dark yellow piss. It was twenty or thirty metres long now, almost at the mouth of a storm-drain further down the street, and scraps of coloured paper were fluttering here and there in the gutter beside it. No. Not scraps of coloured paper. Butterflies were feeding from the piss-stream. As she watched, another came flapping languidly across the street and settled into the gutter, shuffled near the piss-stream, and began to drink.

She heard a tiny *splik*, like the sound of a tear falling to the mirrored floor of the lift, then another. *Splik. Splik.* It was water, falling from the crossing-guard's cunt, landing on the pavement between her jackboots in dark patterns. The ice cubes were melting inside her cunt.

'Has it melted?' she said to the blonde.

This time she nodded, poking out a cold-paled tongue that carried not an ice cube this time, just a cherry.

'Give it to me,' she said. 'No, on my tongue.'

She stuck out her own tongue, bending towards the blonde's face, and the cherry was transferred to her. She flicked it into her mouth and bit it in half. It was still cold, intensely sweet. Its liquid sugars thickened and slowed, starting to melt and flow in her mouth. She savoured it briefly, then chewed and swallowed.

'OK, all of you, stick the ice cubes up your arses,' she said. 'Now.'

The blonde and darkhair blinked, looking unhappy.

'Now,' she said, turning her head and jerking her chin at the redhead. 'Get on with it.'

Slowly, they obeyed her. The redhead came to stand near the blonde. Darkhair, taking ice cubes from their pagodas, slipped a small hand down the back of her trousers and, bending forwards a little, inserted an ice cube up her tight arsehole. She turned back to the crossing-guard.

'Hey, little Miss Pissy, hold your arse-cheeks apart again.'

She took a handful of cubes in her gloved left hand and stepped behind the crossing-guard again, feeling with her bare right hand for the pink arsehole between the firm, rubbery cheeks of her arse. There it was. She rubbed it with her index finger, then pushed, sliding her finger in, deeper and deeper, past the second knuckle and deeper. Christ, she was tight. Tight and hot. She twisted her finger from side to side and heard the crossing-guard moan softly.

She slid her finger out slowly, examined it and wiped it on the white buttock cheeks. Then she bent and started to feed the ice cubes up the crossing-guard's arse. One. Two. Three. Four. Five. Six. Seven. Ice with fire. Ice cubes with curry powder. The crossing-guard moaned again, grateful for the relief of ice in her arse. Droplets of water were still falling from her cunt as the ice cubes inside it melted. When she had pushed the last one deep into the guard's arse, she reached between the thighs and slipped her index finger between the lips of her cunt. Christ. It was freezing inside, running with melt-water and diluted yelm. Her cock had hardened almost painfully as she inserted her finger into the crossing-guard's arse, then throbbed with each ice cube that she had sent into it. She had wanted to fuck her, but up the cunt, not up the arse.

Now her cunt was frozen, not swimming with warm, sugary juices but dripping with cold water. The poor thing. And her arse would be heading the same way. So there was only one thing for it: to fuck her quickly, before the ice cubes in her arse had melted, destroying the heat and tightness. She stood up, loosened her belt and, after letting her trousers drop, she took hold of her cock and wanked at it briskly for a moment. The blonde, redhead and darkhair had finished inserting the ice cubes up their own arses and stood waiting for new orders, shifting uncomfortably from foot to foot, with faint, expressions of wonder on their faces. It must feel nasty: ice cubes melting and trickling inside their tight arse-holes. Poor things. Poor little things. Still, she'd give them something to take their minds off it.

'Get closer,' she said. 'Help me with this. Ginger, kneel behind me.'

The three of them clustered around her and the crossing-guard: the redhead kneeling behind her as she stood with her trousers down behind the bending crossing-guard; the blonde and darkhair standing on either side of the crossing-guard and taking hold of her, adjusting her for the arse-fuck. Each seized a cheek of her firm buttocks and, tugging it open, exposed the pink arsehole between the cheeks. The crossing-guard had stiffened as the hands took hold of her. Now, as she closed up behind her – bare right hand feeling for the bare arsehole, gloved left hand taking hold of her cock and guiding it forwards – the crossing-guard jerked, trying to break loose, suddenly babbling for mercy.

'Come on, take your punishment like a man,' she said. 'It won't hurt much. Not too much. You can hope.' The head of her cock touched the arsehole and she closed her eyes in anticipation.

'Hold her,' she said.

The blonde and darkhair tightened their grip on the crossing-guard, tugging harder at the buttock-cheeks, holding them open like two halves of a fat white door guarding a tiny entrance to a garden of earthly delights. She pushed, jabbing her cock at the arsehole, feeling it resist her. She pushed harder, slowly relaxing her full weight into her groin, focusing it like sunlight into a sharp, blazing point. A laser. A laser to slice through ice with a fierce hissing and cloud of superheated steam. The arsehole was giving way and the crossing-guard was sobbing for mercy, pleading not to be fucked, pleading not to be taken up the arse. It made her feel stiffer, more swollen, more delighted at the prospect of invading the sanctuary beyond the arsehole-gate. She bent forwards and reached up underneath the crossing-guard's body, and took hold of her tits beneath the uniform with her bare right hand and gloved left, delighting in their weight and firmness. She was ready. Push, she told herself. Push. Push.

She pushed and then groaned with surprise and delight, her voice deeper beneath the shriek of the crossing-guard. The arsehole had given way, shouldered aside like the swinging doorway of a saloon as a bullying gunfighter strides in, and her cock had sunk inches deep into the crossing-guard's tight arse. She could feel the ice cubes jostling ahead of it, pushed deeper into the arse-chamber, and there was melt-water swirling in there too, but the walls were still hot, still seething under the curry powder, and so tight and slick that for a moment she thought she was going to come on the first thrust, as the blunt head of her cock slid in triumph into her.

But her balls couldn't deliver their load so quickly, not after three blow jobs. She paused for a moment, gathering her attention, then said, 'Ginger, lick my balls' to the redhead kneeling behind her and started to fuck, battering her body and cock at the slender body of the crossing-guard, at her delicious arse, gasping and grunting like an animal, wanting to leave her sore for days. And yes, there, the redhead had crept closer, put her mouth to the fork of her thighs, and now started to lick and suck her balls, stimulating them, encouraging the slow pooling of spunk for when she would shoot her burning load deep into the icy depths of the crossing-guard's arse.

But for now she was fucking, sliding her cock in and partly out, over and over, hammering at arse-flesh with a cock-hammer, beating it into shape, dominating and subduing it, luxuriating in the contrast between the cold that lay deep inside the arse and the warmth of the redhead's soft tongue on her balls. They must be sweaty too. Sweaty, salty balls, rich with male secretions and odours, slowly licked clean by the redhead's soft, sliding tongue and sucking lips. That would have kept her stiff even if the arse had been no good, had been frigid and watery like the poor, ice cube-packed cunt. But the arse was good, still hot, still tight, but with a shock of ice-water awaiting her cock at the end of each incursion, in the deepest reaches of the arse-chamber.

Now orgasm was gathering, prickling in her fingertips, her nose and lips, tightening the muscles of her thighs and buttocks, hoisting her balls hard to the fork of her thighs so that the redhead had to press her

51

face closer, to lick and suck more vigorously. She tried to press orgasm back, hold it down by force of will, wanting to fuck minutes more, but it was rising too hard. She blinked and shook her head, biting her lip. No good. Unless she stopped fucking altogether it was coming. But maybe –

She released the crossing-guard's right tit and reached for her cunt. It was wet and cold and water was sliding down the smooth thighs, not oozing the way yelm would have done. And the cunt-lips had folded back together, almost as though they had pursed with disapproval at the ice cubes forced between them. She fingered them apart and slipped her fingers inside, sliding them up cold, unresponsive cunt-walls, exploring for the remnants of the ice cubes.

But there were no remnants. The hot cunt had melted ice to become cold itself. No remnants of ice. Only the cherries, clutched between the tightening cunt-walls like little trophies. She fingered one free and lifted her hand back and up to her mouth, slipped it inside and bit into it, still thrusting and relaxing at the crossing-guard's arse, wanting to distract herself from oncoming orgasm with the sweetness and cold of the cherry. Her hand dropped back to the cunt, slipped inside and rummaged for more cherries as she chewed and savoured the first. It was no good. The pleasure on her tongue, the sweetness of fructic sugars, the faint spice of diluted yelm, was seized by the pleasure in her cock, taxed in full to service the payment of her debt, the huge sum she owed the arse in which she was working and that she could only pay in spunk. Torrential spunk. Gallons of it. Gallons of boiling spunk pumped into the arse-chamber. And now it was coming, ready to burst from her hardened, aching balls and boil down her cock and out.

She lifted her hand from the cold, dripping cunt, slipped the cherries into her mouth and held them there for a moment as her hand lifted up the crossing-guard's body and fastened on her right tit again, squeezing it hard as she thrust for the antepenultimate time at the tight arse, for the penultimate time at the tight arse, for the ultimate time at the tight arse.

She came, groaning, hurling her spunk deep into the arse-chamber, biting down on the cherries in her mouth so that sweetness spurted there as saltiness burst inside the crossing-guard's arse. For the first few spurts she thought she was going to faint, the pleasure was so great, the satisfaction of reaching orgasm so overwhelming, but if she lost consciousness she lost pleasure and she hung on, groaning, swearing, blaspheming, paying her debt in full, flooding the crossing-guard's tight arse-chamber with her salary, brine-slime from her aching balls. Her groans had turned into gasps; now her gasps turned into pants, her pants into long, sighing breaths, in and out, in and out, and she slumped forwards exhausted over the crossing-guard's slender back, cock still buried deep in the tight arse, but already starting to soften and shrink.

Five ejaculations in less than an hour. Not bad for a girl who'd never owned a set of cock and balls before today. The crossing-guard would have fallen under her weight if the blonde and darkhair hadn't been holding her up. She was sobbing at what had been done to her, tears dripping to the pavement the way the melting ice had dripped from her cunt, and the sound of it made her cock quiver and stiffen again slightly, trying to ready itself to begin the long gallop to orgasm again. And the redhead was still licking devotedly at her balls.

'Ginger, that's enough,' she said to her and the licking stopped. She pushed herself off the crossing-guard's back and looked down, watching herself as she slid her cock out of the arse. How had something so big fitted into something so small? It must have felt like a train up there, like having the *Titanic* forced up your backside. Her cock glistened as it slid free, smeared with scrapings of arse-wall and rectal mucus, and came free with a final juicy pop. Poor bitch.

'OK, let her go,' she said to the blonde and darkhair.

They let go of the crossing-guard and she slumped to her knees, still sobbing, hands reaching belatedly and uselessly back to shield her arsehole. She wanked at her cock, sliding her hand up and down its full length, wiping it clean, shaking her hand at the pavement. She pulled her trousers back up, and tightened her belt. Her right glove had fallen out and she looked on the ground for it. The redhead anticipated her, stooped for it and picked it up, holding it out to her with a 'Here it is, *Generalissima*.'

'Good girl,' she said. She put it back on, and felt the velvet inside soak up the moisture on her hand. She pushed her cock back into her trousers and zipped up. The crossing-guard was touching her arsehole, sliding two fingers in and out, her other hand buried between her thighs, fingers probing at her cunt. What was she doing? Christ, she was masturbating. And on duty too.

'Hey, stop her,' she said to the blonde and darkhair.

They seized hold of the crossing-guard, lifted her back to her feet, dragged her hands away from her arsehole and cunt, lifted her trousers back up and zipped them. Good. But they still had looks of mild discomfort on their faces and she smiled as she saw that there were small patches of damp on the rear of their trousers, where the melt-water from the ice cubes was trickling from their arseholes.

'Snowy, stop her,' she said.

The crossing-guard was still trying to finger at her arsehole but the blonde slapped at her hand and she walked unsteadily to the pedestrian crossing, ready to press the button. Good. The blonde, darkhair and redhead formed the squad again, ready to escort her across the street. She stood ready, looking across the street to the other crossing-guard and the shops: the newsagent's, the butcher's, the florist's, the video rental, the bank.

'OK, I'm ready to cross,' she said.

The freshly buggered crossing-guard pressed the button and at the top of the pole on the far side of the street the lower half of the sign lit red. DON'T WHIP. She looked up and down the street. No traffic, only the line of drinking butterflies in the gutter along the drying stream of the crossing-guard's piss. The crossing suddenly jingled and on the far side of the street the top half of the sign lit green. No words here, just a pair of crossed canes. She strode across the black-and-yellow stripes of the crossing escorted by her three-girl squad, trying to think of an excuse to punish them. All of them. The blonde, the darkhair, the redhead, the crossing-guard she had just buggered, the crossing-guard who saluted her with the cock salute as she reached the far side of the street.

She stopped on the pavement, eyes narrowing. Yes. She knew. She lifted her right arm and gestured with her gloved hand, feeling it cling awkwardly to her skin with dried fluid from the crossing-guard's violated arse, swinging it up and down the street, to indicate the line of settled butterflies in the gutter.

'I want them stamped out,' she said. 'The whole fucking lot. All of you get over there and wait for the order, now. Soldier, did you hear that?'

The crossing-guard across the street – the one she'd just buggered – nodded.

'Then get on with it, all of you. Now. At the double.'

The four of them on her side of the street hesitated a moment, then trotted off the pavement and on to the street, fanning out as they went, to divide the line of drinking butterflies automatically into fifths: one for the buggered crossing-guard, one for the blonde, one for the darkhair, one for the redhead, one for the as yet unbuggered crossing-guard. They lined up along the gutter, staring down at the butterflies.

'Stamp!' she said.

They started to stamp, butterflies exploding up around their moving boots, jumping left and right, stamping, kicking, their bodies veiled in escaping butterflies for the first few moments.

'Harder!' she said. 'Harder!'

Their boots pistoned at the line of butterflies. Two of the guards were laughing, the darkhair and unbuggered crossing-guard. Fewer of the butterflies were flying up now. Dozens must already have been crushed under their boots, ground into the gutter and the half-dried piss. She smiled, relaxing. That would do it. She strode along the pavement to the newsagent's, pushed the door open and stepped inside. It seemed dark after the sunlight outside and she paused for a moment just inside the door for her eyes to adjust, then strode forwards to the newspapers and magazines. A young Asian woman stood behind the counter, watching her quietly, dressed in dark clothing, her dark hair tied back in a long pigtail. She imagined holding the pigtail as she slid her cock into her from behind. Up her arse or her tight, spicy cunt. Her cock jerked in her trousers and bulged forwards.

She fingered it, knowing the Asian woman would see her doing it, and looked for a morning paper. But there were no papers. Just magazines. Rows and rows of magazines. And all of them, it seemed, were pornographic, sitting neatly arranged by preference and perversion. She strolled down the rows. Blonde women. Redheads. Big breasts. Small breasts. Anal. Lactating. Scat. Golden showers. S&M. She stopped. S&M. She drew one of the magazines out and let it fall upon her gloved left hand, her cock stiffening more, bulging harder under her gently squeezing gloved right hand.

It was a fladge mag with a difference: women being held down and lashed with flowers, firm white buttocks bouncing and reddening in irregular streaks under long-stemmed tulips, chrysanthemums and lilies. She flicked it closed and looked at the cover. *Tsiccû*. Hmmm. She tucked it under her arm and strolled further down the rows, stopped again, drew out another mag, flicked it up. Fladge again, but this time with strips of raw meat. Her cock throbbed and she had the urge to slide her zip down and release it, and start wanking as she leafed through the magazine, staring at the juicy strips of raw meat swinging over and over against firm white buttocks and breasts or being rubbed against pink nipples.

She forced the urge down, slipping the magazine under her arm, then turned and strolled towards the counter to pay. When she reached the counter she put the magazines on it, one on top of the other, then added a large chocolate bar from the display of confectionery. 'Hlid-û Vel' it said on the wrapper. The Asian woman pushed the top magazine off the lower to see the cover-price, face expressionless, then punched numbers into the till.

'Nine pounds fifty,' she said.

She reached inside the pocket of her jacket for the banknotes. One of the larger ones would easily cover it. There, 500,000. She held the note out to the Asian woman, but the delicate head shook once.

'Not OK?' she said.

The Asian woman said nothing, just shook her head again. She frowned, leafing through the handful of banknotes, holding out a 1,000,000, a 2,000,000, a 10,000,000 for Christ's sake, but the woman shook her head each time. Ah, this was why she had the whistle. She reached inside her shirt pocket, took out the whistle, and put it to her lips. She blew hard and it sounded piercingly, filling the shop. The Asian woman cringed behind the counter, putting small, leaf-delicate hands to her ears, then turned and began to reach for a button discreetly set into the wall. She took the whistle out of her mouth and said, 'Leave it!'

Boots were crashing on the pavement outside the shop and the door crashed back violently, a crack appearing suddenly in the lower pane of glass. Here they were, her gallant guards, the redhead, the blonde, the darkhair, the two crossing-guards, tears still shining on the face of the freshly buggered one. They formed a line inside the shop and came to attention, boots lifting and falling with a single synchronised crash, arms jutting out and up in the cock salute. She saluted back, then slipped the whistle back into her pocket.

'What is the problem, *Generalissima*?' said the redhead.

'She won't accept my money for these magazines,' she told them. 'Sort it out, will you?'

'At once, *Generalissima*.'

The Asian woman pressed back against the wall behind the counter, holding the back of one hand to her mouth, eyes wide and fearful. The blonde and redhead marched forwards to the counter, seized the magazines, glanced at them, then walked to the magazine racks and scanned them carefully. The darkhair picked up the chocolate bar and returned it to the display, while the unbuggered crossing-guard wrote steadily in a small notebook. The buggered crossing-guard stood back, still at attention, hands clenching and unclenching by her sides. Her poor arse must still be giving her grief. Oh well. The darkhair returned to a line that only reappeared when she joined it, standing to attention with the buggered crossing-guard. The unbuggered crossing-guard tore the top page out of the notebook and walked forwards to the counter.

'Please contact us at this address when you have the bill for the broken glass in the door,' she said to the Asian woman, whose hand was slowly dropping from her mouth. 'We'll cover it in full, plus 20 per cent for inconvenience.'

She put the page on the counter and returned to the line to stand to attention with the darkhair and buggered crossing-guard. The blonde walked back from the magazine racks, hands empty. Behind her the redhead found the right spot for the raw-meat mag and slipped it back, then followed the blonde. They rejoined the line, standing to attention.

'Good girls,' she told them. 'Now, salute the shopkeeper and apologise for the inconvenience.'

Their shining boots rose and fell again in perfect synchrony, landing crash on the floor, and their right forearms swung across their stomachs and forwards, small fists clenched.

'Hail, Ethnic Minority Shopkeeper! We apologise for the inconvenience!'

'As do I,' she told the Asian woman. 'Good morning. Come on, girls.'

She flapped her hand at them and they marched out of the newsagent's, shiny boots thudding on the floor. Only those boots weren't so shiny now, were they? She smiled and followed them out. The buggered crossing-guard was at the rear of the line, her hands still clenching and unclenching as they swung left right left right, and the wet spot on the seat of her trousers was larger. Her cock stiffened at the sight of it. Had the cherries melted free of ice in her arsehole? Well, she'd soon know. Outside in the sunshine she blinked, letting her eyes readjust before she spoke.

'In a line again, girls,' she said. 'I wish to inspect you.'

They formed a line on the pavement, boots crunching, then silent. She strolled down the line in front of them, redhead, blonde, darkhair, unbuggered crossing-guard, buggered crossing-guard, glancing up and down their uniforms, letting a slight frown on to her face as her gaze reached the redhead's boots, allowing the frown to relax a little as she looked up at the blonde's body, then return as her gaze dropped to the blonde's boots, relax a little more on the darkhair's body, return a little stronger as her gaze reached the darkhair's boots, until by the time she reached the buggered crossing-guard at the end of the line, she was frowning hard. Their faces, concentrated but calm when she had begun the inspection, were now apprehensive. She turned to stroll behind them, tutted half sorrowfully, half angrily, then stopped behind the unbuggered crossing-guard.

'Let's see the soles of your boots, soldier.'

The guard lifted her right calf backwards, slipping her hand under her knee to support it, holding the sole horizontal for inspection. She peered at it and snorted as though in disbelief and indignation.

'Now the other one.'

The guard lifted her left leg. She peered.

'They're filthy,' she said.

60

Silence.

'I said they're filthy, soldier.'

Another moment of silence.

'Yes, *Generalissima*.'

'That's all you've got to say for yourself? How have they got in this disgraceful state?'

Another moment of silence.

'Butterflies, *Generalissima*.'

She paused herself this time, allowing contempt and incredulity to bud on her tongue, then bloom into a bright little flower.

'*Butterflies*?'

'Yes, *Generalissima*. You ord–'

'Shut up. I've heard all I want to hear. Butterflies indeed. I've come across many excuses for slovenliness in my time but this takes the biscuit.'

Further down the line there was a snort of suppressed laughter. She stamped a boot sharply on the pavement.

'Who was that? Who laughed? Own up at once.'

'It was me, *Generalissima*.'

The blonde. She strode further down the line to her, leaving the unbuggered crossing-guard still standing on one leg, the sole of her left boot raised for inspection.

'So, you think it's funny, do you?'

'No, *Generalissima*. I was ... I was nervous, *Generalissima*.'

'Good. You should be nervous. I can promise you a nerve-racking time if your boots are as disgracefully filthy as that idle little slut's back there. Come on, let's see them.'

The blonde lifted her right leg, holding it under the knee, positioning the sole of the boot for inspection. She peered.

'Disgraceful. It's just as bad. Let's s–'

61

She broke off, waited a heartbeat, two, three, then sniffed.

'What's that smell?'

'*Generalissima*?'

'That smell, what is it? You've got something else on the sole of your boot.'

Silence for a moment, then, in a quiet voice:

'It's piss, *Generalissima*.'

'What's that? Speak up, I can barely hear you.'

Silence again, as though she were swallowing, then, in a louder voice, quavering for a moment:

'It's piss, *Generalissima*.'

'*What*?'

'Piss, *Gen*–'

'I heard you, I just couldn't believe my ears. Piss? On the soles of your boots?'

'Yes, *Generalissima*.'

'What about the rest of you? Has anyone else got piss on the soles of her boots? Or "butterflies", like these two? No, shut up, I'll see for myself. All you, now, let's have the soles of your boots up for inspection. Now, d'you hear?'

They all lifted their right legs except the buggered crossing-guard, who started to lift her left, saw that she was wrong, switched to her right, nearly falling over, nearly knocking the unbuggered crossing-guard over.

'If you're *quite* ready,' she said venomously.

They were. She walked down the line, peering, sniffing, redhead, blonde, darkhair, unbuggered crossing-guard, buggered crossing-guard.

'OK, let's see the other foot. Now.'

They put their right legs back on the pavement, lifted their left legs, supporting their knees, holding the soles of their boots horizontal for inspection. She strolled back down the line, buggered crossing-guard, unbuggered crossing-guard, darkhair, blonde, red-head, peering, sniffing. She stopped and turned neatly on the spot, boots squeaking faintly on the pavement.

'I was right,' she said. 'You've *all* got piss on the soles of your boots. Every last one of you. You've *all* got, I don't know, *gunk* on the soles of your boots *and* on the toes. I don't know what you've been up to – and I certainly don't accept this ridiculous story of butterflies – but I know what steps to take now. Shall I tell you? Well, shall I? Ginger?'

'Yes, *Generalissima.*'

'Snowy?'

'Yes, *Generalissima.*'

'Darky?'

'Yes, *Generalissima.*'

'And you, whom I haven't buggered yet?'

'Yes, *Generalissima.*'

'And you, soldier, whom I have?'

'Yes, *Generalissima.*'

'Good. Then I will tell you. The steps I take will be stern ones. Painful ones. I'll teach you to turn out with dirty boots. So, on my word of command, get on to the street. The pedestrian crossing. Let's see. Ah, that's just right. One yellow stripe for each of you. So, move. No! You do *not* need to consult each other, you just need to obey. Do it. Now.'

The line broke and they obeyed her, stepping on to the street, then walking to the pedestrian crossing.

'At the double!'

They moved at the double. Each found a yellow stripe, and stood on it.

'OK, now, all face up the street, away from me. That's right, towards the bank. No, not you just yet, Curry-Bum. You wait for separate instructions. Good. Now, the rest of you, put your caps on the street in front of you. Good girls. Now, bend forwards. Good. Touching the tarmac. Yes, that's right, but back a little, Snowy and Virgin-Arse. I want all fingers resting just on the edge of the yellow. Darky and Ginger, forwards a little. That's right. That's good. Very good. Now, Curry-Bum, I want you to loosen their belts and take their trousers down to half-mast. Can you do that for me? Good, then get on with it. When you've done it, get back into place and do all of that yourself.'

She unzipped her own trousers and helped her semi-stiff cock out, thumbing back the foreskin on the warm, aching head. She could smell it. It smelled warm and salty, almost feral. Spunk and sweat and bum-gunk. The buggered crossing-guard was loosening belts and tugging down trousers, exposing pearly smooth buttocks to her gloating gaze, moisture glistening between the lower cheeks where melt-water had threaded through the tight arseholes. No knickers. None of them were wearing knickers. Her cock rose in salute, ticking on her heartbeat, and she idly wanked at it, waiting for the final belt to be loosened, the final pair of trousers to be lowered to half-mast. There. She stopped wanking.

'OK, good, Curry-Bum. Now, get back to your own stripe and make like the rest. Trousers down to half-mast, bending forwards. Good girl. Very good girl. Now, girls, you can't see me, so I'll tell you what I'm doing. I'm unstrapping my holster. Can you hear it? I'm putting my holster on the pavement. Now I'm loosening my own belt. Listen carefully. I'm sliding it out of its loops. Now it's free. I'm holding it by the buckle, swinging it gently to and fro, feeling how heavy and supple it is. Yes, it's as I expected. It's very heavy and it's very supple. Now, ahead of me I can see, almost glowing in this glorious sunshine, five white bottoms belonging to five disobedient young female soldiers. And I'm afraid I'm forced to put two and two togeder. Or rather, I'm forced to put one and five togeder. One belt, and five bottoms. Disobedience must be punished. Rebellion must be nipped in the bud, or shall I say whipped in the bum? Don't you agree, Ginger?'

'Yes, *Generalissima*.'

'Good, I'm so glad to hear it. So you'll have guessed what I'm going to do, won't you? Eh, Ginger?'

'No, *Generalissima*.'

'Then I'll tell you. I'm going to whip your fucking arses till you're screaming for mercy. Have you got that? Snowy?'

'Yes, *Generalissima*.'

'And you, Curry-Bum?'

'Yes, *Generalissima*.'

'Good. But I'll tell you what, I'll strike a bargain with you. I'm not a cruel woman – well, I'm not an *excessively* cruel woman – and I've decided that waiting in this very heavy and very supple belt of mine are ten potential strokes for each of you. Note my words carefully. Po-ten-tial strokes. But whether those potential strokes become *actual* strokes depends on each of you and your willingness to fulfil your side of the bargain. And what is your side of the bargain, I hear you ask?'

She paused.

'I said, I hear you ask?'

Another pause, then the darkhair said, 'What is our side of the bargain, *Generalissima*?'

'Thank you, Darky. Your side of the bargain, Darky, and Snowy, and Ginger, and Virgin-Arse, and Curry-Bum, is to shit cherries into my mouth when I so instruct you by inserting my tongue in your arsehole. For each cherry you shit I shall leave one potential stroke of the ten currently awaiting you unactualised. Do you understand? Please move your arses from side to side if you do.'

She watched as the five white arses wiggled.

'Good. Now, hold your arses open for me.'

Ten small hands reached behind five white arses, gripping the cheeks, levering them apart, to expose the wet patch of melt-water that had trickled from each pink arsehole. Her cock throbbed, jutting hard and stiff beneath a hollowing stomach. A groan gathered in her throat. She stepped off the pavement, tucking the buckle of her belt inside the back of her trousers so that it hung loose like a satyr's tail, and strode towards the first white arse. Ginger's. The redhead's. She kneeled carefully behind it, lowering her knees one by one on to the hard tarmac, and gazed at the white cheeks, the buttock-cleft levered apart by the clutching hands, the pouting shell-halves of the cunt, fringed with coppery hair, the faintly furred perineum rising to the moist, glistening arse-dell and the faint circlet of silky, coppery hairs that areoled the pink, oozing arsehole.

She closed her eyes and put her head forwards, sticking her tongue out. The tip of it touched moist flesh and she flicked at it, tickled at it, then pressed her face closer, pressing her tongue more firmly to the flesh. More firmly to the arsehole. The moist, cool arsehole. Opening to her probing tongue so that she could slide it deep inside. And it was freezing inside, running with icy moisture from the melted ice cubes. The redhead strained slightly, fulfilling her side of the bargain, trying to discharge her bowels, and little hard shapes brushed her tongue, swimming in icy moisture. Cherries. She drew them into her mouth, sliced them in two with her front teeth, then chewing, savouring their sugariness, swallowed, counting them as the redhead shat them out, and reinserted her tongue fully into the tight arsehole, wriggling it, probing, urging the redhead on.

But her arse was all shat out. She withdrew her tongue and drew back, chewing and swallowing the last cherry. Seven. Seven cherries. So the redhead would be belted only three times. She crawled carefully to kneel behind the blonde and feast her eyes for a moment on the shell-halves of another beautiful cunt, fringed with golden hair, another faintly furred perineum, another moist, glistening arse-dell, another pink arsehole, but hairless this one, perhaps plucked or shaved. What a pleasant task. Plucking the arsehole-hair of a tender blonde, perhaps while she sucked you, her body inverted on your lap, arse presented to your face, mouth sealed hard over your rock-hard cock. Yes. Her cock rose and nodded at the thought of it, cockhead aching for attention, but she forced her lust down and bent forwards, tickling the arsehole with just the tip of her tongue, then licked it, swirling her tongue over it, then pressed her tongue forwards and through to the ice-chilled bowels and the cherries.

The blonde strained, buttocks quivering deliciously around her mouth and cheeks as they fitted between the arse-cleft, presenting her tongue to and through the arsehole, and the cherries started to slide within reach, pumped out in ones and twos. The blonde's bowels were moister, more full of icy melt-water, and she had to let it spill under her tongue and out of the blonde's arsehole, pouring over her chin, dripping *spliksplik* to the tarmac. But cherries came with it and she flicked them into her mouth, split them, savoured them, chewed them, swallowed them, counted them. This time she assisted more, straining her tongue as far into the blonde's bowels as she could get it, feeling the tendon in her mouth stretch and ache, even when she knew all the cherries were gone.

Then she slid her tongue out and kissed the arsehole gently before sitting back. Six of them. Six cherries. So the blonde would be belted four times. She crawled carefully for the darkhair. Ah. Her arsehole was almost furry, ringed with damp silky hairs, and she licked and probed at it in delight for some time, enjoying the soft prickle of hairs on her tongue before she pressed her tongue forwards and through to the waiting bowels swimming with icy melt-water. The darkhair strained, firm buttocks quivering around her mouth, shitting the cherries out for her to slice with her teeth, savour, chew, swallow, count. She withdrew with a last lick and swirl at the arsehole-hairs, and squatted back on her heels for a moment, getting the numbers clear in her head. Seven for redhead, so three belts. Six for the blonde, so four belts. Seven for the darkhair too, so three belts again.

OK. Now the unbuggered crossing-guard. She crawled carefully to kneel behind her. She was a darkhair too, the split shell-halves of her cunt fringed with dark silk, but her perineum was barely furred at all and her arsehole too was bare, inviting pink, like the blonde's. She reached up between the thighs, and ran her fingers over the cunt, slipping her ring finger up between the cunt-lips as she drew her hand back, up over the perineum to the arsehole. She probed at it with her ring finger for a moment, slipping it forwards easily through its moistened sphincter, then withdrew and leaned forwards and pressed her mouth over it. She kissed it, sucked it, then pressed her tongue to it and slid through to the bowels, probing, flickering, urging the guard on. The buttocks quivered and the cherries slid out to her. She split, savoured, chewed, swallowed, counted. Seven cherries again, so three belts.

Now Curry-Bum. She crawled carefully to kneel behind her. Another darkhair, but Christ, look at her arse. Her arsehole was gaping and inflamed, freshly buggered and oozing with moisture, but it wasn't clear moisture, it was brown and slimy, trickling over her perineum and dripping to the tarmac like diarrhoea. Curry powder and spunk. Yuck. Her lip curled and her nose wrinkled, almost as though she could detect a faecal stink. She wasn't anilinguing that. But there were no taste buds in her cock. She stood up and stepped forwards, unbuttoned her trousers and allowed them to drop. Then she peeled her foreskin back fully from the head.

'Steady yourself, Curry-Bum,' she told the guard. 'I'm going up you again.'

The guard quivered for a moment.

'OK?'

'No, please, *Generalissima*.'

'I said I'm going up you again. OK? Well?'

'As . . . as the *Generalissima* pleases.'

'Good girl.'

She stepped to her, and slipped an arm around her waist, presenting her cock to the gaping arsehole, thinking, Poor little thing. Twice in half-an-hour. Then she pushed forwards, groaning involuntarily as her cock rode through the loosened sphincter and up into the moist, spunk-slimed bowels. She started to thrust and relax. Christ, they were warm, almost hot. The curry powder must have inflamed them, maybe set up some kind of allergic reaction so that they glowed fiercely, melting the ice cubes quickly, oozing protective mucus. Warm, loosened bowels. Suddenly, another thought came into her head. Cold, tight bowels. The redhead's bowels, the blonde's, the darkhair's, the unbuggered crossing-guard's. Sitting ready and waiting beyond the four pink arseholes next to her.

Her thrusts slowed and began to stutter. This was good, but fresh arses would be better. And one of those fresh arses would be best of all. She thought it might be the blonde's. The blonde's arse. Yes. At the thought of it she started, foolishly, to thrust harder and faster into the arse she was already fucking, the one she had already decided to desert. Christ. Come on, stop. Stop. She blinked, shaking her head, and managed to prolong the withdrawal from a thrust, to lengthen and sustain it so that her cock slipped out of the guard's arse altogether and she could grab it and hold it back from thrusting forwards again.

She stepped back, gripping her cock hard, admonishing it. There are four tight arses waiting for you so why continue fucking that one? Why pump spunk into that one again? But she had to close her eyes and turn her head from the arse in front of her to convince even herself. The gaping, inflamed arsehole, red-rimmed and inviting, oozing sticky brown slime. She shook her head, eyes still closed, and took a step to the left, so that when she opened her eyes again it was on another arse, on an arsehole that wasn't gaping, wasn't inflamed, wasn't oozing sticky brown slime.

And yes, this one looked even more delicious. Pink virgin arsehole guarding unviolated bowels. She swallowed hard at the constriction in her throat and stepped forwards, tugging her glove off and wiping at her cock with her right hand. She didn't want this too easy; she didn't want her cock to slide in smoothly, lubricated by the buggered crossing-guard's arse. No, she wanted to linger over this, to hear the unbuggered crossing-guard plead for mercy, plead not to be taken up the arse, plead not to be buggered. But she was going to be merciless.

She stood directly behind her unsuspecting victim, and reached down to probe at the arsehole with her right hand. She swallowed at a constriction in her throat again and said huskily, 'I'm going to bugger you, soldier. Prepare yourself.'

The white buttocks quivered juicily and there was immediate panic in the voice.

'*Generalissima*?'

'Prepare yourself.'

'Bu–'

'Yes. Butt. I'm going to butt-fuck you. Prepare yourself.'

Her ears were humming and her cock was sticking up almost vertically, so that she had to press it down to present it to the arsehole sitting between the quivering arse-cheeks.

'Prepare yourself.'

This time she obeyed, bracing her body to be fucked.

'Good girl.'

She slipped her cockhead into the arse-dell and slowly, irresistibly, pushed. And pushed. Harder. And harder. And yes, the arsehole was giving way, opening, admitting her cock to the icy paradise of the bowels. The crossing-guard cried out loudly, like a bird, and she was up her, revelling in the moist juiciness of her bowels, the tightness and the cold, then beginning to fuck firmly but gently, holding her cock on a tight leash, counting off the strokes. Twenty-five, that was all she would allow herself. Just twenty-five, and then she would withdraw and fuck the darkhair, and then the blonde, and then the redhead, and then she would return and fuck the best of the four to orgasm. Just twenty-five strokes and she would withdraw. She had to withdraw. After twenty-five strokes. After twenty-five strokes, damn you. Only twenty-five. I'm only allowing you twenty-five. Only twenty-five. Stop. *Stop*.

But it was no good. The crossing-guard's bowels were too tight, too moist, too juicy, too deliciously cold and pleasure-prolonging, and her cock galloped at them, getting faster, deeper, a thickly veined marrow sliding in and out of the quivering arsehole to the grunts and moans of the crossing-guard.

'Ah. Please. Ah. *Generalissima*. Please. No. Stop. *Generalissima*. Please. Please.'

She couldn't stop. Nothing would convince her cock that anything could be better than this, that one of the white unbuggered arses beside her might offer greater pleasure, tighter, moister, juicier, silkier walls, a more delicious, more pleasure-prolonging cold, and just the thought of the three unbuggered arses made buggering this one more pleasurable, just as a glutton guzzling doughnuts feels his mouth water even more at the thought of guzzling cream cakes.

'*Gener–* ah. *Generalissima*,' the crossing-guard said. 'Please. Please. Naah. Ah. Aaah.' Because she was feeling pleasure now too, her senses gorging themselves on the thick cock churning in her tight arse.

The slut. The little slut. She could feel the arse-walls straining to tighten, to clench on her working cock, to reward the buggerer so that the buggeree was buggered more thoroughly, so that she was flooded more thickly with warm spunk. And she was succeeding. The walls were tighter, the arse clenching on her as she drove herself at it, and that was enough, finally enough. Her final thrust stuttered and faltered, her ears buzzing and vision clouded with orgasm, and she began to come, thick spunk spurting deep inside the crossing-guard's cold bowels. She could hear the crossing-guard babbling thanks, praising her for the warmth and thickness of her spunk, and managed to grunt out a final spurt. There. She was buggered. Virgin-Arse no more.

She slid her cock out of the arse with a juicy squelch and pop and stepped back, knees trembling, feeling exhausted. Look at it. It was gaping now too, its rim reddened, looking inflamed and tender, oozing slime. Both the crossing-guards had been buggered. Good. She looked at the three unbuggered guards, the redhead, the blonde, the darkhair, bending forwards, presenting their white firm buttocks and pink virgin arseholes to her, and was unmoved by them, her cock softening and drooping, smeared with semen and rectal mucus, stained with curry powder. Christ. She wondered if beating them with the belt would re-erect her and thought no, it wasn't possible. Not so soon. Nothing would re-erect her for hours. She was all shagged out. Still, it wouldn't hurt to try. Or at least, it wouldn't hurt her. She reached behind herself and slipped the belt out of her trousers, gripping it by the buckle, and swung it, making it swish.

'Right, girls. Who's first?'

No answer. Hardly surprising really. There was a tremor in the right knee-hollow of the freshly buggered crossing-guard, just visible above the loose crumpled ring of her trousers.

'You, Slut-Bum?' she asked. 'Or you, Curry-Bum? It will be the full ten for you, I'm afraid, my dear, because there's no way I'm licking cherries out of your arse. But I think I'll leave you till later. So how about you, Ginger? Or you, Darky? Snowy? Eh? Cat got your tongues, girls? Well, I'll have to decide for myself then, and I think . . . hmmm . . . *you*, Snowy. Yes, you. So brace yourself, girl. Ten minus six equals four. Four strokes.'

73

Now the blonde's right knee-hollow had started to tremble and, as she walked behind her and positioned herself, a delicate shiver ran through the skin of the blonde's buttocks. A fear-shiver. She swished the belt, not quite comfortable with it yet. Maybe. Yes, this felt better. She looped the buckle-end of the belt around her hand and swished again. Yes, much better. More secure. She could swing it harder now, land it more cruelly on the cringing buttocks in front of her. Another experimental swish and she was ready, shifting her feet apart, rocking her shoulders to relax them. Then she drew the belt back, taking a deep breath, then fed the weight of her upper body into it as it leaped forwards like a giant tongue, eager to lick at the creamy mounds of the blonde's buttocks.

Thwak. It landed with a juicy spurt of sound underplayed with the blonde's involuntary grunt of pain, and she heard the echoes of it rolling back minutely from the flats and the shopfronts. And look, there, on the white buttocks, a broad red track, the lick of a giant leather tongue, seething and singing into the blonde's arse-flesh. She took another deep breath, timing the filling of her lungs to the backswing, held it for a moment, then let it hiss out of her mouth as she swung forwards again, lashing the belt at the red track on the buttocks, almost allowing herself to overbalance as the belt crashed juicily home. *Thwak*. Another involuntary grunt of pain from the blonde, more minute echoes from the flats and shopfronts, and the broad red track on the white buttocks was broader and redder, almost beginning to glow.

Again. *Thwak*. The blonde cried out loudly this time and she felt her cock, impossibly, stir and begin to stiffen slowly as she stared, panting, at the broad red track on the white buttocks, barely broader this time, but definitely redder.

Again. *Thwak*. Another cry of pain from the blonde, another jerk upwards from her cock. She snorted, shaking her head, breathing hard. Four strokes. That was enough. Who next? Slut-Bum. The freshly buggered crossing-guard. She stepped behind her, positioning herself. Ten minus seven equals three. Three strokes. She looked down at her cock. This would stiffen it fully. She would be up and ready to bugger again. To bugger or be sucked.

She rocked her shoulders, twisted her head left and right, swung the belt back, paused, lashed it forwards. *Thwak*. Another juicy spurt of sound, echoing from the flats and the shopfronts. *Thwak*. Marking and reddening the white buttocks. *Thwak*. And yes, her cock was stiff again, jutting forwards, prodding blindly at the air, eager for fresh arse or mouth. Or cunt? Fresh cunt? Tight, hot, juicy cunt? As she walked back along the line of bending guards to stand behind the redhead she noticed that the shell-halves of the blonde's cunt had pouted and when she sniffed she caught a fragment of spice on the air. Hot yelm. Oozing between the blonde's cunt-lips, provoked by the seething glow in her buttocks.

She positioned herself behind the redhead, swung the belt back, lashed it forwards. *Thwak*. Three again. And then three for the darkhair. *Thwak*. Then ten for the crossing-guard she had buggered first. Poor little bitch. *Thwak*. How much she was having to suffer for pissing in the gutter. She walked back along the line, and positioned herself behind the darkhair, glancing at the freshly buggered crossing-guard's cunt. Yes. That had pouted too, the thick lips gaping with pleasure from the belting she had received, from the seething glow in her buttocks.

Thwak. She lashed the belt hard at the darkhair's white buttocks, hoping to hear her cry out on the first stroke. No. Just the involuntary grunt of pain. But maybe. *Thwak*. No, not second time lucky. So – *Thwak*. No, and she had really swung viciously that time, sending the belt whistling forwards, rewarded with nothing more than a third and final involuntary grunt. And the broad red track on the buttocks, of course. Which would seethe and sing into her, loosening and juicing her cunt-lips, levering them apart. While Curry-Bum received ten strokes. Ten strokes of the belt. The poor little bitch.

She walked to stand behind Curry-Bum, shrugging her shoulders, relaxing her muscles. She would have to pace it. Swing the belt steadily and firmly. Not overdo it on the first few strokes, so that she left something in reserve for a final fusillade, just when Curry-Bum thought she had suffered the worst. Oh, yes.

So, to begin. She swung the belt back, paused, lashed it forwards. *Thwak*. One grunt. Ten minus one was nine. So nine more to go. *Thwak*. Two grunts. Well, she'd be crying out by the third. Eight more to go. *Thwak*. Or the fourth. Seven more to go. *Thwak*. Yes. She had. She had cried out softly. Good. Next time. *Thwak*. Yes, it had been louder. The poor little bitch must really be suffering now. *Thwak*. There were still four to go. Time for the fusillade, fast, firm, merciless strokes, heaping pain into the red-slashed buttocks and holding it there. Ready. Steady. Go. *Thwak*. *Thwak*. *Thwak*. *Thwak*.

She let the belt hang loose in her hand, panting, eyes fixed on the abused buttocks ahead of her. Poor little bitch. She could hear her moaning with pain, buttocks quivering and jerking as she clenched and relaxed them, trying to squeeze the sensations of the belting out of them. No good, dearest. No good at all. You'll have to endure it. And it will get worse. Soon you'll have to endure the shame of the effect it's having on you. Of the way it's making your cunt loosen and ooze, swelling and parting your cunt-lips the way it's already made the cunts of all the others swell and part, already made their cunt-lips loosen and ooze and scent the air with yelm-spice.

Yes, she knew what she wanted now. For her seventh ejaculation of the day she wanted to come inside a cunt. But whose? Whose to choose? The redhead's? The blonde's? The freshly buggered crossing-guard's? The darkhair's? Curry-Bum's? One cunt must be best, tightest and hottest, offering the finest pleasures, but she knew that the first she sampled would be the last: she would not be able to restrain herself and she would fuck it to orgasm the way she had fucked the second crossing-guard's arse to orgasm.

Ah, what a delicious dilemma. Five fine furry cunts, hot and tight and oozing with yelm, and she had to find the best knowing that as soon as she started fucking one she would end up spunking inside it. What to do? Could she just use her fingers? Would her fingers be enough to tell her whose was best, whose tightest, whose slickest and hottest? Or might her fingers mislead her? Could she truly read the fleshy lips and silken cunt-walls with her fingers as she would with her cock? Might she choose the second-best with her fingers and cock-fuck it while the best sat nearby, uninvaded, its juicy walls kissing only each other? Or might her fingers even choose the third-best, the third-worst? The fourth-best, the second-worst? The fifth-best, the worst of all?

She began to put her belt back on, circling the problem, poking at it with her mind the way she would have poked at a troublesome tooth with her tongue, reading it, determining where the pain was worst, where perhaps it had began to loosen and could be gently rocked loose. The heart of the problem was her lack of self-control. If she could sample all the cunts one by one with her cock, austerely restricting herself to a dozen or even a half-dozen strokes in each, she could decide which one suited her best. Or which ones. And then conduct a play-off. But she knew that as soon as she began to fuck one, it would be all over: she would fuck it to orgasm and never know what she might have missed in the other four. Lack of self-control. That was the key. As though she were – yes, as though she were Odysseus, planning to sail past the Isle of Sirens, wishing to hear their voices yet knowing that if he did he would lose all self-control and throw himself into the sea to swim eagerly to sacrifice himself to them.

And how had wise Odysseus cracked the conundrum? By having his men first strap him to the mast and then, their ears packed with silencing wax, row the ship past the Isle of Hungry Sisters while their captain, stung to madness by the honey-sweet voices, had raged and blasphemed, shouting to be released, writhing futilely in his bonds. How clever, how cunning. Wise Odysseus indeed. But how could she adapt his plan to her own situation? How could she sample cunts, the way he had sampled the voices of the Sirens, and yet not succumb to the danger therein: being provoked to orgasm the way he would have been provoked to self-destruction? Hmmmm. Her cock had begun to soften as she concentrated on the problem and she folded it back inside her trousers and zipped up. Let's see now. Let's just see. She looked towards the shops, then back at the row of bending young women, the red-striped buttocks, pondering. Yes, they'll be safe enough while I see what I can find.

She strolled towards the shops, looking up and down the row. Newsagent's. Florist's. Butcher's. Video rental. Bank. Video rental. Butcher's. Florist's. Yes, florist's. If what she could see in the window was what she thought it was, it was time to pay a visit to the florist's.

A bell jangled as she pushed the door open and stepped into cool, faintly moist air, her nose tickled by floral scents and pollens. There were great banks of flowers and ferns in front of her, half-screening a tiny counter at the back of the shop, and in one corner, near the window, was a set of wrought-iron garden furniture: two chairs and a table, painted white and decorated with elaborate baroque curlicues and arabesques. There were large stickers on the furniture, OLTSO VE-HRECGÍN!, and crossed-out high prices with lower prices substituted. Yes. Good.

She closed the door behind her and a woman appeared at the counter, slipping through from a curtained doorway behind, white-smocked and still wearing long yellow plastic gloves, as though she had come fresh from a rear workshop, separating roots, mixing compost, snipping flower-heads. She strode down the shop towards the woman, spurs jingling, boots clacking on the floor, hearing the long sigh of air-conditioning and busy trickles of water. The woman raised her eyebrows and smiled. Another darkhair, small, slim, pale-skinned, but with large breasts mounded beneath her white smock. Did she have wellingtons on too? Green wellingtons? Her cock stirred in her trousers, slowly beginning to rethicken with blood.

'Good morning. I'd like to buy one of your chairs and some flowers.'

The woman nodded.

'Certainly,' she said. 'Did you have any particular varieties in mind?'

Her cock thickened faster, straining forwards at her zip. She resisted the urge to finger at the bulge. Such a smooth, quiet voice.

'Lilies,' she said.

'Just lilies?'

She thought for a moment.

'Yes. Just lilies.'

'And how many would you like?'

She thought for a moment again, performing mental arithmetic. Five times six, five more for good luck.

'Thirty-five.'

'Not thirty-seven?'

She frowned a little.

'No. thirty-five is fine.'

'Very well, thirty-five lilies and one garden chair.'

The woman walked along the counter to the till and punched in numbers.

'That will be one hundred and twenty-six pounds and ninety-nine pence,' she said.

She reached inside her jacket pocket for the banknotes. One of the larger ones would cover it. Cover it easily. Five hundred thousand. Yes. But the woman was shaking her head.

'I'm sorry, but we can't accept Euros.'

'It's not a Euro.'

She dropped it on the counter.

'Look.'

The woman barely glanced at it. Her smile was ironic now. Contemptuous.

'No? Then we can't accept that either.'

Her cock unfurled the final inch, fully erect, straining at her zip. She dripped her left hand to it, fingering it openly as she put her right hand into her breast pocket and took out the whistle.

'You can't accept it?'

The woman shrugged and shook her head, not even bothering to reply, looking bored now. She put the whistle to her lips and blew, watching the woman's face. Her nostrils quivered for a moment, as though she had snorted disbelievingly, beginning to organise memories for the tale she would tell later in the day. *Some female lunatic in uniform from the new government. Expected me to accept some ludicrous new currency. I soon put her in her place, I can tell you.*

She lowered the whistle, ears still singing. Outside, in the sunshine, her loyal troops would be hoisting their trousers, buttoning, picking up their caps, settling them on their heads, forming a line, marching swiftly to their *Generalissima*'s aid. She half-turned, so that she could look towards the door but still see the shop assistant out of the corner of her eye. One, two, thr–

The door of the florist's crashed back, its glass splintering in two, no in three places, and yes, the shop assistant had jumped with fright, her hand going up to her mouth. Boots hammered on the floor, then crashed in perfect synchrony as the guards came to attention in a line.

'What is the problem, *Generalissima*?' said the redhead.

She nodded at the shop assistant.

'This insolent bitch,' she said. 'She won't accept my money.'

'Again, *Generalissima*?'

'Yes, again.'

'And your orders, *Generalissima*?'

She looked at the shop assistant while she spoke, sardonically observing the effect of her words.

'Trash the shop. Strip this insolent little bitch and tie her over the counter. Leave her gloves and wellingtons on, if she's wearing any. When you have done that, I will have further orders.'

81

'At once, *Generalissima*!'

The boots crashed; the forearms jerked forwards in cock-salute, and she stepped back as they went to work. The shop assistant had listened with growing fright, small white teeth gnawing once at the knuckle of her hand. Then, as the boots crashed against the floor, she cried out, spun around and ran through the curtained doorway. The redhead and blonde were after her at once. They vaulted the counter easily and ran through the doorway after her. The blonde paused for a moment to wrench the curtains loose, laughing with the pleasure of destruction, wrenching harder as a scream sounded beyond the alcove. The redhead had already got hold of the shop assistant. The curtains tore away and the blonde hurried to join in the fun.

There was a crash from behind her. She turned from the counter and saw that the crossing-guards had thrown one of the garden chairs through the window. The darkhair was trashing the racks of plants, overturning them, lifting pots high in the air before dashing them to the floor, boots stamping briskly at the shattered remains before she went on to the next. The air was thicker with scents already, filled with the rich, almost chocolatey smell of humus.

The crossing-guards joined the darkhair, tugging pots down from the racks, ripping off leaves and flowers. Screams sounded again from the back-room and she turned back to the counter to see the redhead carrying the shop assistant back through the doorway, hoisted over her shoulder, small fists beating in futile indignation on the black uniform, and yes, green wellingtons kicking and swinging. The blonde stepped through the doorway after her carrying a roll of twine that she tossed on to the counter ready for use. The redhead slipped the shop assistant off her shoulder, standing her upright, and she and the blonde set to work, stripping her, tearing the white smock off her to expose pink and filmy silk underwear, knickers and a bra that strained over the large breasts. She watched, her mouth drying, cock straining harder in her trousers. The knickers came down, the shop assistant struggling, trying to keep her legs together to hide the neat black triangle of her pubis, and then the bra was wrenched off to further screams and pleas for mercy, the shop assistant trying to shield her breasts with her hands.

She was stripped, stripped naked but for her yellow gloves and green wellingtons. Now for the tying over the counter. The blonde picked up the twine again as the redhead pushed the naked shop assistant towards the counter. The redhead looked towards her *Generalissima* for a moment, coppery eyebrows raised, and she made a circular motion with her forefinger. The other way around. Arse facing up in the shop, towards the window. The redhead nodded and began to force the shop assistant over the counter. The blonde was biting off lengths of twine with small, sharp teeth, watching jealously as the redhead tugged the shop assistant into position, then clambered up on the counter with her, spread-eagling her over it and holding her down with a knee in her back. Her wellingtons were still kicking, one of them almost off. The blonde, moved from behind the counter, kneeled and pushed it back on before looping twine around the rubber ankle and tightening it hard. The counter had four little legs and the blonde moved from one to the other, tying the feet securely into place, then the gloved hands, so the redhead could slip off the counter at last, panting and flushed, leaving the shop assistant spread-eagled helpless across the counter, breasts crushed to the counter-top, legs apart, pink pussy-lips exposed and pouting, firm white arse quivering as she struggled vainly to free herself. The blonde and redhead stood shoulder to shoulder and saluted, panting and flushed.

'We have finished, *Generalissima*.'

She nodded, flicking off a salute in reply.

'Good girls.'

She jerked and turned as another heavy pot crashed to the floor behind her. One side of the shop was already trashed and the crossing-guards and darkhair were beginning on the other, overturning the racks, smashing pots.

'Girls! Girls! That's enough. Enough, I said.'

Panting, they obeyed her, boots filthy with soil, the palms of their hands streaked green with torn and twisted leaves.

'Good girls. Now, Curry-Bum and Darky, hand me some lilies. Slut-Bum, moisten this little bitch's arsehole with your tongue. Snowy and Ginger, you can hold the cheeks of her arse apart. Lilies, girls. The white flowers. Over there, look.'

She pointed where the lilies were bunched in the unwrecked section of the shop. The blonde and redhead moved forwards to them.

'I don't know. Don't they teach you anything in school these days?'

She turned back to watch the blonde and redhead tugging the shop assistant's buttocks apart and the second-buggered crossing-guard take off her cap and put it on the counter before lowering her face between the buttocks and beginning to work at the arsehole with her tongue. The shop assistant jerked and stiffened as the tongue touched her arse, then started to struggle, swearing loudly.

'Gag her, Snowy. Use her knickers.'

The blonde stooped and picked up the shop assistant's filmy pink knickers, then gagged her, smiling cruelly as she tugged them hard around the small head and knotted them into place. The boots of the first-buggered crossing-guard and the darkhair sounded on the floor behind her and she turned as they marched to her, arms full of lilies.

'Good girls.'

She slid a lily out of the darkhair's arms and turned back to the counter and the spread-eagled shop assistant. The second-buggered crossing-guard's head was still bobbing between the cheeks of her arse as she licked the arsehole thoroughly.

'Is it moistened, Slut-Bum?'

The crossing-guard lifted her head from the arse-cleft.

'I think so, *Generalissima*.'

'Don't think so, know so. Spit into it. Really work at it with your tongue.'

She heard the second-buggered crossing-guard spit, then watched her drop her head into the arse-cleft again. She waited a few seconds, then asked, 'Moistened now, Slut-Bum?'

'Yes, *Generalissima*.'

'Good. Then stand aside.'

The crossing-guard lifted her head, straightened and stood aside. The blonde and redhead let go of the white buttocks and started to move aside too.

'No, Snowy, Ginger, you stay where you are. Keep those buttocks well apart.'

They stepped back, taking hold of the buttocks again, tugging them apart. She walked forwards with the lily.

'What a sweet little bottom this is. And oh, what a very sweet little bottom-hole. Look at it, everyone. Isn't it sweet?'

Someone suppressed a snigger and they chorused dutifully.

'Yes, *Generalissima*.'

'It's so pink and tiny. Isn't it?'

'Yes, *Generalissima*.'

'Don't your mouths water just looking at it?'

'Yes, *Generalissima*.'

'As does mine, girls. As does mine. But I think it lacks a certain something. A certain *je ne sais quoi*. Can any of you suggest what it is?'

Silence for a moment.

'A cock, *Generalissima*?'

The darkhair.

'Well, girls?' she said. 'What do you think? Do you think this dainty pink arsehole lacks a cock?'

'Yes, *Generalissima*,' two or three of them said.

She tutted with disappointment.

'Oh, girls. I'm ashamed for you. How crude. How very crude. What a very revealing insight that is into your barbarous lack of refinement. Really, such a suggestion makes me think you can have no soul at all. No conception of beauty. So come on, think again. What might it be that this dainty pink arsehole lacks?'

Silence, then hesitantly:

'A finger, *Generalissima*?'

The blonde.

'That is better, Snowy, a *little* better, but I still feel it is crude and unrefined. Try again.'

More silence.

'A flower, *Generalissima*?'

The redhead.

'What was that, Ginger?'

'A flower, *Generalissima*.'

'Ah, very good, Ginger. A flower. Now, yes, I like that. Most suitable. But still, just a flower? *Any* old flower? Darky, what do you think?'

'Perhaps a lily, *Generalissima*?'

'But of course! A *lily*. And look, by the most marvellous coincidence, what is this I have in my hand right here?'

'A lily, *Generalissima*.'

'Is that right, girls?'

'Yes, *Generalissima*.'

'Good. Very good. So, we've decided. What this dainty pink arsehole lacks is a lily. And why should it continue to lack when the means of fulfilment is so ready to hand? I see no reason at all.'

She stepped forwards, lifting the lily, fingering the blunt, thick stem, juicy and green. The shop assistant's arse-dell was glistening with the crossing-guard's spittle but would the arsehole admit the stem? Could she slide it deep enough for the flower to sit upright? Only one way to find out. She put the stem into the arse-dell and pushed. For a moment the arsehole resisted and then, with a squeak from the shop assistant, the stem slipped inside. She pushed it deeper, turning it so that the lily was presented to best advantage. There. Would it stay upright? She took her hand away cautiously. Yes. It stayed upright, a white lily sprouting from the shop assistant's arse-hole. But still.

'What do you think, girls? Does it look right?'

'Yes, *Generalissima*.'

'Are you sure? Absolutely sure? Snowy?'

'No, *Generalissima*. I think perhaps it still lacks something.'

'I'm inclined to agree with you. But what? Ginger? Darky?'

The darkhair licked her lips.

'Perhaps another lily, *Generalissima*?'

'Perfect. Absolutely perfect. I take back all I said about your lack of refinement. That is a perfect suggestion. Absolutely perfect. Another lily.'

She turned and plucked one from the bunch held by the first-buggered crossing-guard, then bent over the shop assistant's quivering buttocks, lowered the stem of the new lily into her arse-dell and started to insert it beside the stem already planted in the moistened arsehole.

'Now,' she said, 'I'll have to careful but – Yeees. Yes. Good.'

She leaned back, smiling. The new lily was planted firmly in the shop assistant's arse.

'What do you think, girls? Good?'

'Yes, *Generalissima*.'

'I agree. It looks good. But let's just see . . .'

She stepped to the left, tilting her head, then to the right, tilting her head the opposite way, then tutted.

'Oh dear. It does look good from *certain* angles but from others I'm afraid, well, it's just a touch lopsided. Don't you think? From this angle? And I'd imagine it's the same from behind the counter. Snowy?'

'Yes, *Generalissima*.'

'It looks a touch lopsided?'

'Yes, *Generalissima*.'

'Oh dear, I thought I was right. But what to do?'

'Another lily, *Generalissima*?'

'Snowy, I believe you've hit on it. With *three* lilies it will look good from every angle. A symmetrical anal floral display. So . . .'

She turned back to the darkhair and first-buggered crossing-guard, ticking her hand in front of her like a pendulum, then chose a lily from the bunch being held by the darkhair.

'OK, now, this might be little difficult but . . .'

The arse-dell was crowded now and the arsehole was stretched with the two lilies it was already holding. Would she be able to slip a third in too? It would be very uncomfortable for the poor little bitch:

three thick lily stems up one small arsehole. Still, one must suffer for one's art. At least, someone must suffer. And yes, the third one just managed to slip in, stretching the poor arsehole even further. She slid it deeper, rotating it slightly, adjusting it to the other two lilies. Was that OK? She let go of it and stepped back, tilting her head from side to side, then stepped right, looked, then left, looked. Yes. It was OK. More than OK: perfect. White lilies sprouting from a pink arsehole in a white bottom above smooth white thighs open on a pink-lipped cunt and black pubic hair. Deliciously minimalist.

She looked around at the guards.

'Well, girls? What do you think? Symmetrical now?'

'Yes, *Generalissima*.'

'Sure now? Look carefully.'

They looked carefully, tilting their heads from side to side, saying slowly in ones and twos: 'Yes, *Generalissima*. Yes, *Generalissima*.'

'Good. I agree with you. This time, it *is* perfect. But you know, I have the funniest feeling that someone doesn't appreciate the trouble I've taken with the arrangement. Can you think who it might be? Yes, Ginger?'

The redhead had raised her hand.

'Could it be her, *Generalissima*? The shop assistant?'

'The person who doesn't appreciate my efforts, you mean?'

'Yes, *Generalissima*.'

'Well, to be honest, I think you're right. She *doesn't* appreciate my efforts. Look at her. She's still struggling, even now, and I bet she's saying the most awful things into the gag.'

'There's no pleasing some people, *Generalissima*.'

'True, Ginger. Sadly but certainly true. But I can rest secure in the knowledge that I did my best. Now, there's –'

She broke off, flicking at her lower lip with two gloved fingers.

'Or have I? Have I done my best? Have I really and truly done my best to please this unworthy shop assistant?'

'Why not pissy-whip her, *Generalissima*?'

She turned. It was the darkhair.

'Whatty-whip her, Darky?'

'Pissy-whip, *Generalissima*. With your pistol. It's like pussy-whipping, only with a pistol.'

She clapped her gloved hands softly.

'Marvellous, Darky. What a marvellous suggestion. Pissy-whip her. Why didn't I think of that? Right, I'll do it immediately.'

She dropped her hand to her hip to unbutton the holster, but it was not there. What the fuck? Oh yeah, she'd taken it off when she'd taken her belt off. It was outside on the pavement.

'Darky, just put your lilies down and trot and get my holster, will you? It's outside on the pavement.'

'At once, *Generalissima*.'

'Good girl. Yes, Snowy?'

The blonde had her hand raised now.

'And couldn't we piss in her wellingtons too, *Generalissima*? So it was even more of a pissy-whipping?'

The door rattled as the darkhair went out to get the holster.

'An excellent idea, Snowy. But it might be a little difficult to piss directly into them. Tell you what, you rustle up a flowerpot or a bowl or something and you can all piss into that, then we'll tip the results into her boots. How'd you like the sound of that?'

'It sounds very good, *Generalissima*.'

'You're right. It does.'

The door rattled as the darkhair came back in. She turned to her.

'Thank you, Darky.'

She strapped the holster back on to her belt and unbuttoned it. The blonde had gone into the room behind the counter; now she re-emerged, carrying a clear plastic bowl, unbuttoning her trousers.

'Good girl,' she told her, then turned back to the darkhair. 'Darky, while you were outside Snowy here had the most marvellous idea. To make it even more of a pissy-whipping, you're all going to piss into that bowl and then tip it down her wellingtons once I've finished with her. OK?'

'Yes, *Generalissima*.'

The blonde had walked from behind the counter and put the bowl on the floor. She tugged her trousers down and squatted over it, peering behind herself to see that she was positioned right.

'May I, *Generalissima*?'

'Be my guest, Snowy. Piss at will.'

She slid her pildo out as the blonde started to piss. The clear yellow stream landed in the bowl with a low hiss at first, then spluttered as the bottom of the bowl filled. The redhead was loosening her trousers too, ready to piss next. She pointed the pildo in front of her and pulled the trigger. Bzzz. Bzzz. Good. Now to get to work. She walked to the counter and lifted the pildo between the shop assistant's legs, setting the bulbous muzzle to the lower juncture of her cunt-lips, just where they joined with the perineum. She would start here and work her way up the cunt to the clitoris, firing at will.

Beside her on the floor the blonde had finished pissing and stepped away from the bowl. She could smell warm piss spiced with yelm. The redhead tugged her trousers down and squatted over the bowl, checking that she was positioned right. She waited and then pulled the trigger of the pildo, timing the buzz of it to the splutter of the redhead's piss in the bowl. The second-buggered crossing-guard was loosening her trousers, ready to piss next. She hummed happily, working the pildo slowly higher on the shop assistant's helpless cunt, noting with satisfaction the way the cunt-lips were responding, were uncurling and moistening. Maybe you can please everyone, some of the time. The redhead stopped pissing with a final brisk spurt and splutter and got off the bowl. The first-buggered crossing-guard took her place, starting to piss at once.

'Oi!' the redhead said angrily. She felt something splatter on her boots and looked down, frowning. The crossing-guard hadn't bothered to check her position properly and was pissing on to the edge of the bowl, piss spraying up and around her. Blushing, the crossing-guard shuffled backwards, the clear yellow stream of her piss falling directly into the partly filled bowl now, churning its surface with a low *hash*.

'You know what that means, don't you, dear?' she told her, and returned her attention to the shop assistant's cunt, pissy-whipping it, slowly sliding the bulbous buzzing muzzle of the pildo higher and higher, trying to time its arrival on the shop assistant's clitoris with maximum arousal in the cunt-lips, with maximum juiciness and oozing of yelm.

The first-buggered crossing-guard finished pissing and got off the bowl, replaced immediately by the darkhair, who looked carefully behind her before beginning to piss. She sniffed happily. Warm girl-piss falling into a clear plastic bowl, briefly churned to bubbles. Yelm from a warm aroused cunt, oozing thickly under slow, careful pleasuring.

And look, the lilies were quivering almost like flags as the muscles in the shop assistant's arse tightened with on-coming orgasm. The darkhair got off the bowl and the second-buggered crossing-guard took her place. She glanced at the bowl. Nearly full now, and through the transparent side of the bowl she could see the stream of the crossing-guard's piss falling into the piss that was already there, creating a slanting line of bubbles. She looked back at the shop assistant's cunt and the lilies. Yes. They were quivering almost continuously now. She was near orgasm. A single shot fired directly at her clitoris would do it. But let's just wait a few more moments. The crossing-guard stopped pissing and got off the bowl. That was everyone. The bowl was full almost to brimming, ready to be tipped into the shop assistant's wellingtons. And now was as good a time as any.

'Snowy,' she said. 'You and Ginger lift the bowl and get ready to tip it when I give the order. I think it will be a nice little touch to tip the bowl just as she starts coming, don't you?'

'Yes, *Generalissima*.'

'Good. Get ready then. Two of you mind, and be careful not to spill any. Curry-Bum, while they're getting in position, you can just get down on your hands and knees and lick my boots clean. You pissed on them, you can clean them up. Right?'

'Yes, *Generalissima*.'

The first-buggered crossing-guard started to walk towards her.

'No, get down on your hands and knees where you are and crawl to me.'

'Yes, *Generalissima*.'

The crossing-guard did as she was told, while the blonde and redhead carefully lifted the bowl and carried it to the shop assistant's right wellington. The crossing-guard arrived at her boots, lowered her face to them and started to lick.

'Does the leader taste nice?'

The head shook.

'You've only yourself to blame. Get on with it.'

She lifted the pildo for the last time. One shot to the clitoris and the shop-assistant would be coming like a train. Just soften her up a bit first with – bzzz, bzzz – a few shots to the cunt-lips.

'Are you ready? Snowy? Ginger?'

'Yes, *Generalissima*.'

She looked at the lilies. They were quivering, the white flesh of the flowers rubbing together juicily. Time for the clit-shot. She reached deeper between the shop assistant's thighs, angling the muzzle of the pildo for the clitoris.

'On three,' she told the blonde and redhead.

The bowl of warm piss was poised above the shop assistant's wellington, ready to be poured inside.

'One. Two. Three.'

She pressed the muzzle of the pildo firmly into place, pulled the trigger and held it down. Bzzzzzzz. The lilies vibrated strongly as though in sympathy with the pildo, almost blurring, and she saw the shop assistant's cunt squeeze tight in on itself as though the lips were kissing each other for joy. Muscles were writhing and twisting in the shop assistant's buttocks and back and tendons stood out clearly down the backs of her thighs. The little beast was coming hard, groaning into her own warm, spittle-soaked knickers. There was a funny little noise from the wellington that the blonde and redhead were pouring piss into, a long *kluuurp* rising in pitch. She realised what it meant and relaxed her finger on the trigger of the pildo.

'Look out, it's filling up. Do the other one.'

At her feet, the darkhair had finished licking one boot and started on the other. But there was no piss on that one. Too much zeal, girl. The blonde and redhead stopped pouring piss into the shop assistant's right wellington and carried the bowl around behind her and the kneeling darkhair to the shop assistant's left wellington. She looked at the shop assistant's cunt. It looked as though it was smirking toothlessly on a mouthful of sweets, as thick clear spittle ran from it. The blonde and redhead reached the other wellington boot and started pouring and the long *kluuurp* started again, slowly rising in pitch as the wellington filled with piss. She shuffled her boots impatiently.

'That's enough, Curry-Bum. Snowy and Ginger, if there's any left, tip it over her back then join us outside. The rest of you, come on. No, forget about the lilies. I've decided we don't need them any more.'

She slipped her pildo back into its holster and buttoned it up, then turned and strode from the shop. The shop assistant wouldn't be forgetting this little visit in a hurry. She fingered the bulge in her trousers. But why bother with the door when half the window had been put through? She stepped out of it over the splinters of glass that still jutted upwards in the lower frame. The chair that had smashed the window had cleared the pavement and was lying on its side on the street. Christ, they must have thrown it hard. She turned and stood on the pavement, watching the guards follow her out, stepping through the broken window. Darky, Curry-Bum, Slut-Bum. Snowy and Ginger would be next. Had there been any piss left in the bowl to tip on the shop assistant's back? She hoped so. Yes, here they were. Snowy and Ginger. They all lined up on the pavement in front of her.

'Good girls,' she told them, fingering the bulge in her trousers. 'Very good girls. I'm proud of you all. You acquitted yourself with exemplary coolness and courage in the face of the enemy.'

They were all watching her crotch now, like good girls should, of course. She squeezed it hard, watching the redhead lick her lips surreptitiously. Maybe the blonde too. The darkhair and second-buggered crossing-guard didn't bother to conceal it. She gave her crotch a long squeeze.

'And so, girls,' she said. 'I've decided to award you all a medal. A very special medal. Can you guess what it is? Snowy?'

The blue eyes raised to hers, then dropped back to her cockbulge.

'The Victoria Cross, *Generalissima*?'

'No, Snowy, not the Victoria Cross. But you're thinking on vaguely the right lines. Carry on. Someone else.'

'The Distinguished Service Medal, *Generalissima*?'

'No, Ginger. Not that either. I don't mind giving you a clue, so remember that those are both *British* medals. Perhaps you should try something from overseas.'

'The Iron Cross, *Generalissima*?'

'Oh, Darky. Darky. Don't go there. Don't even think of going there. Try again. Think a *long* way overseas. Or over*sea*. And wounded in action.'

She gave her crotch a final squeeze and took hold of the zip.

'An English-speaking country, *Generalissima*?'

'Yes, Snowy. An English-speaking country.'

She started to pull the zip down, slowly. Five pairs of eyes widened, shining as they watched.

'Concentrate on your suggestions, girls.'

Her zip was down. She reached inside her trousers, groping ostentatiously for her stiff cock.

'The Purple Heart, *Generalissima*?'

'*Excellent* suggestion, Curry-Bum. You're very, very nearly there. Does this give you the final clue?'

She slid her cock out and slowly thumbed back the foreskin, while the first-buggered crossing-guard watched wide-eyed, licking her lips, then raised her eyes to meet hers.

'The Purple Helmet, *Generalissima*?'

'Yes, Curry-Bum. Exactly so. The Purple Helmet. A very special award, for each one of you. Yes, Snowy?'

The blonde had her hand raised.

'But we haven't been wounded in action, *Generalissima*.'

'Haven't you, Snowy? Then tell me, all of you, is it not true that each of you –' she began to lower her voice, watching them lean forwards frowning a little '– between her thighs, carries –' her voice was barely a whisper now '– a gash?'

No response. She let the silence lengthen a moment or two or three longer.

'Well?' she said at normal volume.

Their necks straightened.

'Yes, *Generalissima*,' they chorused.

'I thought so. And as for *other* wounds, I doubt that Curry- and Slut-Bum would agree with you, Snowy. Well, do you, my dears? Curry-Bum?'

The first-buggered crossing-guard blushed, looking down at the pavement.

'No, *Generalissima*.'

'You, Slut-Bum?'

The second-buggered crossing-guard shifted from boot to boot, avoiding her eyes.

'No, *Generalissima*.'

'You see, Snowy? I think being buggered counts as a definite wound, as you would, if it had happened to you. And it nearly did, you know. In fact, I'm seriously contemplating performing it on you now.'

The blonde shivered delicately and stiffened.

'What do you think of that, eh?'

The blonde shivered again, then moistened her lips slowly.

'The *Generalissima* is always right, *Generalissima*,' she said in a low voice, her eyes lowered demurely.

She laughed.

'You little slut. You want it, don't you? Your tight arsehole is hungry for meat. Well, it can remain hungry. The Purple Helmet will not be awarded to arses on this occasion, girls, it will be awarded to cunts. So, Snowy and Ginger, get that chair set upright on the middle of the street. Curry-Bum, Slut-Bum, go into the butcher's and buy some strips of meat, about so wide by about so long.'

She indicated with her gloved hands.

'Here, this should cover it.'

She reached inside her jacket pocket and pulled out the roll of banknotes, peeling off two 1,000,000s and a 5,000,000. The first-buggered crossing-guard took them, asking, 'But what if she doesn't accept them, *Generalissima*?'

'Then take whatever steps are necessary, Curry-Bum.'

'Yes, *Generalissima*.'

They saluted, small white fists jutting in the sun-light, then turned and ran for the door of the butcher's. The blonde and redhead stooped over the garden chair, lifted it upright, carried it into the middle of the street and put it down.

'As for you, Darky,' she said. 'You can make sure I don't subside while I'm waiting.'

'I am to suck the *Generalissima*?'

'Yes, Darky. You are to suck the *Generalissima*.'

'Now, *Generalissima*?'

'Beware of insolence, Darky. It is not yet too late to change my mind and decide to award you the Purple Helmet intra-anally. You are not a big girl and I can promise you that it would be most painful.'

'The *Generalissima* is always right, *Generalissima*.'

'Yes. And the *Generalissima* wishes to be sucked. Now.'

'Yes, *Generalissima*.'

The darkhair walked in front of her and kneeled down, looking up at her.

'To orgasm, *Generalissima*?'

'No. You know very well that I do not wished to be sucked to orgasm. You are merely to retain the erection in optimum condition for the medal ceremony. No bobbing, no fancy tricks, just a straight-forward, slow-paced suck and lick.'

'As the *Generalissima* pleases.'

The small soft hand closed around her shaft, adjusting the cockhead. Warm moist breath puffed at it, once, twice, then the mouth slowly closed and began to suck. She breathed in hard through her nostrils and had to swallow before she could speak again.

'A straight-forward, slow-paced suck and lick. Nothing more.'

The darkhair mumbled something around her cock. It sounded like 'Yes, *Generalissima*.'

'Good girl,' she started to say, but she was interrupted by a sudden crash of breaking glass as something came through the window of the butcher's, landed on the street, bounced, then rolled irregularly to end up in the gutter on the far side. It was a sucking pig. The darkhair continued to suck as though nothing had happened, sliding her mouth slowly back and forth on her cock. She can concentrate, that girl, she surely can. Something heavy went over inside the butcher's and there were shouts of female anger and indignation, suddenly muffled, then cut off altogether. The crossing-guards were using their initiative. She heard boots on the tarmac next to her and looked to see the blonde and redhead returning from setting up the chair, jealousy ill-concealed in their faces as they avoided looking at the kneeling darkhair.

'Good girls,' she told them.

Something else went over inside the butcher's and more glass smashed. She heard one of the crossing-guards swear inside the shop and there was the sound of a firm blow landing on flesh. The darkhair sucked, unperturbed. More crashes, more smashing glass.

'Snowy, Ginger, go and see if they need help.'

'Yes, *Generalissima*.'

But even as they turned to obey the order the female voice began swearing inside the butcher's again and a boot was kicking out shards of glass still jutting from the frame of the butcher's window. The crossing-guards stepped out, grinning, long strips of raw, dripping meat hanging in their hands. The swearing continued in the shop behind them and there was the sound of someone struggling on the floor. Tied up. She wondered what the shop assistant inside the butcher's looked like and felt her cock throb in the darkhair's mouth. But no time for that now. It was nearly time for the medal ceremony instead. A Purple Helmet for each of her gallant girls. The crossing-guards stood to attention in front of her, smiles fading a little. They were jealous of the kneeling fellatrix too.

'Is it beef, girls?' she said.

The smiles strengthened.

'Yes, *Generalissima*.'

'Good. For fuck's sake, I can't hear myself think. One of you, go and shut that bitch in the butcher's up. Gag her with one of those strips of meat if you have to.'

'Yes, *Generalissima*.'

The second-buggered crossing-guard trotted to obey, stepping neatly back over the shards of glass. The voice continued for a moment more, then suddenly yelped and was cut off. A few seconds later the crossing-guard reappeared, grinning, stepping out through the window, and marched to stand in front of her again.

'Good girl. Now everything *is* ready. Darky. Darky dear. That's enough. You've kept me wonderfully stiff but now it's time for the medal to be awarded. Come on. Off you get. Snowy, Ginger, get her off.'

The blonde and redhead stepped eagerly to obey, gripping the darkhair's shoulders and tugging her gently backwards. She opened her eyes wonderingly, looking up.

'That's enough, dear. Time for the medal ceremony.'

The darkhair's mouth came off her cock reluctantly with a moist pop and the blonde and redhead hoisted the darkhair to her feet, her eyes fixed on the glistening head of her cock. The Purple Helmet. Due to be awarded to all five of them very shortly. Very shortly indeed.

'Good girl. Good *girls*. All five of you have, as I said, been most gallant today. Curry- and Slut-Bum have just once again shown exemplary courage and coolness in the face of the enemy, though I am sure I take nothing away from their achievement when I say that any two of you could have conducted themselves equally well. You are all worthy of the medal and you are all going to receive it. And so, if you would all follow me.'

She stepped on to the street and walked to the wrought-iron chair, tugging her gloves off. She tossed them on to the seat and began to unbutton her shirt. The guards lined up beside her, watching her. She slipped her arms out of her shirt and draped it over the back of the chair, and fingered her nipples for a moment. They were stiff too, like her cock. She bent over her boots, tugged them off one by one, propped them against the legs of the chair, then unbuttoned her trousers and slid them off. The guards' eyes were on her, wide and admiring, flickering between her cock and breasts, the nipples jutting up, stiff and lengthened like little echoes of her cock. She brushed the gloves off the seat of the chair and sat down. The iron was hard and cold beneath her arse and she slid herself to and fro on it for a moment, then bounced on it, making her cock jump between her thighs. She sat still and jerked her head at the line of guards.

'In front of me, girls, and I will explain how the ceremony will be conducted. Curry- and Slut-Bum, when I give the order you will bind me to the chair with those strips of meat. Hands and feet, tight. A little later, you will also blindfold me with one of the strips. In between, you will all chew pieces of meat and insert them in your ears. When you are ear-plugged and I am blindfolded, you will all strip completely and form an orderly line in *random* order. One by one, you will mount the chair and straddle me. When I nod, you will lower yourself on to my cock and take the Purple Helmet deep into your portable medal-case. You will conduct six squats to polish your Purple Helmet. Exactly six. I may try to suggest by some means that you are to continue. You will ignore this and perform exactly six squats. You will then return the Purple Helmet for polishing by the next in line. Do you understand?'

'Yes, *Generalissima*.'

'Good. Any questions?'

The redhead raised her hand.

'Yes, Ginger?'

'Even if you order us to continue, we don't?'

'You will not be in a position to receive direct orders, Ginger, because you will be ear-plugged with meat. I may suggest that you are to continue, with facial expressions or head-shaking. Whatever I do, you must ignore it. Exactly six squats. In this way, I can ensure that all of you receive the Purple Helmet. Is that clear?'

'Yes, *Generalissima*.'

'Good. Any more questions? Darky?'

'You said in random order, *Generalissima*. What did you mean, exactly?'

'I meant what I said. I must not know what order you receive your Purple Helmets in. That is why I will be blindfolded. When you have all received your Purple Helmet for the first time, you form another line in a *different* order, random once again, and repeat the process, once again performing exactly six squats. When that is complete and you have all received the Purple Helmet for the second time, you will do it all over again once more, performing exactly six squats. When that is complete, you will remove my blindfold and your own ear-plugs and await further orders. Is that clear?'

'Yes, *Generalissima*.'

'Good. Any more questions? Ginger?'

'Squats are all we perform, *Generalissima*?'

She thought for a moment.

'You may also lick my nipples.'

'Yes, *Generalissima*.'

'Good. Now, any more questions?'

Heads shook.

'No, *Generalissima*.'

'Excellent. Then we can begin. No, hold on. One last thing to remember. You will all strip completely but for your caps. Understood?'

103

'Yes, *Generalissima*.'

'Good. Then now we *can* begin. Curry- and Slut-Bum, tie me to the chair with strips of meat.'

They hesitated.

'Now, I said.'

They came forward, fumbling with the strips of meat they were carrying.

'Organise yourselves, girls. Curry-Bum, you do the tying; Slut-Bum, you hold the meat.'

The second-buggered crossing-guard took hold of all the strips of meat and the first-buggered one kneeled to begin tying her to the chair. Hands first. She grimaced involuntarily when the first strip touched her skin. It felt clammy and cold. Raw meat. Trickles of blood ran down her hand as the guard looped the strip of meat into place, binding her wrist to the back of the chair, then tightened it, tied it, then started on her other hand. She tested the knot and felt it start to slip.

'Not good enough, Curry-Bum,' she said. 'Tighter, girl. Tighter. Use two strips if you have to. You've got plenty.'

'Yes, *Generalissima*.'

The first-buggered crossing-guard returned to her tied hand, looped another strip of meat into place, tightened it, tied it. She tested the knots as the crossing-guard waited anxiously. It was good. She could barely move her hand at all now.

'That's fine. Carry on.'

'Yes, *Generalissima*.'

The crossing-guard set to work on her other hand. She looped a strip of meat into place, tightened it, tied it, added a second, tightened it, tied it. She tested the knots. Even better.

'Very good work, Curry-Bum. Now my feet.'

The crossing-guard kneeled in front of her, and was handed a strip of meat by the meat-holder. Her eyes

104

fixed on her erect cock for a moment, then lowered as she looped the strip of meat around her ankle and a chair-leg, tightened it, began to tie it, her eyes drifting up again, settling on her erect cock. She licked her lips, her eyes lifting a little further, meeting hers.

'Two here as well, *Generalissima*?'

'Yes please. And don't worry, I can promise you that it will feel even bigger inside you dan it looks.'

The crossing-guard blushed slightly.

'Yes, *Generalissima*,' she said, almost whispering. She looped another strip of meat around her ankle, tightened it, tied it, then shuffled on her knees to set to work on her other ankle. She tested the knots. They were solid, her movements only making blood run out of the meat and on to her foot, tickling. She could smell it – the wet iron smell of fresh blood. A new strip touched her other ankle and tightened around it. The crossing-guard's eyes were back on her cock as her fingers knotted the strip, then took another and looped that into place too, tightened it, tied it. She tested the knots, trying to kick her foot loose. No good. Which was very good. She was tied and immobilised. The crossing-guard had kneeled for a few moments more, waiting for her to test the final knots.

'Perfect,' she told her. 'I'm absolutely helpless. Very good work.'

'Thank you, *Generalissima*.'

The crossing-guard rose to her feet. The other crossing-guard still had several strips of meat in her hand.

'Now, girls, the ear-plugging. Slut-Bum, bite pieces off one of those strips you've still got and hand them out. Each of you is to chew two pieces thoroughly and insert them in her ears, one into each. You mustn't be able to hear a thing. Understood?'

'Yes, *Generalissima*.'

'Good. Then get on with it.'

She watched as the second-buggered crossing-guard – the one with the strips of meat – lifted one to her mouth, grimaced a little, as she drew the end in, biting with small white teeth, then spat a morsel of meat into her hand and held it out to the blonde. Then she raised the strip of meat to her mouth again, to bite, spit and hand another morsel of meat to the redhead. The blonde was already chewing, looking disgusted, and the redhead slipped her morsel into her mouth and began to chew as well. The crossing-guard bit, spat, handed out, and the other guards chewed, blood from the raw meat starting to spill down their chins. The blonde had finished chewing her first morsel and took it out of her mouth with two fingers, inserted it into her ear, screwing it home with her index finger, and stepped back to the crossing-guard to receive a second morsel for her other ear.

The redhead did the same, then the darkhair, then the first-buggered crossing-guard, then the second-buggered crossing-guard, who had bitten off a final morsel for herself and not spat it out, just chewed it. They looked like a convention of military vampires, red blood spilling down white chins beneath black caps, chewing, spitting out meat, inserting it into their ears, screwing it home. The blonde had finished both ears now.

'Snowy,' she said. 'Snowy! Can you hear me? SNOWY!'

Good. It had worked. The redhead was about to insert her second piece of chewed meat.

'Hold on, Ginger, before you muffle yourself completely. Remember, next you blindfold me, then you line up randomly, receive your Purple Helmets, polish them with exactly six squats, then line up randomly again, receive, polish, line up again, receive, polish, then take off my blindfold and take out your earplugs, and await further orders. You are now in command during my temporary abdication. Understood?'

She nodded.

'Yes, *Generalissima.*'

'Good. Then carry on, Lieutenant Ginger.'

The redhead swung her forearm across her stomach, then jutted it forwards, fist clenched, boots coming together with a clap on the smooth tarmac.

'Yes, *Generalissima!*'

Then she inserted the chewed meat into her ear and screwed it home. Everyone else was finished; they were all standing looking at each other, wondering what to do next.

'Girls!' she shouted. 'Girls!'

Nothing. The redhead took command, gesturing to the crossing-guards, pointing at her head, pretending to tie a blindfold into place around her own eyes. The crossing-guards nodded and walked over to stand behind her. She closed her eyes and waited. Yuck. A strip of raw meat settled over her eyes, was looped quickly around her head, tightened, knotted. She could feel trickles of blood run out of it down her cheeks and around her ears. The trickles of blood on her hands and feet had started to dry in the warm sun, itching a little. What were they doing now? Lining up? Yes. She could hear boots shuffling on the tarmac. How many possible combinations were there?

Let's think. There are five guards, so that was five possibilities in the first place in the line, then four in the second, three in the third, two in the fourth, one in the fifth and last. Five times four is twenty, and twenty times three is sixty, and sixty times two is one-hundred-and-twenty, and that's it. One-hundred-and-twenty possible combinations of cunts. And she would sample three of the combinations, having her Purple Helmet polished by the supple sugary walls of five cunts three times over. Her cock lifted higher at the thought of it, ticking as her heart began to beat faster. Had they lined up yet? Yes, she thought so. But what was that? Popping sounds. Ah, it was boots. Tight boots being tugged off white feet and shins. Now buzzing sounds, like sleepy wasps. Yes. Zips coming down. They were unzipping their trousers, slipping them down, stepping out of them, unbuttoning their shirts, dropping them to one side. Stripping completely, but for their caps.

She imagined white naked bodies, slender fingers stroking restlessly at excited cunts, levering pink lips apart, squeezing delicately at stiffened clitorises, preparing the cunts for penetration. Another sound. Bare feet shuffling almost inaudibly on tarmac. The line was inching towards her, the first guard in it preparing to mount the chair, straddle her, then, on her nod of command, take the Purple Helmet she had been promised deep into her velvet-lined medal-case and perform six squats on it. Her breath was coming faster with anticipation. When? When? Now. She felt the chair shake faintly and moving air brushed her skin. Her cock strained upwards. She was being straddled, white thighs opening above her stiff cock, pink-lipped cunt gaping between it, capped by blonde hair? Red? Black?

She nodded, then jerked as hard nipples descended against her bare breasts and began to rub up and down against her own hard nipples, then she gasped as hot stickiness touched the head of her cock and its whole length was slowly sheathed in hot, slick-walled cunt. But did that count as one squat? The nipples worried at her nipples, then lifted away and she felt hot breath sear her breasts for a moment. Then a tongue licked, a mouth closed, sucking hard. She gasped again, then almost groaned as the cunt lifted and sank again, lifted and sank again, lifted and sank again. Three squats. The mouth sucked harder, sharp teeth nibbling at her, then lifted and settled on her other nipple, sucking, licking, nibbling. The cunt lifted again, even more slowly, seeming to suck and ripple along her cock as it went, then sank back, then lifted again, sank back. It was too much.

'Carry on!' she said. 'Carry on, you bitch! Keep fucking me. I order you. As your commanding officer, I order you. Keep fucking me.'

The cunt lifted on her cock, paused for a moment as the head lodged between the lips, then lifted completely off. She groaned with frustration, snorting air eagerly through her nostrils. Cunt-scent. Hot yelm. Hot cunt-lips and cunt-walls, oozing yelm. Whose was it? Whose cunt had that been? It must be the best. It had to be. The chair quivered again. The cunt's owner, blessed among women, was climbing off the chair, making way for the next cunt. For an inferior cunt. It had to be inferior. That had been the tightest and hottest and slickest cunt in the world. A jewel beyond price. A light unto the nations.

The chair quivered again. Another pair of white thighs was opening above her, exposing another pink-lipped cunt, ready to descend and sheathe her glistening, grieving cock. To try to console it for its loss. And fail, of course. No cunt could match the first cunt. Surely. But she could feel blood congesting in her throat again and her mouth drying. Surely. She nodded. Hard nipples descended against hers, nudging, teasing, and the head of her cock kissed hot stickiness again, then sank between welcoming cunt-lips, received into paradise. Honey-throat, she thought incoherently. Honey-throat. Honey-cunt. Pink sugar. Pink sugar. The hard nipples jousted at hers, sliding on the spittle left by the first guard's mouth, and then the fresh new cunt began to lift and sink. First squat. She groaned with frustration. This was delicious too. Maddeningly delicious. The cunt lifted and sank. Teasing her. Gripping her cock between velvet walls. A strong cunt with velvet walls. Lifted and sank. Three squats. Three more to go. Do them slowly. Please. Do them slowly.

They were slow, lingering. The cunt lifted and sank. Lifted and sank. Lifted and did not sink. Her frustration was so acute that she thought for a moment she was going to start coming, hurling spunk into the air after the departing cunt, wasting her seed without a vessel to pump it into. But no, she managed to hold orgasm back, forcing it back into her aching balls. The chair quivered. The owner of the second cunt was climbing off, making way for the owner of the third. The trickles of blood on her hands and feet and down her face, around her ears, had dried completely, tugging at her skin as she tried to move. The chair quivered again. A third pair of white thighs was opening above her, exposing a third pink-lipped cunt for her cock to rise into. Hard nipples brushed her chest, met her hard nipples, jousted with them.

She nodded without consciously willing it, her whole body stiffening with anticipation of the third hot sticky kiss of cunt-lips on the head of her cock. It came and she groaned, lengthening the groan as the cunt slid over her cock, a velvet sheath for her steel stump, gripping her full length, rippling on it, sucking at her cock without moving an inch. The bitch. The bitch. She was going to make her come, defeat her cunning plan to sample all five cunts three times over in random order before making her choice. But surely this was the best. It had to be. It was working at her cock by sheer muscular effort, the velvet walls rippling and shivering along her cock, gripping it, milking it.

Then the bitch lifted to make the first squat, her cunt dragging her cock with it as it lifted, almost lifting her buttocks off the seat of the chair, then letting it go with a sudden slurp of released pressure, the head sliding delightedly past the slick, sugary cunt-walls, then sank back down on it, accepted the cock fully into itself again, lifted off it, dragged it up with the cunt, released it again, sank down on it, firm muscles in the velvet walls gripped fiercely at it.

It was too much: as the cunt lifted again, sucking her cock with it, she groaned and began to come, snorting as she spurted what seemed like gallons of hot spunk into the hot slick cunt-cylinder that had tormented her beyond endurance. The best-laid plans of mice and men. Of gerbils and *Generalissimas*. The cunt paused as though in surprise, then sank swiftly back down again over her fountaining cock, sucking hard at it again, rippling along it, prolonging and heightening her orgasm. Greedy cunt. Oh, greedy, greedy cunt. But whose was it? Whose was this cunt of cunts, this *vagina vaginarum*? Her cock throbbed and spurted for the last time, then lay still, clasped in the velvet arms of its lover, still rock-hard, stiff as a post, inserted fully into fleshly paradise.

'Christ,' she said. Spittle had dribbled freely down her chin and she could feel it dripping on to her chest. 'Christ. That's enough. That's enough now.'

Slurping, popping, the cunt rose off her cock. The chair quivered.

'Enough, girls,' she said. 'I've had enough.'

The chair quivered again. She was being straddled. White thighs were opening above her, exposing a fourth pink-lipped cunt above her still erect cock.

111

'Enough,' she said. 'That's fucking enough. Enough, do you fucking hear? Are you fucking d–'

She stopped. Yes, they were fucking deaf. And they were under orders to fuck her three times each, in random order. Straddle the chair, descend on her cock at the nod of command, perform six squats on it, get off. Three times each. And only then would they take her blindfold off and remove their earplugs. But there was an easy enough way out of it. She wouldn't nod. She would just shake her head. They would get the message. She shook her head vigorously. No. I don't want any more. She gasped. Hot stickiness had touched the head of her cock again, then a cunt descended fully, accepting its Purple Helmet for conspicuous gallantry in the face of the enemy. She groaned.

'No, you insubordinate bitch. No. Stop. Now.'

She shook her head again. The cunt began to lift. Had she understood? No. It paused, then sank again. See-sawing on her cock. Her poor cock. Her poor stiff cock. Congested with blood. She was going to do herself an injury if she stayed erect much longer. And her balls. They were aching, protesting at having to gather spunk for her ninth or tenth orgasm of the day as the cunt lifted and sank maddeningly, tormenting her poor stiff cock. A hot mouth closed on her nipples and sucked. Who was this? Who was doing this to her? Who had been so obtuse as to misread her unmistakable head-shaking and begin the squats? The cunt lifted and sank, lifted and sank. Six squats. Over.

The chair quivered. The guard was getting off.

'That's enough!' she shouted. 'I don't want any more. Enough!'

The chair quivered again. Hard nipples brushed her chest, circling her breasts, spiralling in on her own

112

nipples. She shook her head. No. No. That's enough. Hot stickiness kissed the head of her cock. She was still erect, her cock throbbing with congested blood. If she could force it to go down they couldn't continue. A cock can't accept a flaccid cunt. She shook her head. What was she thinking? A cunt can't accept a flaccid cock. She strained, trying to force her cock down by sheer will-power, but it defied her, staying stiff as ever as the fifth cunt of the day sank down over it, sucking at it, gripping it with sturdy velvet-lined walls. Oh Christ. Another one. Another cock teaser. Her balls were going to explode if she was provoked to orgasm again. She knew they were. They would go off between her thighs with fleshly little crumps, throwing mincemeat up in little fountains. The cunt lifted, sucking her cock with it, released it with another pop, then sank, sucking at her cock again. Bitch. Oh, you bitch. You sadistic bitch. Or was it the same guard? Had it been the same guard all along? Were the others watching her and laughing, ears long-ago unplugged, whispering their despicable plot to each other just out of hearing?

'Bitches,' she snarled. 'If you're fucking –'

She groaned as the cunt lifted and sank again.

'Please, stop. It is I, your *Generalissima*, begging you to stop. For the sake of sanity, in the name of all humanity. Stop. Stop.'

The merciless cunt lifted and sank, gorging itself on the meat of her cock. She heard a buzz and felt a puff of air on her sweat-damp forehead, then a light brushing of tiny feet. A fly. A fly had landed on her, attracted by the smell of her sweat or the smell of raw meat. Or both. She felt its tongue probing at her skin, drinking her sweat. It moved, the feet tapping out unreadable signals into her skin, as the cunt lifted and sank for the fourth time. She groaned, blowing futilely upwards, trying to frighten the fly off her face. Another buzz, another puff of air, and another fly was on her face, marching to and fro before beginning to drink. The cunt lifted and sank for the final time. Her balls ached fiercely. The cunt lifted off her cock with a lingering slurp. The chair quivered. Now it was all going to begin again.

Stroke III

It was half-an-hour early, but what the fuck. He left his desk and went to get his jacket before going to lunch. As he took it off the rack he sniffed, frowning a little. Perfume. An odd heavy perfume, sweet, almost creamy in the upper registers but with a base of musk, and sexually disturbing, almost feral, as though a female animal on heat had been crouching by the door, waiting to be serviced.

He sniffed again but it had gone, perhaps wafted to nothing on the air disturbed as he took down his jacket. He slipped the jacket on and went out to lunch, reaching inside the inner pocket to check his wallet. And here was his second surprise of the day: there was a slim book sitting in his pocket with his wallet. He took it out, still walking. It looked like a bank book, dark blue and on the front cover elegant, old-fashioned gold lettering above and below a picture of a gold fountain with silver spray. Above the fountain it said *The Merridew Bulling Society*. Below the fountain it said SEMPER SPUTAMUS.

Bulling? He opened it, feet rattling down the first flight of stairs, and began to leaf through it. His lip curled. Ah, he might have known. It was fucking Matt up to his old tricks again. It was a bank book and it was in his name and address: *John Thomas, 68*

Lincoln Parade, Orrell SX1 5FN. It looked completely genuine except for the fact that the paper was black and the ink white. Black pages ready to be filled, though oddly there was no column for withdrawals, just a column for date and time and cashier and deposit. He was about to close it and put it back into his pocket as evidence for when he confronted Matt in the pub later in the week, when he noticed that the first line for deposits had been filled in. Date 11/5, time 12.07. Typed in neat white ink. That was today, nearly. He looked at his watch. Twenty minutes away. And the cashier was 'Susie' (handwritten in white) and the amount 20cc (typed in neat white ink again). Twenty cents?

He shook his head, closed the book and put it in his pocket. Matt had never before gone in for mind-games with his practical jokes, but there was a first time for everything. He trotted down the final flight of stairs, nodded to the security guard at the desk and left the building. Tuna sandwich today, he thought, then maybe he'd see if Hilary was on the bench at the park today. On again, off again. Maybe on again today. He rounded the corner of the offices and began to walk down Irving Street, glancing up for a moment to absorb the weak sunshine on his face. It might be a fine weekend. They were due one. Now, which sandwich shop was he going to patronise today? The one down by the river or the one up on Salmouth Hill? He'd have to run to get back to work on time if he went to the one on Salmouth Hill, and maybe the effort would tip a cosmic balance somewhere and earn him a fine weekend.

He crossed the street, glad that he'd got out of the office before the crowds started, and glanced to the left without knowing why he'd done so. Not until he saw it. Between the shoe-repair shop and the café.

Dark glass, a picture of a gold fountain with silver spray and elegant, old-fashioned gold lettering over the door. *The Merridew Bulling Society*. But no motto underneath. He suddenly saw himself reflected in the glass, standing still and staring. What had been there before? He thought it had been a fishing-tackle shop. Hadn't it? He didn't know and this couldn't be Matt. A practical joke doesn't go as far as hiring and decorating an empty building. It would cost hundreds. Thousands, for Christ's sake. Unless the window was all there was, nothing behind it. But then how had Matt known he'd be walking *this* way today, after finding the book?

He walked up to the window and tried to look inside, face pressed to the glass, hands cupped around his eyes. He couldn't see anything. But whoever was inside would have been able to see him trying to see in. Well, didn't he have a perfect right to? After all, he *was* a customer. He glanced at his watch. 12.02. He looked up and down the street. He wanted to grab a passer-by, force them to look at the window, ask them if that really said *The Merridew Bulling Society*. I mean, does it really say *Bulling*? Is this really real? A bell jangled sharply right next to him and he turned and saw a man in a suit stepping inside the society, his right hand emerging from inside his jacket with a dark blue book. The bell jangled as the door closed. He sniffed. That perfume again. As though it had wafted from inside when the door opened.

He looked at the window again and read the words above the door for the sixth or seventh time. *The Merridew Bulling Society*. Fuck it. He reached inside his jacket pocket, slipping the book out as he walked to the door, glanced at the cover and opened the book one-handed. *The Merridew Bulling Society*. And his name inside. The bell jangled as he pushed the door open and stepped inside. When he saw what was inside he thought: Thousands of pounds? Tens of thousands, at the very least. This was nothing to do with Matt, unless he'd won the lottery and taken up practical joking on a monumental scale. Or was it Josiah Beagle? Was he being filmed right now, set up for the prime-time piss-take slot?

Inside it was exactly like a bank or building society – an old-fashioned one with dark carpet and minia- ture palms in heavy pots. A long line of tellers' booths down one wall. Fifteen or sixteen of them. Dimly lit. Discreetly lit. But there didn't seem to be any customers and he couldn't see the man in the suit who had entered just before him. And where did you queue?

He pushed the door shut, hearing the bell jangle again, and walked forwards. He could see waiting shapes and name cards in the windows of the tellers' booths above an odd bubble of glass at about waist height. All the names were female. JULIA MARY. REZAH. SUSANNAG. FIONA. CHARLOTTE. ZUFIA. DAISY. Where was the queue? No queue. No booth marked ENQUIRIES. So what did he do? He walked to the nearest booth. JULIA. A brunette in dark uniform turned away from a white computer and keyboard and smiled at him, eyebrows raised.

'Yes, sir? How can I help you?'

'I'm not sure,' he said. 'I –'

'Perhaps your book will help, sir. May I see it?'

He slipped it into the little tunnel beneath the window. What was the glass bubble for? It sat just in front of his crotch and he noticed that it had a little sliding window in the middle of it, with two little holes on either side. And there were handholds on either side of the booth, like something on an underground train, as though customers were supposed to clutch them as they stood there. What for? The brunette had opened his book, still smiling. Her smile broadened. She looked up, closing the book.

'Ah, yes, sir. You've got an appointment with Susannah. Just down the line. She's ready and waiting for you now, sir.'

'Thank you,' he said, feeling slightly dizzy. Maybe that was what the handholds were for. The smile and the flawlessness of her skin. And hadn't he seen her somewhere before? She slipped the book back to him and he picked it up and walked down the line. In a painting, somewhere? More dazzling smiles met him as he passed MARY and REZA. Blonde and Asian and somehow familiar. Like SUSANNAH. Susie. Her smile broke over him, making him feel dizzy again. Jet-black hair with slow, almost oily highlights. Full, moist, red lips, flawless skin (was it something in the coffee?), heart-shaped face, long pale throat accentuated by the dark collar of her uniform, and what looked like large, firm breasts, with the company logo over the right one. The golden fountain with silver spray. Above it said in embroidered gold lettering *merridew bulling society*; underneath it said SEMPER SPUTAMUS. The company motto.

'Good afternoon, sir,' she said. 'You have an appointment?'

'Uh, yes.'

Christ, he had an erection. Bulging in front of the glass bubble, exactly in front of the little sliding window.

'And you'd like to make a deposit, sir?'

'Uh, yes. Yes, I suppose so.'

'May I see your book, please, sir?'

'Uh, certainly.'

He slipped the book into the little tunnel and she picked it up. Long white fingers. No rings. And he

119

could smell that perfume again. Sweet and creamy but with an undertone of musk. Not sexually disturbing, sexually provoking. It's her cunt, he suddenly thought. It's her fucking cunt. She had opened the book, still smiling, and her smile broadened.

'That's fine, sir. If you'd like just to unzip ...'

What? What had she said? She pushed her chair back and stooped under her desk. What was she doing? Her face suddenly appeared in the glass bubble, smiling up at him, and he felt his hips shift guiltily. She'd see the bulge in his trousers. He started to edge back. She was tugging at the little window in the bubble, sliding it open.

'Sir? If you'd like to come forwards and unzip?'

'Unzip'? Had she said 'unzip'? Well, his cock thought so. It was poker-stiff in his trousers, straining forwards at the zip, jerking even stiffer as he saw what she was doing. She was putting her face to the little window, little dimples of amusement at the corner of her lips. Her hands slipped through the little holes to either side of the window, gesturing him forwards.

'I'm waiting, sir. I promise you, it won't hurt a bit.'

He glanced sideways, at JULIA and MARY and REZA. At FIONA and CHARLOTTE and ZUFIA, on the other side. FIONA was blonde and CHARLOTTE was black and ZUFIA was an Asian and they were all beaming at him, like JULIA and MARY and REZA.

'I don't understand,' he said.

'Sir?'

'You want me to –' he swallowed '– unzip?'

'Yes, sir. Of course. You want to make a deposit, don't you?'

'I, yuh. I ... yes. I do.'

'Then please unzip.'

'I ... unzip?'

'Yes, sir. But if you like, I can do it for you.'

'For me?'

'Yes, sir. Would you like that?'

'I . . . yes. Yes, I would.'

'Then please come forwards.'

He swallowed and took a step forwards. Her hands fluttered in the little holes, urging him on. He noticed that the fingernail on the ring finger of her left hand was trimmed short. Why? He took another step. Nearly within reach now. He looked sideways, groaning a little at the row of gleaming smiles that met him. He closed his eyes and took the final step forwards, left leg, right leg.

'Thank you, sir.'

Delicate hands touched his trousers, fluttering at the outline of his erection, sliding up and down his cock.

'Oh, sir. You are a big boy, aren't you?'

The fingers began to probe and palpate, tapping at his erection, tickling through at his cockhead.

'A *very* big boy.'

He moaned. His zip buzzed for a moment.

'May I, sir?'

He blinked, opened his eyes, looked down. She had started to lower his zip. He nodded, swallowed hard.

'Yes. Yes, please.'

His zip buzzed fully down. He looked away and closed his eyes again. The hands brushed at the open slit in his trousers, tugged it apart, slipped inside, to slide up and down the outline of his erection in his underpants. His cockhead was bulging against the hem of his underpants, almost pulsing with arousal, and he could feel a trickle of pre-come building in his urethra. The hands – light and delicate inside his trousers as butterflies – took hold of the hem of his underpants and tugged it slowly down, allowing the head of his cock to slip free and jut upwards in his

121

trousers. A fingernail brushed the neck of his cock, scratching very gently at it.

'There you are. You didn't want to hide yourself in the dark all day, did you? A big boy like you?'

The smooth, cool-skinned finger rubbed the neck of his cock, just below the head, then slid deeper, trying to crook around his full erection.

'A *very* big boy like you. So come on, out you come.'

The finger began to tug gently, slowly pulling his cock forwards so that it could slip through his trouser-slit.

'Come on, Mr Stiffy. It's *so* much nicer in the open air. Ah, *there* you are.'

The head of his cock brushed the trouser-slit and jerked forwards suddenly. He moaned again, feeling his knees melt and tremble, so that for a moment he thought he was going to fall over. He opened his eyes to try and keep his balance and noticed the hand-holds on either side of the booth. That was what they were for. He took hold of them, swallowing hard, and looked down. His cock was out of his trousers, jutting forwards, held steady by her right index finger as she smiled dazzlingly at it. She cooed for a moment, almost chuckling with admiration.

'And a very good morning to you, Mr Stiffy. You are a fine specimen, aren't you? But you haven't taken your hat off yet. Shall I take it off for you?'

His knees loosened again, trembling hard.

'Well, dear? The strong silent type, are we? Yes? Well, I don't mind. Still, I *will* just slip it off, so I can get a better look at you.'

Her thumb came up on the other side of his cock and her other fingers lined up beneath her index finger, gently gripping, slowly sliding his foreskin fully down to expose the ripe plum of his cockhead.

A transparent pearl of pre-come had gathered in the cockslit, glittering as his cock moved under the delicate pressure of her fingers.

'There. That's *much* nicer, isn't it? You can feel the air on your lovely bald head now, can't you? But darling – have you got a cold? Your poor little nose is running. Would you like me to wipe it clean for you? Oh, I forgot. You're the strong, silent type, aren't you? Well, just nod then. Just nod if you'd like me to wipe your poor little nose clean.'

He gathered tension in his hips and tried to jerk his cock.

'Oh! I felt you move then, but was that a nod? Do it again. Once for yes, twice for no.'

He did it again. Once.

'Ah, so you do want me to wipe your nose clean. Good. I'm glad. It looks so unhygienic, that bead of snot hanging there. And if I'm not mistaken, it's getting bigger all the time.'

He groaned involuntarily at what he was seeing, a low rumble filling his throat. She was pressing her face forwards to the little window, her mouth opening and red moist tongue creeping forwards between her plump lips. She was swinging the tip of her tongue, making it sway through the air like a little snake, slowly creeping forwards for the ripe plum of his cock and the glittering little pearl of pre-come. Then her tongue slipped back into her mouth.

'I can't reach you, darling. You have to move forwards a little. Come on.'

His feet took him nearer without conscious decision, sliding his cock almost through the window in the glass bubble.

'Good boy,' she breathed. '*Very* good boy.'

Puffs of warm air slid over the head of his cock and he felt the ache in his balls harden and begin to pulse.

'Now, where were we? Oh yes, your poor little nose. It's running, isn't it? And you said that I could clean it for you. OK, here we go then.'

The mouth opened again and the tongue slid forwards, not swaying this time, just sliding forwards, stretched taut so that the tip was narrow and sharp. He was looking almost vertically down now, watching the gap between the tip of her tongue and the pearl of his pre-come narrow millimetre by millimetre. Almost there. Almost there. Yes. The tipmost tip of her tongue had just touched the pearl of pre-come and the perfect sphere of the pearl broke, flowing forwards.

'Mmmm,' she murmured. Her hand tightened on his cock, holding it rock-steady, cock-steady, then the tongue-tip slid forwards another millimetre and flicked upwards, taking away most of the pearl, then slid forwards again, slipping just between the lips of his urethra, flickering, cleaning out the remaining traces of pre-come. He strained to suck the sensation into his cock, the barest contact of her tongue on his cockhead, then almost groaned with frustration as her tongue slipped back to her mouth, running along the lips, left and right, before slipping back inside.

'Do you know, dear, I'm not sure that was snot, after all? It didn't taste like snot. In fact, you know, it tasted rather *nice*, really. The sort of thing one could almost acquire a taste for, now I think about it. Have you got any more for me to try, hmmm? Oh, yes, you have. I can see that it's starting to build again in your little nose. Or is that the nose? I thought it was, because I thought that stuff was snot, but if it's not snot, then maybe that's not a nose. Maybe it's a mouth? A little mouth? Yes, maybe it is. It does look like one, after all, and it is in the right place in your lovely bald head. A little mouth. So that makes me wonder . . .'

Her hand tugged at his cock, lifting it upwards to expose the underside.

'Oh, yes. I was right. It is a mouth, because I can see that it's got a lovely long throat leading up to it. I can *just* see it running all the way up the underside of your great big neck. But does that mean . . . ?'

Her left hand swung across, index finger raised. He felt her press the fingernail to his urethra down near the root of his cock, just above his balls.

'That stuff that was – that *is* – leaking out of your little mouth. It must be coming up your throat. So if I press my fingernail to your throat and slide it upwards, like *this*. Oh, yes. Look.'

The regathering pearl of pre-come at his slatch had suddenly swelled into a perfect little sphere again, then swelled beyond that, beginning to ooze forwards under its own weight. Her fingernail had paused about a third of the way up his cock

'I was right. Your throat is full of that lovely stuff. So if I . . .'

Her tongue slipped through her lips again and came forwards until the tip touched into the pearl of pre-come. The pearl broke, flowing on to the tip of her tongue. Her fingernail began to slide slowly up the underside of his cock again and the pearl swelled, more of it flowing on her tongue. Her fingernail reached the top of his cock and she lowered her left hand, her tongue tip slipping forwards between the lips of his slatch again, flickering for the remaining traces of pre-come, then withdrew, slowly licking left and right across her lips before slipping back into her mouth.

'Yes. I *am* acquiring a taste for it. Isn't that naughty of me? Because if it isn't snot, it must be spit. What a naughty girl I am, liking the taste of your spit. And look, it's coming back again.'

The pearl of pre-come was starting to regather, swelling through the lips of his slatch.

'Your mouth must be watering like billy-o, dear. You must be looking forward to some big treat, something *really* delicious. Are you, dear? Is that why your little mouth is watering so much? Oh, I can't resist it.'

Her right hand tightened on his cock and her left hand lifted to it again, pressing the fingernail of the index finger up against his urethra, beginning to slide it up as her tongue slid from her mouth again, the tip making contact with the reswelling pearl of pre-come. Her fingernail almost hurt this time, she was pressing it so hard into the underside of his cock, sliding out the pre-come in his urethra. It reached the top and her left hand fell away, hovering ready for something else, the fingers flickering slowly up and down as though she were slowly practising scales on a keyboard. Her tongue-tip slid to the lips of his slatch again, probing deep between them this time, flickering for the remaining traces of his pre-come. Then her tongue slipped back to her mouth, licking left and right along her lips, slipping back inside.

'Mmmmm. I have definitely acquired a taste for your spit, dear. Isn't that naughty of me? But I wish you could tell me why your mouth is watering like that. What treat are you expecting? It must be very, very delicious. Look. Your mouth has started to water again. Your throat must be full of spit again *already*. But . . .'

Her lips pursed, pouted, as though she were suddenly thinking hard.

'If it *is* spit, why it is climbing your throat? Spit is made in mouths. It can go *down* throats, but it doesn't come *up* them, surely. So maybe it isn't spit, either. Not snot and not spit. So what on earth can it be?'

126

She was silent for a few seconds.

'No, I can't guess. But maybe I can find out. After all, if it's coming *up* your throat, it must be coming up *from* something. You must be hiding something else in your trousers. What can it be?'

She put on a different voice to reply, lisping slightly, a little Susie talking to a big Susie.

'I don't know, Susie. I really don't know.'

'Well, then, why not find out?'

The big Susie voice.

'Find out?'

The little Susie voice again.

'Yes. Reach inside his trousers and see what else is in there.'

'Reach inside?'

'Yes. What's so difficult about that?'

'Well, nothing, I *suppose*. But are you sure it's safe?'

'Of course it's safe. You've already done it, haven't you? And look what you found: this lovely big gentleman.'

'You're right. I did. And he is a lovely big gentleman. A lovely great brute. Gosh, do you think there might be another one in there? Maybe even bigger? Even more brutish?'

'Well, no, I don't think *bigger*. I think *he* is about as big as they get, don't you? But there might be something *almost* as big or even just as exciting, in a different way.'

'You're right.'

'So go on then.'

'What?'

'If I'm right, reach inside his trousers again. See where all that lovely pr– um, that lovely not-snot and not-spit is coming from.'

'OK.'

'Well, get on with it then.'

'I said OK. I'm just *preparing* myself.'

'You're prepared already. Do it.'

'OK, OK, no need to rush.'

Her left hand stopped playing scales and slipped forwards for his trouser-slit. His body stiffened. What was she going to do? The hand slipped inside his trousers, gently felt around the root of his cock and slid down into his underpants.

'Oh, it's all *hairy*. I can feel hair. And what's – what's this?'

The hand was deep in his underpants now, just starting to brush the top of his scrotum, sliding deeper, the fingers probing gently, scratching a little.

'There's a big bag hanging around his neck. It feels warm and a little bit moist and it's *wrinkled*. Oh! And it moves when I scratch at it. And there's – there's something inside it. I can feel them sliding over each other.'

'What do they feel like?'

The big Susie. The Susie in charge.

'They're *hard*. Like stones. Hard and smooth.'

'How hard?'

'Very hard. When I squeeeeze them –' he jerked a little and groaned '– they don't seem to be affected at all. But there's a squidgy bit at one end. When I squeeze *that* . . .'

He jerked again, gasping with pain.

'Yes, that bit isn't hard at all. What funny things they are. But hang on.'

'What? What have you found?'

'There's a kind of tube leading out of the squidgy bit.'

'Where does it go?'

'I'm trying to find out. To *feel* out. Hmmm. It leads up towards his cock an–'

'Oh, Susie, you silly little thing.'

'What? What have I done?'

'You've really let the cat out of the bag now.'

'What? How have I let the cat out of the bag?'

'You've said the word you're not supposed to say.'

'What word?'

'The c-word.'

'What c-word?'

'The c-word you said just then when you were describing how the vas deferens led out of the epididymis.'

'The what led out of the what?'

'The vas def– Oh.'

'Ah-ha. See? You've done it too. And that was *much* worse than the c-word. Much, much worse. *You*'ve let the cat and kittens out of the bag. The tiger and the tiger-cubs.'

'Well, so what? He knew we were playing. He likes it. Don't you? See, he does. He's nodding.'

She had made the head of his cock move up and down.

'OK. Does he like me squeezing his balls? Like this?'

The left hand rummaged in his underpants, closing around his balls one after the other, squeezing. His cock paused, then nodded.

'Oh, Susie, first the c-word, now the b-word. You're spoiling *everything*. But in answer to your question – Yes. He likes that too. But not *too* hard, I think he's trying to say.'

'What about the squidgy bits? Does he like me squeezing them?'

He felt her feeling for his epididymies again and flinched, waiting for the stab of pain as she squeezed them. But it was OK: his cock was shaking its head.

'No. He doesn't like that. He says they're too tender to be squeezed. You can't squeeze his squidgy bits, only his b-words.'

'His balls, you mean?'

'Yes. His b-words.'

'Good. I'm glad. I like squeezing his balls. I like squeezing his squidgy bits too.'

'But *he* doesn't.'

'Who doesn't? Him or *him*?'

'Who's "*him*"?'

'Mr Stiffy, of course.'

'I see. Well, neither of them like it.'

'OK. Then what else *does* he like? Does he like me stroking his balls, like this?'

His cock nodded.

'Yes. Mr Stiffy likes that.'

'Tickling them, like this?'

His cock nodded.

'Yes. Mr Stiffy likes that too.'

'You try something too.'

'OK. Well, Mr Stiffy, do you like this?'

Her right hand tightened on the neck of his cock and began very gently to wank him. It stopped.

'Do you like that, Mr Stiffy?'

His cock nodded.

'Does he?'

'Yes. He does.'

'I can think of something else he might like.'

'What?'

'I'll whisper it.'

'No. He might not hear it then. Say it aloud. What else might he like?'

'No. It's too rude to say.'

'Say it. Or I'll tell him what you *really* want to do.'

'I would. So say it.'

'Bitch.'

'Say it. What else might he like?'

'Bitch.'

'*Say* it.

130

'He might like – a kiss. A kiss on the top of his bald head.'

'Who? Mr Stiffy?'

'Yes. Go on, ask him.'

'No. It's a silly suggestion. I've decided he wouldn't like it after all.'

'He might do. You won't know till you've asked him.'

'No, he definitely wouldn't like that. It's girly stuff. Kissing. He's a big boy now. He's outgrown all that sort of stuff. It's soppy.'

'*Ask* him. I think he *will* like it.'

'And I think he won't. So I'm not going to ask him.'

'Then *I* will.'

'No, you won't. I ask the questions. But I'm not asking this one.'

'OK, then. You ask the questions and I ask the question. And the question is: Mr Stiffy, dear, would you like a kiss on the top of your head? There. What did he say?'

'He didn't say anything.'

'Then what did he *do*?'

'He. Well, he . . .'

'*What*? Tell me.'

'He nodded. But not so as you'd noticed.'

'Then how did you notice if he did it not so you'd notice? Ah, got you there, didn't I? I bet he nodded a lot. I bet he really really likes the idea of having a kiss on the top of his head. So admit it. He nodded a lot, didn't he? Admit it.'

She blew a raspberry to herself, ripe lips pouting and vibrating, and he had to grip the handholds tightly again.

'Admit it. He nodded a lot, didn't he?'

'Yes. OK. He did. But maybe he didn't hear what you said properly.'

'Then I'll ask it again. Mr Stiffy, dear, would y–'

'Shut up. I'll ask this time.'

'Go on then. Ask him.'

'I will. Mr Stiffy, you wouldn't be so soppy and girly as to like a kiss on the top of your head, would you?'

She paused, then said, 'Oh, dear.'

'What?'

'He would. You were right. He would like a kiss on the top of his head.'

'Then give him one.'

'No. He might like the idea, but I'm *sure* he wouldn't like the real thing.'

'How will you know until you try? Go on, give him a kiss. Kiss the top of his head.'

'Shut up. I don't want to.'

'But he does want you to. So do it. Now.'

'Bitch.'

'Do it.'

'OK, I will. But he won't like it, I bet.'

He gripped the handholds again, watching her mouth come slowly forwards, lips pouting reluctantly, preparing to plant a kiss on the bald head of his cock.

'Are you doing it?'

She sighed with exasperation.

'Yes, I *am*. I said I was, didn't I? So shut up and stop interrupting.'

The kiss resumed, ripe red lips pouting. He shivered, feeling his knees tremble again. And there, yes, delicate as a falling petal that brushed the head of his cock in passing, she had kissed the head of his cock and withdrawn.

'Well, have you done it now?'

'Yes.'

'And did he like it?'

'I haven't asked him yet. I don't need to. I already know what the answer will be.'

'No, you don't. Ask him. Ask him whether he liked it. I bet he did. I bet he really really liked it. I bet he wants you to do it again.'

'I bet he doesn't.'

'OK then. What do you bet?'

'I bet. I bet. I don't know, I just bet.'

'No. Put your money where your mouth is. If you're wrong, you have to do whatever I say.'

'No. That's too much. You'll make me do things that aren't nice.'

'Scaredy-cat. You know I'm right. He did like it. You're just scared to admit you're wrong.'

'I'm not wrong. He didn't like it. I can tell by the way he quivered when I did it. He was disgusted.'

'I bet you he wasn't.'

'And I bet you he was.'

'Good. Then the bet is on. And if you lose, you have to do anything I say. Anything at all.'

'Bitch. You tricked me.'

'Shut up and ask him. Or I'll do it for you.'

'Bitch.'

'Ask him.'

'No.'

'OK, I will then. Mr Stiffy, dear, you liked being kissed, didn't you? OK, so what's he doing?'

'Bitch.'

'Ah-ha. I was right. He's nodding, isn't he?'

'Shut up, you dirty cheat. You cheated. You tricked me into betting.'

'No, you agreed to do it of your own free will, so now you have to do *whatever* I say. And I say, first of all, that you have to kiss him again.'

'No.'

'Do it.'

He stiffened with anticipation. The lips brushed his cockhead again, petal-soft, and withdrew.

'Have you done it?'

'Yes.'

'Properly?'

'Yes. Of course.'

'OK, then carry on doing it. Kiss his head all over. And kiss it hard.'

'But he doesn't like it! I know he doesn't! He's only saying he does because he doesn't want to hurt our feelings.'

'Bollocks. You're only saying that because you don't like doing it.'

'I do. I like it. It's nice. I like kissing his head. It feels nice and warm.'

'Then stop causing trouble and *kiss*. Kiss his head all over. Hard.'

'OK, I will.'

He tightened his grip on the handholds again as her right hand tightened on the neck of his cock, pulling him a little nearer, and her mouth came forwards, lips pouting. She began to kiss the head of his cock all over, little darting kisses at first, trickling in a petal-soft line up the broad upper surface of the glans, then darting left and right over the cock-warts, the sensitive papillae that studded the curve of his cockcrown, growing harder and more lingering, fanning back down his cockhead, over the wings of the upper surface. The pearl of pre-come was back in his slatch, swelling, beginning to droop forwards and down. It would drip soon. Drip to the floor. Now she was kissing towards the tip of his cock, lips trembling teasingly as they pressed to the hot, smooth glans-skin. And then a kiss landed right on top of his slatch, squashing the pre-come pearl flat. Her face jerked back in mock surprise, the centre of her lips moist with his pre-come.

'Yuck. What's that?'

'What's wrong?'

'There was something sticky on the head of his cock. It's all over my lips.'

'It's pre-come, silly. Don't you remember, you were licking at it a little while ago? You said you liked the taste.'

'Oh, yeah, so I did. And . . .'

Her tongue emerged, licking at the patch of pre-come on her lips.

'Yes. I still like the taste of it.'

'Keep on kissing him.'

'OK, OK. No need to . . .'

Her voice trailed off as her mouth came forward again and began kiss the head of his cock again. Now she was concentrating on the underside, pushing his cock upwards with her right hand, trickling soft kisses up and down the under-rein, the *fraenum praeputii*, then left and right in the cock-ditch, the *cervix penis* that circled his cockhead below the cockcrown, the *corona penis*. The fingers of her left hand stirred in his underpants, tickling at his balls again. He jerked. She was trying to speak while still kissing the head of his cock, puffs of hot breath teasing it.

'What?'

She had pulled her mouth back.

'I was saying, that's enough.'

'Enough what?'

'Enough kissing. You can do something else now.'

'What? It mustn't be anything disgusting. I'm not doing anything disgusting or dirty.'

'This isn't disgusting or dirty. Not that it matters anyway, because you lost the bet and I can tell you to do whatever I like.'

'Not if it's disgusting or dirty.'

'No. Anything at all.'

'Shut up. Tell me what it is.'

'OK. That's enough kissing, so now you can *lick* the head of his cock. I know he'll like that.'

'Yuck. No, I'm not doing that. I'm definitely not. And he won't like it anyway, so there.'

'Yes, he will.'

'No, he *won't*.'

'He *will*.'

'*Won't*.'

'Shut up and do it.'

'Shan't. Because besides being something he won't like, it's dirty and disgusting, so I'm not doing it.'

'If he says he likes the idea of it, will you do it?'

'He won't, because it's dirty and disgusting.'

'Ask him.'

'No.'

'Ask him.'

'No.'

'Then I will. Mr St–'

'Oh, shut up. I'll do it. Mr Stiffy, sir, please tell me: you don't like the idea of me licking your head, do you? That's really dirty an–'

She tutted sorrowfully.

'What? He's nodding, isn't he?'

'Yes.'

Through clenched teeth.

'I *told* you he would. So do it. Lick him. Lick him *all* over until I tell you to stop.'

'Bitch.'

'Do it.'

He gripped the handholds again. There. Her mouth was coming forwards, glistening lips opening, tongue sliding between them. Then the tongue slid back.

'Do I *have* to? *All* over?'

'Yes, you have to. All over. Go on, do it.'

The lips pouted sulkily, then the tongue slowly re-emerged. She leaned forwards and he felt a shiver run through him. He closed his eyes and waited. As the tip of her tongue touched his cockhead he jerked, almost swinging his hips back, almost moving his cock out of reach. Almost *wanting* to do it. Because this was going to be almost painful.

Breath hissed out of his mouth. She had started. Started to lick his cockhead. Hot, moist, velvety tongue. Sliding teasingly to and fro on the surface of his cockhead, the tip of it probing into every gully and crease, reading every cock-wart, sliding and circling the cockditch. Flicking and flickering. Teasing him. Then her tongue left him. He could feel her spittle drying on the head of his cock.

'Well?'

She sounded a little breathless.

'Well what?'

'Did he like it?'

'Yes. I think he did.'

'Is he nodding?'

'Yes. Kind of.'

His cock was nodding: ticking up and down faintly on his pounding heartbeat.

'OK. Then *now* you can *suck* him.'

'OK.'

'What, you'll just do it? Just like that?'

'Yes.'

'Slut.'

'I know. And isn't it fun?'

Her mouth came forwards again, lips curling open, her right hand tightening hard on the neck of his cock, pooling blood in his cockhead, super-sensitising it, so that when – he gasped, clenching at the handholds – she drew it into her mouth and began to suck, his knees melted again, his whole groin liquid

137

with the sensation of her moist mouth sucking. Pausing. Sucking. Pausing. Sucking. A rhythmic suck, silent at first, but gradually beginning to slurp, as though her mouth were watering at the taste of his cockhead in her mouth, as though his cockhead were a giant purple sweet. A gobstopper. A giant purple gobstopper. Just sucking. No tongue. Just lips and suction. And just his cockhead in her mouth. It was a noisy blow job now. Slurping esuriently. Sucking and pausing. Sucking and pausing. While the fingers of her left hand were busy tickling his balls, gently stroking them, tickling, scratching. Then her lips popped free and his cockhead came out of her mouth. She sighed with satisfaction.

'Did he like it?'

'Yes.'

'And did you like it?'

'No. I *loved* it.'

'Suck him again. But take him much deeper this time.'

'Deep throat?'

'Not just yet. And to be honest, I don't think he will last that long. I very much fear, from the state of his b-words, that's he's about to blow any moment.

'Wanna bet?'

'Yes.'

'What do you wanna bet?'

'Your knickers. If he doesn't come during the next suck, he gets to sniff them.'

'Hmmm. OK, then.'

Warm breath flickered over his cockhead and he clenched tight at the handholds as she let go of him with her right hand and began to suck him in again, but very slowly, lips sealed over his cockhead, slowly sliding up and over it, the tip of her tongue trembling in his slatch, as the fingers of her left hand started to massage his balls. Squeeze them. What had she said about her knickers? That he would get to sniff them? Get to sniff her knickers? Still warm from her arse and thighs and cunt? Still warm from her pussy? Her dark-pelted pussy? Whence cameth that creamy musk of arousal? O God, he wanted that. He wanted to sniff her knickers. But if he came during this suck, he wouldn't be able to. She would lose the bet against herself and he wouldn't get to sniff her knickers. No. It was unfair. Horribly unfair. How could he restrain himself? His cockhead was inside her mouth now, slowly being sucked deeper, the blade of her tongue working at it now, sliding up and down, waggling happily underneath it, like a puppy's tail. And her fingers, working in his underpants. Squeezing at his balls. Relaxing, then squeezing. She was trying to make him come. The bitch. The *bitch*. She didn't want him to sniff her knickers.

But he was going to. He was *going* to. He clenched his eyes tighter shut, trying to tug himself away from the delicious sucking that was drawing his cockhead deeper into the moist paradise of her mouth. To tug himself away from her torturing fingers in his underpants. He wasn't here. He wasn't in this bank. He wasn't being sucked to orgasm by one of the most beautiful women he had ever seen in his life. He wasn't. He wasn't. But he was. And he could feel orgasm being sucked out of him like a yolk. It was thirty seconds or less away, building in his abused balls, gathering and towering in his head, ready to burst from him like a milky *tsunami*, flinging itself from him in spurts of thick salty spunk-slime, copious enough to choke her. Because that's what he wanted to do. He wanted to come into her mouth so hard that she choked, that she gagged on it. He wanted to come harder into her mouth than anyone had ever come before.

She had sucked his cockhead deep inside her mouth now, tilting forwards over it so that it was sliding against the ridged velvet of her palate. Her fingers stopped tickling in his underpants and he almost gasped with relief. Her mouth began to rock gently, sliding the palate back and forth over the head of his cock, millimetres forwards, millimetres back. No sucking now, just the rubbing. She was trying to make him come. Just from the rubbing. Millimetres forwards, millimetres back. Because that way her victory would be greater. She would have defeated him with gentleness. Just a gentle rocking, rubbing her palate gently at his cockhead. Not a ferocious sucking, with slurps and pops, her mouth fucking him hard and her fingers jabbing brutally into his balls so that he came in seconds, groaning with pain. No, not that. Just a gentle rocking, with his cockhead pressed to her velvety palate deep inside her mouth.

He breathed out and in, emptying his lungs, then filling them. If he could hold out he would get to sniff her knickers. So hold out. Hold out. She won't keep it up for long. He smiled at the double entendre. That was good. He was relaxing. He could think about other things than the fact his cock was inside the mouth of one of the most beautiful women he had ever seen in his life. Than the fact that one of the most beautiful women he had ever seen in his life was employed to suck cocks all day with fourteen or fifteen of some of the other most beautiful women he had ever seen in the life. Employees of the Merridew Bulling Society. Yes. He was relaxed. Orgasm was still thirty seconds away, but it wasn't coming any closer. It was hovering at a distance, not sliding closer with every second of sucking. No, he was relaxed.

So that she nearly caught him out. Very, very nearly. When her gently rocking mouth suddenly woke on his lulled cock, suddenly began to suck furiously at it, sliding forwards over it so that it hung on the entrance to her throat, then sliding back, then forward, then back, sucking loudly and moistly, while the fingers of her left jabbed brutally into his balls. He was nearly caught out by it, nearly forced to come, spluttering with surprise and pain, but she wasn't excessively cruel. She didn't keep at it till he did come – and he would have come very soon – she stopped after a second or two or three, sliding her mouth off his cock, relaxing her fingers on his balls. Pop. Her mouth was off his cock and he could feel her spittle cooling almost all the way along its length now. And Christ, his balls were aching.

But he hadn't come. He hadn't come. So he would get to sniff her knickers. She was panting, trying to find the breath to start the conversation with herself again. She started it, still out of breath.

'Well?'

Panting again. Swallowing.

'Well what?'

'Did he come?'

'You know he didn't.'

'Then I win the bet and he gets to sniff your knickers.'

'OK. OK.'

'Take them off then.'

'Give me a minute to recover.'

'No, take them off now. He wants to sniff them, so why should he wait?'

'Because I want a minute to recover.'

'No. Take them off, give them to him and suck him again. This time he'll come in about, oh, I'd say, oh, about fifteen seconds. Because he'll have your knickers over his head and he'll be sniffing them. I won't even need to squeeze his balls. Just a straight suck will be enough. Well?'

'Well what?'

'Have you taken them off yet?'

'Give me a fucking minute to recover.'

'You've had a fucking minute to recover. You've had two fucking minutes to recover. You've got all day to fucking recover, after this. So get them off and give them to him and get sucking. Now.'

'Bitch.'

He felt her left hand give his balls a final little squeeze and slide out of his trousers. What was she doing? He opened his eyes and looked down. Her right hand was gone and her left hand was slipping back through the handholes in the bubble. Now her head moved back. Where was she? He went up on tiptoes, trying to peer inside the booth. She seemed to be crouching on the floor, lifting her skirt. Yes. She was doing it. She was sliding her knickers off, stepping out of them. She stood up suddenly, something white folded tight in her left hand.

'Here you are, sir,' she said with another dazzling professional smile. She dropped the white something in the little tunnel underneath the window and he let go of one of the handholds and reached in and picked it up. Oh God. It was her knickers. Soft and warm. Her head dropped behind the window. She was kneeling back on the floor, pushing her head forwards into the bubble again. Quick. He let go of the remaining handhold and quickly unfolded her knickers and tugged them open. He lifted them to his mouth and nose and sniffed. Oh God. Yes. That scent – it had been her cunt. Her dark-pelted pussy. The crotch of the knickers was saturated with it and when he pressed his lips there he could feel that they were sticky and moist. Her pussy-lips had been unfurled and oozing against them.

'Suck him.'

He jerked as though an electric shock had run through him and looked down. Her head was back in the bubble, her right hand reaching through the handhold again to tug his cock forwards on to her opening mouth. He slipped the knickers over his head, quickly adjusted them so that the crotch sat directly over his mouth and nose, and breathed in deeply and happily, putting his hands back to the handholds and gripping them tight. Her right hand took hold of his cock and guided it towards her mouth. He breathed out, then in again, savouring the perfume that her pussy had moistened the knickers with, the creamy musk above the scent of body-warmed cotton and a sprinkling of talcum powder.

Her mouth closed over his cock and started to suck. No pauses this time, just a continuous suck. No fingers working inside his underpants, squeezing and teasing his balls. Just a suck. A long, slow suck. With his mouth and nose pressed hard into the warm, pussy-soiled knickers of one of the most beautiful women he had ever seen in his life. He felt her left hand sliding back into his trousers and his balls tensed, ready to be assaulted again. But her hand slid underneath them, slipping between his thighs and pressing up against his buttock-cleft. What was she doing? Her ring finger was probing at him, tickling through his arsehole hairs, touching his arsehole, pushing at it.

It slid easily inside, lubricated with her yelm or his own sweat, and curved, probing at the lower wall of his arse-chamber, feeling for his prostate. This was why the fingernail was trimmed. Yes. This was why. It pressed hard as she sucked eagerly on his cock and he felt his cock throb in her mouth, his balls tightening painfully to the fork of his thighs. This was it. He couldn't hold back any longer. He was boiling up, boiling over. He came, spurting torrentially into her warm, welcoming mouth, expecting to hear her choking on it almost at once. But she didn't. She received it in silence, tongue working busily under his cockhead, encouraging him on. He thrust himself at her, pulling himself on to the bubble by the hand-holds, pushing his cock deeper into her mouth, wanting to slide it into her throat and continue coming there, so that she would have to acknowledge the volume he was flooding into her, so that she would have to choke and splutter.

But she didn't. Not a sound. Because, after all, this was her job. And now he couldn't reach her throat in time anyway, because he had finished coming. Her mouth slid silently off his cock and her ring finger slipped out of his arse, work over. He took a deep breath through his nose, then through his mouth, comparing the smell and taste of her pussy-soiled knickers. Her left hand left his trousers.

'Mmmm,' he heard her say with her mouth full. She was back behind the window.

He let go of the handholds and lifted the knickers off his face. She was smiling at him again, lips closed on a mouthful of spunk.

'Mmmm?' she said, gesturing with one hand.

'Your knickers?'

She nodded. He put them back into the tunnel underneath the window and she picked them up, standing up to slide them back on. He watched her, his cock slowly softening. She sat back in her chair.

'Mmmm mmm,' she said. 'Thank you.'

She pressed a button on the desk in front of her and a little vertical tube opened in front of her. Eyes still fixed on his, she bent forwards and put her mouth over the tube. She smiled again, lips relaxing so that spunk gleamed between them, and began to dribble spunk into the tube, letting it slide from her mouth in little spurts and drips, thick and slimy and full of bubbles, glistening obscenely in the low light inside the booth. His cock stopped softening. That was his spunk inside her mouth. Christ, look how much there was. He had nearly filled her mouth with spunk. It was still spilling out of her. OK, *some* of it was spittle and some of it was just air (look at all the bubbles) but most of it was spunk. Pure, thick, salty spunk. And he had done it.

She was blowing now, fuffing spunk off her lips, her cheeks working as she gathered what was left inside her mouth and spat it out. *Ptu. Ptu.* A thought struck him. He waited. She ran her tongue over her lips and inside her mouth, over her teeth, opening her mouth wide so that he could watch, her eyes still on his, watching his reaction. Then, she leaned down even further, to wipe her tongue on the edges of the tube, sliding it up and down.

She sat back, reaching under the edge of the desk in front of her.

'We try to clean out every drop, sir,' she said. Her hand came back from under the desk, tugging up a long plastic tube with a little bent end. Something started to suck and he jerked involuntarily, reminded of a dentist's chair. Yes. It was a dentist's sucker or whatever it was called. She slipped it into her mouth, sliding it between her teeth, along her gums, eyes still on his, extracting every last drop of spunk in her mouth. When she had finished she put the tube back under the desk, then leaned forwards, finally looking away from him, pressing buttons on her computer terminal. Her eyebrows went up.

'Oh, sir, I did say you were a big boy, didn't I? And you've certainly proved it.'

She picked up a silver fountain pen and opened his bank book. She wrote carefully in it, then blew gently on the page before slipping it back into the tunnel beneath the window. He picked it up. The '20' in the deposits column had been neatly crossed out and replaced with a '28'. He looked up.

'It was only an estimate, sir. It quite often happens, on the first visit, that our cumstomers exceed the estimate, so we don't make estimates for the second visit.'

She smiled happily.

'We just wait and see what comes up.'

'Yes,' he said.

'Well, sir, I think that's everything for the first visit. You've made your first deposit and I look forward to seeing you again soon. All you need to do now is choose a girl for your next visit and start counting the days. Yes, sir, anyone you like. Except me, of course. You can't have the same girl twice in a row. It's against company regulations. Goodbye.'

She stood up in her chair, reaching for the top of the window with her left hand so that her right breast flattened against the glass, the golden fountain and the silver spray just a few centimetres from him, and the motto. SEMPER SPUTAMUS. Something rattled. She was pulling down a blind with writing on it. The writing said: ORIFICE CLOSED. He looked sideways. The other assistants were all smiling at him again. And she had said he could choose one of them. Christ. Well, he'd seen JULIA and MARY and REZA and SUSANNAH and FIONA and CHARLOTTE and ZUFIA and DAISY. He walked further up the line of booths. More dazzling smiles met him. Asians, blacks, Chinese. Flawless skin, flawless teeth. He shook his head. He couldn't choose. He'd have to start at the beginning and work his way down the line visit by visit. He walked back to the first booth. JULIA.

'Your book, sir?'

146

He passed it to her and she typed at her terminal for a moment, then put the book into a slot underneath it. It slid inside.

'Cumstomers often take this way out, sir,' she told him.

'This way out?'

'When they can't choose any particular girl for the second visit.'

'Ah.'

'But I promise you, sir, I won't disappoint.'

The book had slid out of the slot underneath the computer terminal. She picked it up and put it on the desk, then picked up a silver fountain pen like the one Susannah – Susie – had used and wrote in it, then put it back into the tunnel beneath the window. He picked it up. '13/6', neatly typed. 'Julia', handwritten in white ink.

'Thank you,' he said.

'Thank *you*, sir.'

'See you on the, uh, thirteenth.'

She beamed.

'Yes, sir. I'm looking forward to it. Oh, and, sir, one other thing.'

'Yes?'

She nodded downwards.

'Zip yourself up before you leave. Cumstomers often forget, on their first visit.'

Stroke IV

1. To play the game you need a coin, preferably one dated with a prime number: 1901, 1907, 1913, 1931, 1933, 1949, 1951, 1973, 1979, 1987, 1993, 1997, 1999, or 2003. You start in a small dressing room with two doors: a green one and a red one. There's a naval uniform hanging on the wall: black silk shirt, black silk trousers, black silk underpants; a heavy greatcoat of black leather; gleaming black boots; and a black officer's cap that says HMS BUM. You put the uniform on, noticing something inside the pockets of the greatcoat. You reach inside and pull out a small shaving-kit with a nearly finished tube of shaving cream and what looks like a blunt razor. You examine the other pockets and find a whistle.

If you want to leave the room by the green door, go to 42.

If you want to leave the room by the red door, go to 50.

2. You've chosen one of them and can now cunt-fuck her. Her sisters lift her under her thighs and hold her up for you with her legs wide apart. You order them to spit on their free hands and moisten her cunt for you, though she's already started to juice. Her sisters obey, spitting on to their free hands and rubbing the spittle into their sister's cunt. You

wank at your cock slowly as you watch, then step forwards to fuck her. You can smell spicy female sweat and feel the heat pouring off their smooth skin. You take hold of your cock with one hand and with the other vee her cunt-lips apart as her sisters adjust her for you. As you slide home, she gasps with pleasure and her sisters pout a little with jealousy. But they're conscientious young women and don't let this stop them doing their duty to the best of their ability, and so they keep their sister admirably positioned as you get into your rhythm and start fucking her properly. She's tight, hot and slick, and you feel almost as though you're fucking all three of them at once as you put your hands around the waists of her sisters and haul yourself forwards, sending your cock into her up to your balls, then sliding out, over and over. She gasps at every thrust and her sisters are starting to pant with the effort of holding her up and steady for you. She's got her arms around her sisters' necks and as you approach orgasm you put your mouth and nose into one of her exposed armpits, sniffing and licking at the hot, fresh sweat streaming from it. It's all you need and you gasp into her armpit as your cock starts spurting inside her hot, tight cunt. You slide out of her, knees shaking.

The girls still want to thank you for rescuing them. Go to 67.

3. Groaning, you awake to find yourself tied face-down on the filthy bed in the apelike creature's underground chamber. Hairy fingers are exploring your arsehole. You start to scream and struggle but it's no use: you're about to be buggered and your adventure is over. Go to 1 if you'd like to play the whole game again.

4. You start climbing using the technique you mastered earlier, sliding your index and ring fingers

149

and big toes deep into arseholes and gradually working your way up. Below you, you hear turds splattering on the floor and an occasional rush of water as the floor is washed clean from the large holes you noticed at the foot of the wall. You're getting tired but keep climbing, pausing occasionally to rest and look above you. You notice a pale patch on the wall of the shaft about fifteen or twenty degrees to your left and as you get nearer to it you realise that it's an open doorway. You climb sideways towards it, your wrists and shoulders really starting to ache now. Suddenly your sweat-moistened fingers start to slip out of an arsehole and you think you're going to fall. Toss your coin.

If you get heads, go to 12.

If you get tails, go to 52.

5. You steer for the poolside and pull up alongside it, pushing the superstructure up so that you and the woman can get out. It's hard work and her arse bounces and jerks on your cock, but finally the superstructure's up and she can stand, sliding her arse off your cock and then climbing out of the ship as you wrench at her ankle-chain where it's attached to the ship. It comes loose suddenly and you can climb out too, your knees trembling and your cock soiled with rich-smelling spunk and shit.

The game is over. If you want to play again, go to 1.

6. You've decided to creep across the chamber and hope the apelike creature doesn't notice you. You have to pick your way carefully through the bones thickly strewn across the floor. Toss your coin.

If you get heads, go to 8.

If you get tails, go to 31.

7. You choose to unchain one of the women, then push her over to the open trapdoor and order her

down the stair. Reluctantly she obeys. You cautiously walk down the stair after her, straining to see the treads in the light shining through the trapdoor above you. Suddenly the trapdoor slams above you and you're plunged into complete darkness. The woman screams ahead of you and you hear something growling. A light flares up from below and you see that the stair below you are empty. The woman's screams are suddenly cut off.

If you want to climb back up the stair to try and open the trapdoor, go to 44.

If you want to continue down the stair, go to 18.

8. You've nearly reached the open doorway on the other side of the chamber when you trip on a bone and fall to the ground heavily. You hear an enraged growl from the bed behind you: the creature has spotted you. You pick yourself up and run desperately through the doorway, but you've twisted your ankle and can't move very fast. You run down a long corridor into complete darkness, hearing the creature's growls echo off the walls behind you. Suddenly you crash into a door. Toss your coin.

If you get heads, you're knocked unconscious. Go to 3.

If you get tails, you manage to pick yourself up and try to open the door. You discover that it's bolted. Go to 65.

9. The ship is slicing through the piss and you tense yourself, wondering what will happen as the prow rams into the poolside. In the last couple of seconds the woman notices what is happening and cries out. She asks you to steer out of trouble, but you ignore her. With a crash the ship rams the end of the pool and you're driven forwards against the woman's back, your cock sliding even deeper into her tight arse, making her cry out with surprise and pain. It's

all you need to start coming, and the woman whimpers in time with each spurt of your spunk into her arse. Suddenly you feel cold liquid on your feet: the ship has been holed by the collision and piss is starting to pour in. You'll have to steer for the poolside. Go to 5.

10. You press the button that sucks milk from the woman's breasts, charge the guns, then begin to fire them, learning how to judge range from elevation. Suddenly you notice that the other ship is close behind you, closing in to attack. You turn the ship, and order the woman to pedal at top speed, but when you press the button to charge the guns again, the woman cries out as the tube sucks uselessly on her tender nipples. You realise she's out of milk and decide to try and ram the enemy ship instead. Go to 21.

11. You apologise for interrupting him and he grunts surlily before turning back to the helpless woman. As you continue along the corridor you hear, with perfect clarity through the now open door, the cane strike the woman's buttocks again and another cry of pain. Then you hear the door slide shut and the next cane-stroke is muffled. Go to 62.

12. Your worst fears are realised and you slip, sliding helplessly down the wall to the floor far below. You clutch desperately at the buttocks, trying to slow yourself, but you're only half-successful and land very heavily. Go to 25.

13. You choose the one you want to cunt-fuck and kneel in front of her while she's still chained to the wall. Her hands and feet have been chained wide apart so that her armpits and thighs are open and unprotected, and you have unrestricted access to her pussy. You sniff at it, noting that she's dry but fragrant, then begin to kiss her inner thighs, slowly

working upwards on each until you plant a kiss directly on to her pussy-lips, which slowly start to swell and part. She struggles a little, her flesh trembling under your lips. You start to lick her inner thighs too, tasting her skin, working your way upwards again until you lick teasingly at her pussy-lips, tickling them with your tongue. She swears at you, telling you to lick her properly, but you ignore her and work at her inner thighs with your tongue again before raising your head and putting your tongue into her bellybutton. She swears at you again and you reach up and run your fingers over her breasts, noting that they're hot and firm and her nipples have hardened. You squeeze her nipples, twisting and tugging them until she cries out with pain, then you lower your head back to her pussy. You sniff at it again, savouring its muskiness while you insult her, telling her that it smells of fish, that she's a dirty, unwashed slut. You press your nose directly into her pussy, working it between her pussy-lips, feeling it smear with pussy-juice. You rub your lubricated nose up and down her pussy, pressing the tip on to her clitoris, then starting to lick her again, working your tongue up and down her pussy-lips, exploring every millimetre of them, savouring their warmth and flavour. She starts to moan as your face grows wet with pussy-juice. When you think she's ready you stand and unzip your trousers, then push forwards against her, telling her to lick your face while you fuck her. Her chains rattle as she pushes herself out at you, begging you to insert your cock into her as she kisses and licks your pussy-juice-smeared face. You finger her pussy, fingers splashed with hot pussy-juice, forcing her pussy-lips even further apart as you put your cock to her and slowly slide it in. She groans with pleasure, praising your size and solidity, and you start to fuck her, making her chains rattle rhythmically, forcing her firm arse to flatten against the cold wall of the shaft. Her pussy pulses on your delighted cock, seeming to suck at it, before reluctantly releasing it for the out-stroke, then drawing it deeper on the in-stroke. You squeeze and torment her breasts and nipples, forcing your tongue deep into her mouth, which tastes hot and sweet. She moans, her tongue battling back against yours, then you take your mouth off hers and start licking her exposed armpits, savouring her musky sweat as you thrust harder and harder at her, still squeezing and tormenting her breasts. You rub your mouth and chin in her armpits, coating your own skin with her sweat, then start kissing her again, ordering her to lick her own sweat off your skin as you release her breasts and lower your hands to her waist, slipping them between her buttocks and the wall as you stop thrusting for a moment, then start again, feeling your hands crushed between the wall and her firm buttock-flesh. You dig your fingers into her buttocks, gasping now as orgasm boils up in your balls. She thrusts herself out to meet your strokes, begging you to fill her with spunk, and you gladly oblige, spurting thickly and heavily inside her tight pussy, crushing your chest against her breasts, feeling the hardness of her nipples even through your clothing. You slowly slide out of her, your cock still stiff. Go to 69.

14. You've decided to cane one of the girls with an unmarked arse. You step behind her, gloating over her white skin, imagining how the first cane-stroke will bite into her flesh, making her bark with agony, then plead for release. You rotate the shoulder of your caning arm, loosen it for the first stroke, taking a few experimental swings, making the cane swish through the air, clenching your free hand to keep it

154

from your cock as you watch her buttocks tighten with fear. Then you steady yourself for the first stroke, take a deep breath, release it and take another. You swing your arm back. Go to 61.

15. The buttocks start protruding from the wall at just the right height for you to bugger one, and you circle the shaft making your choice, sticking your fingers into their arseholes and testing for tightness and heat. You find one to your liking, unzip and move up close to it, fingering the arsehole apart and fitting the head of your cock to it. Another pair of buttocks is at just the right height for you to kiss and lick it and you begin doing so as you slide your cock slowly into the pair of buttocks below, gasping. You start to bugger the lower pair of buttocks. Another turd splatters on the floor behind you but you continue to bugger and lick the arses you have, reaching out and fingering other arseholes too or slapping buttocks with your hands. Your strokes get deeper and faster and suddenly you groan and start coming, pumping spunk into the hot arsehole you chose. Your knees feel weak as you slowly withdraw, releasing your cock from the arsehole with a pop. Toss your coin.

If you get heads, go to 24.

If you get tails, go to 51.

16. You examine the trapdoor but it's held shut by a small but sturdy combination-lock. You ask the three women, all of whom are chained to the wall, what the combination is and they tell you it's been tattooed underneath their pubic hair, one number for each of them. You try to see what the numbers are by fingering through their pubic hair, tugging it apart to see what is tattooed on the skin beneath, but the hair is too thick for you to see properly. You realise you will have to shave them. You take out the

shaving-kit you found when you dressed in the naval uniform and begin to lather the first of them, using as little shaving foam as possible from the tube, which is nearly empty. Then you start to shave her, being careful, but still making her squeak and complain, because the razor is even blunter than you thought. The number is slowly exposed as you shave away a central patch of her pubic hair. She's excited by the shaving and you're able to supplement the shaving foam with her own pussy-juice. Finally the number is exposed: 1. You go to the next woman, leaving the one you've just shaved begging you to fuck her. The tube of shaving foam runs out as you lather the second woman's pubes for shaving and you have to be more careful than ever with the razor. She squeaks and complains, but she's excited by the shaving too, and you're able to supplement the shaving foam again with pussy-juice. The number is slowly exposed as you shave away a central patch of her pubic hair. You think it's 3 but it might be 2, so you have to shave a little more. You were right: it's 3. To prepare the third woman you have to scrape shaving foam off the pussies of the first two and carry it across to her. She squeaks and complains when you start to shave her but as before she is excited by it and you're able to supplement the shaving foam with pussy-juice. When you're moistening your fingers with it, she complains that the shaving foam already on your fingers makes her pussy sting. You shave a patch of her pubic hair off and uncover the third number: 5.

If you want to use the number immediately and open the trapdoor, go to 33.

If you have been excited by the shaving and want to have sex with one of the women, go to 69.

17. You've decided to cane the girl already caned. You step behind her, gloating over her red-striped

156

arse, imagining the pain already seething through it and how your fresh cane-strokes will add to it, heaping pain upon pain. You rotate the shoulder of your caning arm, deciding not to take any practice strokes so that the first stroke is a complete surprise. You swing your arm back. Go to 61.

18. As you climb down the stair the odd growling gets louder, the musky odour gets stronger and the dim light gets brighter. You realise you've reached the bottom and are standing in the doorway of a large circular chamber lit by the evil glow of luminescent fungi growing on bones scattered on the floor. You pick out the shape of a large bed where a giant apelike creature with matted white fur is sleeping, growling to itself as it dreams of unspeakable pleasures. You notice an open doorway on the other side of the chamber and decide to try and creep across without waking the apelike creature. Go to 6.

19. You let go with one hand and reach down to unbutton your trousers. Toss your coin.

If you get heads, go to 41.

If you get tails, go to 54.

20. Suddenly you smell burning. Milk has hit your ship and ignited the special chemicals impregnating the wood your ship is made of. You try to keep your prow aimed at the enemy but the woman is frightened and her arse has tightened convulsively on your cock. You struggle to concentrate on the battle, but the ship is rocking on the waves already caused by the battle, making your cock bounce inside her arse and pushing you to the brink of orgasm. Flames are rising from the deck of your ship now and you realise you'll have to steer for the poolside quickly or be forced to scuttle the ship while you and the woman are still aboard. Toss your coin.

If you get heads, go to 60.

If you get tails, go to 43.

21. You've decided to ram. You aim directly at the enemy but even as you move towards it, you see its forward guns swinging to cover you. They quiver and you know they're firing milk at you. Toss your coin.

If you get heads, go to 20.

If you get tails, go to 63.

22. You've chosen one of them and are ready to bugger her. Her sisters prepare her for you. They make her bend over and pull her buttocks apart while one of them moistens her arsehole with her tongue. She moans a little as her sister's tongue works at her arsehole, asking her to push it deep inside. When she's well-moistened, her sister moves back and you can step forwards to service her glistening arsehole. Her two sisters hold her buttocks apart for you, almost like a door, and you put the head of your throbbing cock to her arsehole, feeling the sticky spittle. You push but she's an anal virgin and very tight. You push harder but she doesn't open and you have to ask her sisters to hold her steady. They're happy to obey, but she cries out as you push harder at her, forcing your cock against her arsehole. Panting, you draw back a little and ask one of her sisters to moisten the head of your cock with saliva. They both move to do it and you smile, then let both of them lick at the head of your cock, their smooth hot tongues making you groan with lust. Then you ask them to hold their sister's arse open for you again and you move forwards with renewed confidence to take her anal virginity. You put your cock to her arsehole and push again, harder and harder, and she cries out on a rising note that breaks into a scream of pain as your cock suddenly jumps forwards in her arse, sinking through the tight sphincter into the juicy depths of her virgin arse. You almost come at once,

but you bite on your lower lip and manage to hold orgasm back, feeling the walls of her violated arse throb on your cock. Then, slowly, you begin to bugger her, revelling in the sense of possession, in the soft cries of pain she releases in time with each thrust, the soft grunts of relief with each half-withdrawal. Gradually you start to fuck her faster, your balls tightening to the fork of your thighs, galloping at her in a long, tightening rhythm, faster and faster until you're suddenly coming, hurling hot spunk into the depths of her arse, thrusting your cock deep into her, chasing the spunk with your cockhead. She gasps and shudders, telling you it's like being flooded with molten cream, and you hear her moan with disappointment as you slide your cock out of her arse, knees trembling, ears delighting in the thick pop of extramission as your cock finally leaves her arse.

The girls still want to thank you for rescuing them. Go to 67.

23. As you turn back your feet slip on the floor and you start to slide down the corridor faster and faster. You scrabble to stop yourself but it's no good: the floor is getting steeper and more slippery all the time and the smell is overpoweringly strong now. Suddenly your feet slide into space and you're left scrabbling to hang on to a lip of oozing rock, nearly vomiting at the stink of shit that rises from beneath you.

If you decide to have a final wank before letting go and falling into the shit that undoubtedly waits beneath you, go to 19.

If you decide to get it over with and let go now, go to 47.

24. You're ready to try and climb up the shaft. The wall is slick and damp but the buttocks are close enough for you to think you can climb it by sticking your fingers and toes into their arseholes. If you haven't

159

already done so, you take your boots off and push them into the pockets of your greatcoat, then start experimenting and discover that by inserting the index and ring fingers of one hand deep into an arsehole, you can start to pull yourself high enough up the wall to put the index and ring fingers of the other hand into a higher arsehole and repeat, holding yourself steady by lodging your big toes in arseholes lower down. But inserting your fingers into tight hot arseholes excites you, and your cock has stiffened and is throbbing eagerly (again).

If you decide to climb the walls of the shaft despite the state of your cock, go to 4.

If you decide to bugger one of the protruding buttocks before you start climbing, go to 15.

25. Still dazed, you start struggling to your feet. However, you're still on your knees when water starts to flow from the large holes in the wall you noticed earlier, streaming down the floor towards the central hole. The flow gets stronger and stronger and you realise it's starting to sweep you down the floor towards the central hole. You scrabble desperately to keep in place. Toss your coin.

If you get heads, go to 40.

If you get tails, go to 64.

26. Milk splashes harmlessly in the piss beside you and flames are already starting to lick towards the superstructure of the enemy ship. You've beaten him. Go to 5.

27. You unchain them from the altars one by one, your cock stiffening as you smell the fresh sweat rising from their skin. While one of them squats to piss on the face of the hairy, muscular man lying chained on the floor, the other two thank you again, firm young breasts bouncing, and say that they want to reward you for your help. Go to 67.

28. You want to be sucked but you can't decide which mouth to stick your cock in first, so you decide to run a little competition. You ask the girls to kneel in front of you in a semi-circle, then tell them that they each have to compose a six-line rap about fellatio, the best of which will win its composer first suck on your cock. They giggle, looking hungrily at your stiff cock, and one of them puts up her hand to begin. You nod and she raps: 'I said to my sis' as I went down south,/"All I want now is a cock in my mouth."/My sis' said, "Sis', you ain't nothing but a slut",/I said, "In the mouth's better than the butt";/My sis' said, "Yeah?" "Yeah," I said, "that's right,/'Cause the mouth's full of spit, not full of shite."'

One of her sisters snorts with derision and puts her hand up for her turn. You nod and she raps: 'A cock in the mouth's worth two in the bush,/When push comes to shove and shove to push,/'Cause a cock in the mouth's placed just right/To be licked and be sucked all the way through the night;/That way you fulfil what's a young girl's dream:/A gut packed tight with hot fresh cream.'

The final sister shakes her head sorrowfully and puts her hand up for her turn. You nod and she raps: 'This homie comes to me and he's packing some heat,/'Bout a nine-inch rod of solid meat,/He laughs and says, "Girl, I'm outa your class,/This won't fit neither your cunt nor your ass."/I said, "You don't need no conventional fuck/From a girl equipped with a hurricane suck."'

Her sisters shake their heads and snort too. You muse over the raps, asking for one of them to be performed again, then you choose the one you like best and nod to the composer. She shuffles forwards a little on her knees and closes her mouth over your cock, sucking eagerly. Her sisters watch jealously, mouths open and leaking saliva, but you've no intention of neglecting any of them and after a few seconds you order the winner to give them a turn too. She slides her mouth off your cock and another mouth closes eagerly over it, dark eyes fixed upwards on yours. You breathe in deeply, controlling yourself, then tell them to start performing the raps again, sharing the lines between each other so that a new mouth closes over your cock at the end of each line. They obey and start rapping and you close your eyes to savour the lyrics and the change-over of mouth at the end of each line, but the combination of pornographic lyrics and fellatio rapidly proves too much for you and before the second rap is halfway through you start spurting. The girl who's sucking your cock swallows your spunk greedily and noisily, and when you open your eyes and look down at her she smiles up at you like the cat that got the cream. You clear your throat and thank her, your voice shaky with pleasure.

The girls still want to thank you for rescuing them. Go to 67.

29. You choose the one you want to bugger and find the key that unlocks her chains. You release her, then spit on to your fingers. You order her to bend over and hold the cheeks of her arse apart. She obeys and you kneel behind her, your cock throbbing up against the zip of your trousers as you see her pink arsehole revealed between her splayed white cheeks. You rub spittle into it, working it deep with your fingers, and hear her murmur involuntarily with pleasure. When she is well-moistened, you unzip your trousers and lower them, ordering her to crouch on the floor with her arse in the air. As you close up behind her, she starts trembling. You reassure her, feeling for her arsehole with one hand while you

162

guide your cock towards it with the other. Her arsehole feels hot and slick on the head of your cock, but when you push forwards she cries out softly, her sphincter resisting your advance. You try again, forcing your cock hard against her arsehole, telling her to open to you. The pressure mounts and she moans, then screams as your cock slowly slides into her. She's tight and hot and you pause for a moment to savour her before beginning to fuck her, getting deeper with each thrust until your pubic hairs are brushing the stretched rim of her arsehole and your cock is deep in her arse. She's babbling and moaning, begging you to stop, but you notice that she's thrusting back involuntarily against you with every stroke, part of her revelling in her buggery, and when you come, spurting thickly and heavily inside her, she groans with pleasure. Panting, you slide your cock out of her, hearing it come free with a pop. When you've recovered, you chain her back to the wall. Go to 69.

30. You climb cautiously down the stair, smelling the musky odour get stronger and stronger. Suddenly you hear a sound: a low growling that rises and falls; and you notice that a dim light has started to shine ahead of you.

If you decide to climb back up the stair and unchain one of the women to send ahead of you, go to 7.

If you decide to continue climbing down by yourself, go to 18.

31. You reach the doorway safely and slip through it. You walk down a long corridor, hearing the sounds from the chamber slowly dwindle behind you. It's too dark to see but you keep your hands in front of you and suddenly touch another door. It's closed and bolted but you cautiously start to slide the bolt open. Toss your coin.

If you get heads, go to 65.

If you get tails, go to 55.

32. You order the woman down on all fours on the poolside with her arse in the air, then kneel behind her, adjusting your cock to slide it into her arsehole. Smoke and heat from your burning ship pass over you in gusts as it settles deeper into the piss. Though you haven't noticed it yet, the ship that beat you is manoeuvring to pull up along the poolside too, a few metres behind you. As you slide your cock into the woman's arse and start slowly buggering her, gasping with pleasure and sliding your hands under her smooth belly to take hold of her firm breasts, you suddenly feel something splatter on your back. For a moment you think it's piss again, but it's warm and when you turn and look behind you, you see that the enemy ship is firing at you again, splattering you with milk. You continue to bugger the woman as the milk is fired at you, splattering on your back and buttocks and trickling down over your flanks and balls. You feel orgasm build and start to bugger her harder, making her grunt and moan as you drive your cock into her tight arse and dig your fingers into her breasts. You come with a groan, firing warm spunk into her arse as warm milk splatters on your back. There's a sudden hissing and spluttering from the pool as your stricken ship finally slides under.

The game is over. If you want to play again, go to 1.

33. You use the combination to open the lock and pull the trapdoor open. Underneath it, a narrow stair descends into darkness, though there seems to be a dim light far below. You sniff suspiciously, thinking you can detect an odd musky odour.

If you want to climb down the stair immediately, go to 30.

If you want to unchain one of the women and send her down first, go to 7.

34. You've turned to the left and walk up the sloping corridor. Suddenly you hear a muffled sound through one of the walls: it sounds like a cane or whip landing on flesh, followed by a cry of female pain. You stop and put your ear carefully to the wall, trying to ignore the cold moisture that touches your skin. You hear the sound of the cane or whip on flesh again, followed by another cry of female pain, and this time there's no mistake. You step back and look carefully at the wall and think you can see the outlines of a door. You step forwards and start running your hands over the wall, pressing and tapping, trying to find the mechanism that opens the door. Start tossing your coin. When you've got three heads or tails in a row, go to 48.

35. You've decided to fight him for possession of the caning-chamber and step inside glaring at him belligerently. He laughs and swings to face you, raising his cane higher before slashing at you with it. You dodge the blow and jump closer to him, aiming a kick at his groin. Toss your coin.

If you get heads, go to 49.

If you get tails, go to 56.

36. You choose the one you want to suck you and find the key that unlocks her chains. You release her and she kneels in front of you. You order her to unzip your trousers and take your cock out. She obeys, her hands trembling as she unzips you and manoeuvres your cock through your trouser-slit. You watch her open her mouth and blow gently on the head of your cock, which twitches with pleasure. She slowly puts her head forwards and begins to lick the head of your cock, curling her tongue around it, putting the tip of her tongue in your slatch and

wriggling it from side to side. Then she slides your cock into her mouth, sucking hard, and her head begins to bob backwards and forwards, mouth-fucking your cock. Her mouth is warm and moist and she's an expert fellatrix, heightening your cock-joy with well-judged slurps and murmurs of admiration and gratitude. You run your fingers through her hair, ordering her to suck harder or move her mouth faster or slower, and she obeys, staring up at you each time you speak. When you're ready to come you ask her whether she spits. She shakes her head, her mouth jerking sideways on your cock. You ask her whether she swallows. She nods, mouth jerking up and down on your cock. You tell her she has to swallow every drop, then you start fucking her mouth hard, sliding your cock further and further inside. She responds eagerly, gasping for breath between your thrusts, sliding a hand into your trousers to fondle and squeeze your balls. You groan as you feel yourself starting to come. Your spunk starts to spurt into her mouth and she gulps it down eagerly, squeezing your balls expertly so that you feel as though you're going to discharge every drop they contain. When you've finished spurting, she cleans you so that you don't leak in your trousers afterwards, massaging your cock from the root to force all the remaining spunk out of it. She licks at your slatch, absorbing every drop. When she slides her mouth off your cock it's still hard. You chain her back to the wall.

Go to 69.

37. You walk along the corridor to the right, and notice an increasingly bad smell and that the torches are starting to flicker and go out. The floor is slowly beginning to slope and get slippery. As you pass the entrance to another corridor you've had enough and you turn back. Toss your coin.

If you get heads, go to 23.

If you get tails, go to 62.

38. You start manoeuvring to make your attack, trying to close the range to fire. The other ship responds and you notice that its guns are turning on you. Your own guns are charged with milk but you think the range is a little too great. Toss your coin.

If you get heads, go to 59.

If you get tails, go to 20.

39. You let go of her left breast and grab for the joystick, ordering her to pedal in reverse. Her arse jerks and writhes on your cock, making it hard for you to concentrate as you try to prevent the collision. Somehow you manage to do it, steering the ship to port as the propeller spins in reverse, cutting the ship's speed slowly away to nothing. Collision avoided, you decide to steer for the poolside. Go to 5.

40. You manage to make it to your feet and struggle back to the wall. Go to 4.

41. Your other hand slips as you try to unbutton your trousers. Go to 47.

42. You open the green door and walk down a long, dimly lit corridor. Torches are flickering ahead of you and you reach another long corridor at right angles to the first with a slippery, steeply sloping floor. The corridor slopes up to the left, down to the right.

If you decide to turn left, go to 34.

If you decide to turn right, go to 37.

43. It's no good: the woman's arse is giving you too much pleasure and you start to come, groaning as your thick hot seed spurts up into her. You lose control of the ship and by the time you've recovered flames are rising too high in front of you for you to steer. Go to 66.

44. You climb back up the stair and desperately push on the trapdoor. It doesn't move. Suddenly

you're surrounded by the musky odour and what seems to be hot air playing around your ankles. You look down but you can't see a thing, only sense some unspeakable presence. You scream as wiry but immensely strong arms suddenly seize your legs and you're dragged back down the stair. Mercifully, your head strikes a tread of the stair and you're knocked unconscious. Go to 3.

45. You continue down the stair and realise that it leads to a brightly lit circular chamber with a large bed. The woman has already been tied face-down on the bed and is being buggered by a giant apelike creature with matted white fur. You see an open doorway on the other side of the chamber.

If you decide to climb back up the stair and open the trapdoor, go to 44.

If you decide to creep across the room while the apelike creature is busy buggering the woman, go to 6.

46. You choose one of them by saying 'Eenie-meenie, minie, mo, catch a slapper by her toe, if she squeals, swell her woe, eenie-meenie, minie, mo.'

If you want to cunt-fuck her, go to 2.

If you want to bugger her, go to 22.

47. You plunge downwards, feeling the air suddenly get hotter around you, and land with an enormous splash in what seems like a bottomless lake of shit. For a few moments you think you're going to drown in it and then your feet suddenly touch a stony bottom and you realise that you can stand with your head just out of it. Your face is streaming with shit and you've already vomited, but you cautiously feel your way forwards, and discover that the stony bottom is sloping upwards and the shit is getting shallower. Finally you struggle ashore completely soaked in shit. You see a dim light ahead of you and stagger towards it, occasionally stopping to throw up.

Your adventure is over. Go to 1 if you'd like to play the whole game again.

48. Suddenly the wall slides open under your hands and bright torchlight floods out on to the corridor with a rush of hot, moist air charged deliciously with female sweat. You peer blinking into the light and see that the door has opened on a square chamber in which three naked women are chained over three altars, white buttocks raised invitingly to the air. Dozens of torches are flaring and spluttering and there's a rack of canes and chains along the far wall. A short, muscular, hairy man in black leather shorts, black leather waistcoat and black leather jackboots is standing over one of the women with a cane raised in his hand. He's glaring over his shoulder at you in outraged surprise and beneath his raised arm you can see three red cane-strokes on the woman's buttocks.

If you want to apologise for interrupting him and continue on your way down the corridor, go to 11.

If you want to fight him for possession of the caning-chamber and women, go to 35.

49. As you aim the kick, your other foot slips on the damp floor and you fall on your arse with a tooth-loosening thump. He's on you in an instant, slashing at you with the cane, and you have to roll backwards in humiliation through the door and back on to the corridor. As you pick yourself up, panting and rubbing at the cane-strokes on your arms and flanks, the man stands in the door for a moment grinning in uncouth triumph, then spits sardonically and steps backwards. The door slides shut again and after a few moments you hear the caning begin again inside the chamber. You try to retrigger the mechanism that opens the door but it doesn't seem to be working any more and, after a frustrating couple of minutes,

169

you continue on your way down the corridor. Go to 62.

50. You open the red door and walk down a long corridor that ends in a circular room about five metres across. Three naked women – a blonde, a redhead and a shwarts – are chained like stars to the walls, breasts, armpits and pussies bare and unprotected. A key is hanging on a hook midway between each pair, three keys in all, painted white, red or black. There's a trapdoor in the middle of the floor. Go to 69.

51. As you step back from the freshly buggered buttocks, trying to decide what to do next, something moist and heavy strikes you on the head and you fall over. You realise you've been hit by a falling turd. Go to 25.

52. You manage to recover and climb the last few metres to the open doorway. As you drag yourself over the edge, you hear a final turd landing on the floor far below. You smile and sit on the floor for a few moments as you take your boots from your pockets and pull them on. Then you stand and walk down the dark corridor that stretches ahead of you. You come to a partly closed door and push it open. Go to 58.

53. You've decided to cane the girls rather than release them. First of all you examine the buttocks of the girl you heard being caned through the wall of the corridor, bending close to them and feasting your eyes on the red weals across her white skin before beginning to knead and stroke her arse. She protests, begging you to release her and her sisters, but you don't reply, and continue to paw at her arse with one hand while wanking yourself slowly with the other. When you feel you're getting ready to come, you stop reluctantly and go over to examine her sisters, and

knead and stroke their arses too, glorying in the firmness and weight of their buttocks and the silken smoothness of their moist, sweating skin. Your wanking hand itches for your cock, but you exercise rigid self-control and complete your examinations before strolling over to the rack of canes. The hairy man chained on the floor has started to recover from the kick to his balls and threatens you hoarsely as you make your selection from the canes. You ignore him and lift down a long, supple cane of golden bamboo. You swing it thoughtfully, making the strokes harder and harder, your cock stiffening even more as you see the apprehension in the faces of the chained triplets. Then you stroll behind them to examine their buttocks and decide which girl to cane.

If you want to cane the girl already caned, go to 17.

If you want to cane one of her unmarked sisters, go to 14.

54. You manage to unbutton your trousers and take hold of your cock, which has already started to stiffen. You squeeze at it and get it fully erect, then start wanking cautiously, still hanging on with your other hand. You feel your other hand starting to slip and wank harder. Just as you're starting to come, your other hand finally slips. Go to 47.

55. You manage to slide the bolt fully open. You pull the door open and slip through it, gasping with relief as you find a bolt on the other side and slide it firmly home. You then turn and find another long corridor in front of you. Light is flickering at the far end and you walk cautiously towards it. When you get to the light you discover that it comes from torches blazing along the walls of another corridor at right angles to the one you're on.

If you choose to take the new corridor to the left, go to 34.

If you choose to take the new corridor to the right, go to 37.

56. Your foot thuds into his groin and he grunts with pain, dropping his cane and clutching at his balls as he sinks to the floor of the chamber, moaning. You take a set of chains from the rack along the far wall and chain him up before turning your attention to the three women. As they realise what has happened they start babbling with gratitude, telling you how grateful they are that you've rescued them. You realise that they're identical triplets: dark-haired young women with fresh young faces and firm, rounded bodies.

If you want to confirm their gratitude and release them, go to 27.

If you want to spurn their gratitude and cane them, go to 53.

57. You order her to pedal faster again and feel her bouncing deliciously on your cock as you steer the ship down the pool. You gasp with pleasure as sweat trickles down her naked back from the effort of pedalling the ship, moistening the meld of your cock and her arse. You let go of the joystick and reach in front of her for her breasts, tugging the plastic tubes off the nipples and squeezing them hard in both hands. They're warm and soft, moistened with sweat, and you can make milk squirt from her nipples by squeezing them between your index and ring fingers. She moans as you work at her breasts, her arse tightening on your cock as she pedals harder and harder, driving the ship faster and faster through the piss. Suddenly you realise that it's going to ram the end of the pool.

If you decide to carry on regardless and let the collision ram your cock deeper into her arse, go to 9.

If you decide to try and manoeuvre out of trouble, go to 39.

58. You pass through the door into a huge brightly lit shed that reeks with piss. The smell gets worse as you walk towards what looks like a giant swimming pool which stretches to the far end of the shed. Three naked women are standing to attention at your end of the pool by three shapes that you can't recognise. As you approach them one of the women – the one in the middle – squats and begins pissing into the pool. You can see now that the shapes are huge models of battleships from the early twentieth century. They're about fifteen feet long, with two sets of guns near the bow and a third set on the stern, and are ready to slide forwards into the piss. You come to the edge of the pool and look into it. It's full of piss and seems to be about ten or twelve feet deep, light rippling through its yellow depths. Small waves are travelling down it from the far end and splashing up over the edge, splattering your boots. The woman who was squatting on the edge of the pool and pissing into it has finished now and stands. You notice that she is attached by her ankle to the middle ship by a thin stainless steel chain. She salutes you but you ignore her for the moment and examine the ship. It's called *HMS BUM* and you discover that the grey-painted wooden superstructure swings back to reveal two moulded seats inside. The forward seat partly overlaps the aft seat, so that whoever is sitting in it will be pressed against whoever is sitting in the aft seat. There's a set of pedals in front of the forward seat. Your cock starts to stiffen in your trousers and you finger the bulge thoughtfully. You look at the other two ships. One of them is called *HMS RUM* and the other *HMS CONCERTINA*. Their superstructures are hinged and lift back to reveal seats designed in the same way.

* * *

Now you order the woman in the middle to stand fully to attention so that you can examine her. Her breasts look large and swollen and when you finger her nipples they feel hot and tender. She moans and bites her lips. You squeeze the right nipple and a thin jet of milk spurts from it and splatters on your leather greatcoat. Your cock stiffens to full erection. You squeeze her left nipple and a jet of milk squirts from that too. You wipe the trickles of milk off your greatcoat with your fingers and tell her to lick them clean. She obeys. Her tongue feels warm and soft and your cock throbs inside your trousers. You examine the other two women, and find that their breasts are full of milk too. You order them all into the ships and they climb aboard, pulling their chains with them. They sit in the forward seats, resting their small bare feet on the pedals. You order them to start pedalling and propellers start turning in the bows of the ships. You order them to stop and take out your whistle. You blow it and bare feet – big ones – sound on the floor behind you. You turn around and see three naked black men walking towards you, big dicks swinging. All three of them are wearing boots and two of them are wearing naval caps too. One cap says HMS RUM, the other HMS CON'TINA. You order the two wearing caps into the ships behind the women, but they stand beside the ships first to have their cocks sucked to full erection. You get undressed and leave your clothes in a pile well back from the edge of the swimming pool, then walk towards your ship and climb aboard, sliding into your seat behind the woman, still wearing your cap. The men are still having their cocks sucked by the women in the ships, black dicks pushed into white faces, but they're fully erect now and you order them to get aboard. You haven't adjusted yourself properly in your seat yet

174

and you realise that you will have to stick your cock up the woman's arse to do it. You reach forwards to finger her nipples again, and make milk dribble from them to moisten your fingers. Then you order her to raise herself a little and slide your cock underneath her. You moisten her arsehole with her own milk, and hear a sudden cry from the woman inside *HMS CONCERTINA*. You realise that one of the men has just slid his big cock up her arse and you wince at the thought of it. You order your woman to sit on your cock and she obeys. Your cock slides smoothly into her milk-lubricated arsehole and she whimpers as she pushes herself back against you. The woman in *HMS RUM* cries out too. You ask the men if they're ready to launch and they nod, grinning as they clutch the women to their naked bodies. The women have pained expressions on their faces. You turn your head and order the third man to close the superstructures and launch the ships, but he tells you that the breasts aren't connected to the guns yet. You ask him what he means and he comes forwards and shows you, tugging forward a harness and a pair of plastic tubes. He adjusts the harness over the woman's shoulders and connects the plastic tubes to her nipples, then points out a little control panel beneath your right hand. He tells you how to control the guns and you experiment for a minute or two, making them swing left or right and elevate or fall. Then he tells you how to charge them with milk. You press a button and the woman whimpers, milk flowing forwards in the tubes, sucked from her breasts. He tells you that the guns are now charged and ready to fire. You press the fire-button for the number one guns and they shudder a little. After a second or two you see splashes in the pool about fifteen or twenty feet away where the milk has hit the piss.

The man tells you that the wood of the ships has been treated with a special chemical that will start burning if it is splashed by breast-milk. He then points out the joystick beneath your left hand that controls the rudder. There's an emergency button on it that will scuttle the ship if you're hit and on fire. You thank him for the lessons and he swings the superstructure shut over you and the woman. There are eye-slits in it forward, starboard and port, and a system of mirrors allows you to see astern too. Suddenly the ship shudders and you feel the keel scraping on the edge of the pool. The man is pushing it into the pool. The woman whimpers again as your cock bounces in her arse, then cries out as the ship suddenly lurches forwards, its stern dropping into the pool with a heavy splash. Now it's afloat, wallowing a little without steerage way. You order her to start pedalling and gasp as she does so, because the movement makes her arse ripple deliciously on your cock. Slowly the ship begins to move forwards. You hear another splash from port astern and realise that *HMS CONCERTINA* is afloat. You look in the mirror and see it wallowing on the pool, slowly beginning to move forwards. *HMS RUM* is being pushed into the pool, too, by the panting third man. You experiment with the joystick, learning how to steer but keeping a careful eye on the other two ships. There's another splash and *HMS RUM* is afloat now too, but almost immediately something seems to be wrong: it's wallowing in the piss, gradually beginning to settle deeper. The superstructure swings open and you see the woman struggling to get off the man's cock and slip overboard. The man tries to stop her, continuing to bugger her until the ship is nearly half-submerged, when he releases her and allows her to jump overboard and she starts dogpaddling to shore, trailing the broken chain. Then the man follows, his still-erect cock shining as though polished as he lowers himself into the piss and starts swimming for shore.

If you want to test fire the guns again, go to 10.

If you want to attack the remaining enemy ship immediately, go to 38.

59. You press the button that fires your guns and suddenly notice puffs of smoke rising from the enemy's prow. You sigh with relief as you realise you've hit him with milk and ignited the special chemicals impregnating the wood the ship is made of. His guns are firing now too. Toss your coin.

If you get heads, go to 26.

If you get tails, go to 20.

60. You manage to keep orgasm down and steer for the poolside. The other ship closes in again and you see its guns swinging to cover you. They fire again but you hear splashes in the piss close by as the milk misses. You manage to draw up along the poolside and try to lift the superstructure and get out. Flames are licking all along the prow of the ship now. You order the woman to help you and she shoves upwards at the superstructure too, making you gasp as your cock is driven even deeper into her arse. Finally you manage to get the superstructure up and order the woman off your cock as piss splashes inside the ship, splattering your body and face. She stands and your cock uncorks from her arsehole with a pop. She scrambles out of the burning ship on to the poolside and you notice that she's still chained by her ankle to the ship. You manage to wrench the chain loose and follow her, smiling to yourself as you realise that, though you've lost the battle, you've still got a stiff cock and a tight female arsehole to slide it into.

If you decide to play the whole game again immediately, go to 1.

If you decide to bugger the woman before playing again, go to 32.

61. *Thwak.* Your arm lashes forwards, licking the long golden tongue of the cane at the defenceless buttocks before you. The girl barks with agony and her chains rattle as she struggles to break free of them. It's no good: she's too securely held and she has to remain exactly where she is, a fresh cane-stroke glowing across her white arse. You swing your arm back again. *Thwak.* Your arm lashes forwards and the long golden tongue of the cane licks greedily at the buttocks, the crisp sound of its cruel kiss sounding clearly through her almost feral cry of pain. Another fresh cane-stroke is glowing against her silken white skin. You suddenly sniff, smelling cunt-juice and, when you step forwards and look between her half-parted thighs, you see a gleam of moisture. She's started to leak. You step right up to her, put your free hand up between her thighs and finger her cunt, coating your fingers with cunt-juice before stepping back to continue the caning. You anoint the head of your cock with her moisture and slowly start wanking, swinging your arm back again. *Thwak.* Your arm lashes forwards and the long golden tongue of the cane leaves another red stroke glowing against that marvellous arse, its crisp cruel kiss sounding through her cry of pain once again. It's nearly too much for you: your hand is pumping at your cunt-juice-lubricated cock and you have to drag it away, closing your eyes and clenching your teeth to stave off orgasm. You take deep breaths, trying to stay calm, then slowly open your eyes and let the cane fall to the floor of the chamber. You walk to the remaining sister with the unmarked arse, and stand in

front of her, your swollen cock ticking almost in her face. You order her to suck you or be caned herself, and she obeys, taking your soiled cock into her mouth and sucking at it as she stares up at you with wide, fearful eyes. A few seconds of her hot, moist mouth is all you can endure, and you slide your cock out reluctantly and return to the girl you've just caned. You slide one hand over her red-striped arse, revelling in the heat you've awakened in it, rummaging between her thighs with the other, moistening your hand before beginning to wank at your cock again. You wank slowly but it's no use: five or six strokes in and you start coming with a groan, hurling your spunk across the curves of her arse like a rich salty sauce across the sugary mounds of a trifle. You almost black out with the violence of your orgasm and the sound of blood in your ears almost drowns the soft splashes of your spunk landing on her arse. Then, gasping, you step back, distractedly noting that her inner thighs are glistening with cunt-juice almost as far down as her knees. You tell her she's a slut, but she laughs and tells you that it hurt but it was fun and she wants you to please unchain them now. You shrug and say you will. Go to 27.

62. You walk along the corridor until you reach another door. You open it and step through into a dark room, leaving the door open so that the light from the torches helps you see what is inside. The floor is damp and you nearly slip over as you walk directly across the room, staring up at the walls, which are lined with curious spirals that you can't quite make out in the dim light. Suddenly you stop in your tracks, your heart pounding. You have nearly walked forwards into a wide hole in the middle of the floor: it's only the stink of shit rising from it that alerted you in time. You walk back, and your eyes

become accustomed to the dim light. Now you can see that it's another circular shaft, rising to an unguessable height above, and that the curious spirals on the walls are made up of protruding female buttocks. They're arranged by colour, so that a spiral of pale buttocks is next to a spiral of lightly tanned coloured buttocks, which is next to a spiral of medium-tanned buttocks, and so on. You notice a series of large holes all around the wall where it meets the floor. Suddenly something splatters on the floor to your left and when you walk there you find the remains of a large turd splattered over a patch of floor.

If you decide to try and climb the walls of the shaft, go to 24.

If you decide to bugger one of the protruding buttocks, go to 15.

63. You hear splashes in the piss beside you and realise that the milk has missed. The enemy ship makes frantic attempts to manoeuvre away but it's too late: your prow strikes it heavily, caving in part of the bow and driving your cock even further into the woman's arsehole. You order her to pedal backwards, gasping as her pumping legs make her arse ripple on your cock. As you slide back from the rammed ship you notice that it can't steer properly and is starting to settle deeper into the piss. It's sinking and the man aboard evidently decides to steer for the poolside. Go to 57.

64. The flow of water is now too strong for you and you're swept helplessly towards the central hole. You clutch desperately at the edge, reasoning that if you can hold for a few seconds longer the water will stop. Gradually the flow of water stops, but you're not able to climb back on to the floor, and so you hang by your aching arms from the edge of the hole.

If you decide to have a final wank before letting go and falling into the shit beneath you, go to 19.

If you decide to get it over with and let go now, go to 47.

65. The bolt screeches loudly as you slide it open and you hear growls coming down the corridor. You pull frantically at the bolt but it keeps sticking and you can hear the monster pounding down the corridor behind you. Toss your coin.

If you get heads, go to 55.

If you get tails, go to 68.

66. You press the button on the joystick that scuttles the ship and cold piss suddenly starts washing around your feet. You struggle to push open the superstructure and get out, but the woman screams. You remember that she is chained to the ship and the piss is ten or twelve feet deep. Piss is rushing into the ship through the holes torn in the keel by the scuttling mechanism and you scrabble to find where the woman's chain is attached to the ship. It's taking too long: the ship is going under and the piss is rising above your waist, then your shoulders. You find the place and tug desperately at the chain, trying to tear it loose, your cock still inserted deep into the woman's arse. The piss is lapping at your chin, rising higher and higher. You take a deep breath and hold it as the piss rises above your head and the ship begins a long swooping descent to the bottom of the pool. Desperation makes you stronger and you suddenly feel the chain tear loose. The woman's arse throbs on your cock with relief as you shove desperately at the superstructure, trying to swing it back so you can both get out and swim back to the surface. The woman helps you, thrusting up at the superstructure too, forcing herself further on to your cock so that even as the two of you struggle beneath the cold

181

piss you realise you're on the way to another orgasm. Suddenly the superstructure loosens and slowly begins to swing up. You try to open your eyes but the piss makes them sting and you have to pull yourself out by touch, your cock finally sliding out of the woman's arse. You feel as though you can't hold your breath any longer but you finally get out of the ship and kick frantically for the surface, clutching the woman by the waist. Gasping, you both break the surface and swim feebly for the poolside, ears and nostrils full of cold piss. When the two of you reach the poolside you drag yourselves out of the piss, gasping and spitting.

The game is over. If you want to play again, go to 1.

67. The girls want to thank you for your help: in other words, you can have sex with one of them. You swallow and make your decision.

If you want to refuse their kind offer and continue down the corridor, go to 62.

If you want to be sucked, go to 28.

If you want to cunt-fuck or bugger one of them, you need to choose one of them first. Go to 46.

68. A hairy body crashes into you from behind, throwing you forwards against the door and knocking you unconscious. Go to 3.

69. If you want to bugger one of the women, go to 29.

If you want to cunt-fuck one of the women, go to 13.

If you want one of the women to give you a blow job, go to 36.

If you have the combination of the trapdoor and want to open it, go to 33.

If you want to have a look at the trapdoor, go to 16.

Stroke V

Even though he was listening for the knock on the door he barely heard it. A mouse-tap, timid pale knuckles on the hard dark wood of his door. Mouse-tap with pearl-knuckles. Should he pretend not to have heard it, wait and let her knock again? But what if her courage failed her completely and she ran from the surgery, tears beginning to form in her dark eyes, those pale knuckles pressed to that small soft mouth, bitten by her small teeth as she tried to keep back her sobs? And anyway, even if she was going to knock again, he didn't want her to; he didn't want to wait the few seconds it would take. His cock was filling his trousers too solidly for that.

He cleared his throat.

'Come in,' he called.

Nothing for a moment. Had she taken fright and run away? He was staring so hard at the handle of the door that when it trembled he wasn't sure it had, his desire to see it moving was so great. Had it moved? Was her small hand beyond the door, clutching the handle, tightening, turning?

Yes. Thank God. It trembled again, then turned. She was there. She was coming in. He hurriedly looked down at his desk, at the notes he had casually arranged there, and even found the calmness to pick up his pen and begin to make a note. The door opened and he heard her step inside the room. His heart thumped and he longed to look up at once, to smile at her reassuringly, to welcome her into the room. But he knew he couldn't. He made the note and said, still not looking up, 'Close the door, please.'

Using, as before, the masculine form of the imperative. Oh, the sheer devilish cunning of it, the trickery, the deceit. The poor innocent fly walking into the spider's parlour. The little fly and the big spider. The very big spider. Bigger all the time. Sitting in its web of dark hair in his trousers. He heard the door close and prepared the look of surprise on his face for when he looked up. He heard her feet crossing the floor.

'Sit down, please,' he said, still looking at the notes, paused for a moment more, then put his pen down and looked up. Masculine imperative again.

'Now, what – ah, what can I do for you, Miss?'

The look of mild surprise rose on his face as he saw her – as though he had expected to see a man – then it faded almost at once. An everyday doctor's mistake. Expect a man, receive a woman. Her mouth opened. She was about to speak. He was about to hear her speak. For the first time. Oh, dear God, let me savour this moment. Let me savour it for ever. But her mouth hung open for a moment, moist, perfect, then closed. Such a sweet mouth. A rosebud. A rosebud in that lily-pale oval, with that mouse-button of a nose, those coal-dark eyes, those slender strokes of the eyebrows. Speak, my sweet. Speak to me. Then he had to fight to keep from groaning aloud with ecstasy and delight. She was colouring, the lily-pale oval of her face flushing to rose, her eyes pleading with his. Blushing. She was blushing. Oh, the taste of her was on his tongue, sweet as the urine of a diabetic. Her mouth opened again.

184

'I . . .'

A whisper, a silken thread of sound snipped short.

'My dear?'

Her eyes dropped.

'I – Dr Tsemmfa sent me to see – he said – a letter.'

Her face was dark rose now, full of blood, and he realised he was gazing at her too greedily, wolfishly almost, and when her eyes raised to his again she would see his lust in his face. He dropped his eyes to his notes again, drew in a long, silent breath and released it.

'Ah, yes, I remember now. Dr Tsemmfa. Let me see. The letter.'

He pretended to look for it, biting his lip a little as he moved papers back and forth and saw that his hands were trembling with excitement. Calm yourself. Breathe in, breathe out.

'Yes, here it is.'

He lifted the letter and pretended to read it.

'Let's see. He says – ah. Yes. Hmmm. *Hmmm*. I see.'

He put the letter down, still pretending to read it, carefully arranging his expression for when he looked up again. A foundation of professional interest, with perhaps a sprinkling of disbelief? A *soupçon* of sternness? He looked up, but it had all gone for nothing again, for her eyes were demurely lowered, the blush in her face faded to pale pink. He sniffed, hoping to see her eyes lift again to his, and said, 'Yes, Miss, Dr Tsemmfa wrote to me last month telling me of the, uh, unusual features of your case. The most unusual being, of course . . .'

He allowed his voice to trail off, wanting her to look up. Ah, she did almost. She raised her eyes if not her face, and lowered them at once when she saw that he was looking at her, the blush rising again. He coughed discreetly.

'The most unusual being, of course, the means by which you contracted the condition. Because he tells me that you insist you have not caught it, well, my dear, how shall I put this? You insist that you have not caught it in, ah, the usual fashion. Is that correct?'

Her eyes were still lowered and he watched a little bolus of anxiety rise and sink in her throat.

'Yes.'

So quiet. So shy. So cock-stiffening.

'Are you certain, my dear? Because this is a serious condition, you must realise. It can go through a population like – what is the phrase? – like wild fire. Like very wild fire indeed. We must nip it in the bud, even – or should I say especially? – when the bud is so very pretty a one as yourself. Do you realise that when the condition enters its infectious phase, with a mere two, ah, partners a month you could be responsible for the infection of half the population of the island in a mere six months?'

Her eyes lifted again, flicked back down, lifted. Timidly, she shook her head.

'No, Doctor. I – I would not be.'

'My dear Miss, I beg to differ. It is a matter of clear epidemiological fact, well-established by numerous field studies. I myself contributed a paper to a venereological journal of some repute only two years ago clearly establishing –'

But her head was shaking again. Ah, so there was some spirit there. Some rebellion in that tender pale body.

'No, Doctor. In general, that may be true. In my case, no.'

'Hmmm?' he said, slowly working his hand over his lap towards the bulge in his trousers.

'For you see, I intend to have no more . . . partners. Since the death of my husband –' his hand reached the bulge and began, very slowly, to squeeze '– I have been chaste. It is difficult, yes, but I have been so. For two years now.'

'Yes?'

Christ. He could hear the excitement in his voice. Stop pawing yourself, you fool. Stop it. He clenched his hand into a fist and slid it up his leg, resting it on his knee.

'Yes, Doctor. I promise you.'

'And, Miss, of course, I believe you. Dr Tsemmfa believed you. That is why your case is of such exceptional interest. He and I are writing a p–'

She was blushing again.

'But you knew, of course?'

She nodded once and he had to clench his other hand to keep it from crawling to the bulge in his lap.

'Yes, Doctor.'

'Then as I say, with the strictest preservation of anonymity, he and I are writing a paper on your case and have the highest hopes of it. This is the first recorded case of – how shall I put it? – ah, extra-venereal infection with the condition. It is of unusual interest and may offer most valuable insights into the nature of the dis– of, ah, the condition. Perhaps point the way, in coming years, to the possibility of a cure.'

'Yes, Doctor.'

'It may be some consolation to reflect that through your suffering others may be healed.'

'Yes, Doctor.'

'But, of course, it is better that you suffer not at all. And that is why Dr Tsemmfa has sent you to me. I have had some success in treating the condition over the years and – though I must be careful not to raise your hopes too high – I feel some measure of confidence that I can – if not cure you completely – ameliorate some of the more, ah, distressing symptoms.'

187

'Yes, Doctor. Thank you, Doctor.'

'Then, my dear, if we might begin. If you would like . . .'

He held his hand out flat, pointing at the screen in one corner of the room.

'Yes, Doctor. At once, Doctor.'

Ah, good, Tsemmfa had accustomed her to the routine. Clothes off, then on to the couch, ready for the examination. She slipped off her chair and walked behind the screen. He said, raising his voice a little, 'Of course, my dear, you are continuing to take the medicines Dr Tsemmfa recommended?'

Her voice was slightly muffled when she replied.

'Yes, Doctor.'

'And the, ah, discoloration is still evident?'

'Yes, Doctor.'

'I see. Please inform me when you are ready, my dear.'

But if she were still taking the medicine, of course the discoloration would be present. Tsemmfa knew what he was doing: he could have had her pissing all shades of the rainbow, and for a time they had debated it. A different pill every day, so that she pissed red on Monday, orange on Tuesday, yellow on Wednesday, green on Thursday, blue on Friday, indigo on Saturday, violet on Sunday. But pissing rainbows might have sent suspicion trickling into even her innocent and trusting head, so in the end they had decided that she would piss a simple and discreet violet. Certainly enough to disturb her, hopefully enough to distress her too, but not enough to make her suspicious. No, nowhere near enough to make her suspicious.

'I am ready, Doctor.'

He shivered with pleasure. She was ready. Waiting for him behind the screen, skirt and knickers off, slim thighs still pressed together, pale-lipped vulva sealed between them. He pushed back in his chair and got to his feet, looking carefully at the screen. No, she was completely concealed. He reached into his trousers, tugging his erection vertical, tucking it behind his belt, buttoning up his white coat over it.

'Good. I would like to have a sample myself, for tests, if I may?'

'Doctor?'

'A sample, my dear. Of the discoloured, ah, *fluid*.'

'Yes, Doctor.'

He began to walk to the screen, holding his hands out in front of him. Had the trembling subsided?

'Do you think you will be able to supply one for me, my dear?'

'Yes, Doctor. I think so. I will try.'

He reached the screen, his erection arrowing harder in his trousers, but pointing straight up, so there was no tell-tale bulge. He silently inhaled and stepped behind the screen, forcing himself to glance casually at the neat little pile of clothes on the chair and the shoes side-by-side beneath it, then at the foot of the couch, forcing his eyes to travel casually up her body, over her small, slim feet and ankles, her shins, her knees, her thighs, her stomach, her small breasts still tucked in their green bra but with her slim hands folded protectively over them nonetheless.

'Thank you, my dear. You are used to the routine, by now, of course?'

'Yes, Doctor.'

He crossed to the sink on the wall near the foot of the couch and began to wash his hands.

'But I will need to examine your, ah, chest too, my dear, so if you would . . .'

A pause, then: 'Yes, Doctor.'

He tugged a square of paper from the dispenser above the sink and dried his hands, then dropped the crumpled paper in the bin beneath the sink. He picked up the little packet sitting between the taps and turned back to the couch.

'Thank you, my dear.'

She was unclipping the bra, blushing again, knees pressed harder together as though to compensate for the exposure of her breasts. The bra-catch clicked open and the cups dropped half-away from her breasts. He closed his eyes for a moment, not able to breathe. She drew the cups away from her breasts and laid the bra on the couch beside her. He found it impossible to stop his tongue momentarily moistening his lips. Oh, they were perfect, perfect. Creamy little mounds topped by the daintiest little brown nipples in perfectly circular areolea. Oh, he would have to measure them at her next appointment. He would *have* to.

'Thank you, my dear.'

Her hands folded over them, fluttering like small wings, left laid on right in a pale fan, and he looked away and began to open the packet, annoyed with himself when he saw that his hands were trembling again. Stop it, he told them. They stopped. He pulled the tightly folded rubber gloves out, shook them loose, dropped the wrapper to the floor, then tugged them on, dropping them crisply into place over his wrists with a sound like tiny pistol-shots. She jerked nervously on the couch and he hid a smile, feeling himself relax. He was in control. She wouldn't notice a thing. He stepped up to her.

'This is the third week, you say?'

'Yes, Doctor.'

He tutted sympathetically and leaned forwards to begin.

'Another most unusual feature of the case.'

He gently put a fingertip on her right knee and pushed.

'My dear?'

She paused a moment, then swung her legs apart. One of his knees trembled momentarily.

'If, ah.'

Damn. He had to cough before he could begin again.

'If you could swing them just a *little* wider.'

Better. Calm and professional. She swung them a little wider.

'Ah, Miss, though when I said a little wider, I meant, ah, a lot wider.'

'I am sorry, Doctor.'

She swung them wider, opening the pale inner planes of her thighs to him. And her pussy. Yes. Some girls have cunts, but she, she definitely, she pre-eminently, she had a pussy. A beautiful little pussy. Its pale lips were tightly closed, meeting in almost sculptural perfection, like a *yoni* carved in pale jade. But it was flesh; it would be warm beneath his fingers, and no *yoni* carved in stone had a slim crescent of black silk arching just above it, almost dusted on the skin.

'Thank you, my dear. May I?'

He looked at her and as their eyes met there was another explosion of blood in her face. Such a delicate and sensitive register of her emotions. Her eyes dropped and her mouth opened, trembling, moist.

'Yes, Doctor.'

Whispered. She might have been put on the earth to say that to him. To make his cock throb and strain upwards even harder behind his belt. His treacherous knee trembled again for a moment and he clenched his hands below the edge of the couch. Don't tremble, he ordered them. But her eyes were lowered to her fanned hands on her breasts and she wouldn't see.

When he unclenched them and raised them they were steady. He reached between her thighs.

'A little wider still, my dear. And this time –' allowing self-deprecation to seep into his voice '– when I say a little, for once I mean a little.'

'Yes, Doctor.'

She was smiling. His gloved fingertips brushed her pussy. She stopped smiling. He gently explored her, running his fingers up and down her pussy-lips, folding them back from the hidden cleft of her vagina, folding them forwards over it.

'And now, Miss. If I may begin the, ah, internal examination?'

She nodded without speaking. His heart thumped in his chest as he slowly prised her pussy-lips apart and began to work a finger up into her. Oh, she was tight.

'You're a little tight, Miss. If I may?'

She nodded again. He raised his gloved hands from between her legs, and lifted them to her mouth. She released one hand from her breasts and propped herself on it as she leaned forwards to meet his gloved hands, opening her mouth, to allow him to push the fingers inside one by one. She licked at them, nose wrinkled a little at the taste of the rubber, moistening them conscientiously and carefully. All five on his left hand, all five of them on his right.

'Thank you, Miss. Dr Tsemmfa has you well trained.'

She laughed nervously, not sure if he was making a joke. She leaned back, her hand coming back over her breasts. Well, he wasn't. It was true. Tsemmfa did have her well trained, the delicious little bitch. He put his gloved hands back between her legs, and prised the lips of her pussy open again, working her own spittle into the gap between them, trying to insert his fingers again. No. He lifted his hands again.

'A little more, Miss. And when I say a little more this time, I mean, ah, quite a lot more.'

She released the hand from her breasts and leaned forwards, accepting his gloved fingertips into her mouth again, as she worked spittle up in her mouth, licking harder, moistening them thoroughly. After all, this was helping her as much as it was helping him. Her nose was wrinkled again, but not so much this time. Can you taste yourself on them now, you little slut? The taste of your own pussy? Is it good? Is it sweet?

'Thank you, my dear.'

He dropped his hands quickly to her pussy, not wanting any of her spittle to drip too soon. Yes. Rub it in again. Rub it in well. Work it between the pussy-lips and try again. Ah. Good. Easier this time. But was that entirely due to the spittle? He was into her beyond the first knuckle, sliding deeper. No, not entirely due to the spittle. Her pussy-lips were unfurling a little and her pussy-walls were not entirely, ah – how shall I put this? – unmoist. She had tasted herself on the gloves, second time around. And it had excited her. Second knuckle now. He could begin probing. Any second now.

Yes. His fingertip had brushed it. Something hard, deep in her pussy. He pushed his finger deeper, probing the outlines of the thing. It was smooth and hard. Circular. Tubular. About twice as thick as his finger, less than half as long. He worked his finger down beneath, deliciously deep into her, the tip of his tongue curling just between his lips as he concentrated. No, he needed two fingers and more lubrication. He slid the finger out, and raised his hand back to her head.

'Just a little more, Miss, if you please.'

Hand slipping off her breasts again, propping her up as she leaned forwards, small mouth opening to

193

admit his fingertips, one by one. And had she done it more quickly this time? More eagerly perhaps? Did her mouth linger on the fingertips as he pushed them between her lips, releasing them reluctantly? He thought so. Because she could taste herself more strongly now. The tang of pussy-flesh on his fingers. Particularly on the ring finger of his right hand. Would she linger most of all on that one, working her tongue at it more than thoroughly? Yes, maybe. He thought she did. She could taste herself, and she liked it. A tele-auto-cunnilinctrix. Licking his fingertips one by one, longing to taste herself on them, and liking it. Licking them and liking it.

'Thank you, Miss.'

He put his hands together as though in prayer and dropped them back between her legs. Oh, yes, she liked it. Her pussy-lips had peeled wider, the gap between them beginning to glisten with a fluid that wasn't her spittle. She was juicing up. He breathed in through his nose slowly and furtively. Yes. Juicing up very nicely. He put his hands back on her pussy, rubbed the spittle in well, then slid two fingers into her, deep into the velvet groove. This time she shivered as he slid them in. She was liking this more and more. He found the little metal tube and took hold of it, ready to begin sliding out. But there was something he must do first.

'I've found Dr Tsemmfa's pessary, Miss. Has it been any good?'

She was silent for a moment. He looked up at her and her eyes skated under the contact of his, flickering timidly to the left, then returning, before flickering to the right.

'I . . . I don't think so, Doctor.'

'No? But he assures me in the letter that this time he used the maximum safe dose. Surely it has had some effect?'

She shook her head.

'None at all?'

'No, Doctor. Because you see – I can feel it happening again.'

'*Now*?'

She nodded, swallowing, beginning to blush again. He looked away from her, lowering his head and looked hard between her legs, glorying in the sight of his two fingers buried in her pussy.

'Oh dear. Oh dear, oh dear. I'm afraid it may be more serious than Dr Tsemmfa gave me to understand. If just a simple examination can trigger the reaction, well . . .'

She sobbed quietly, just once, and he had to purse his lips hard to prevent himself smiling.

'But my dear, you mustn't take it so hard. I am *sure* there is something I will be able to do for you. If you don't mind me saying so, your, ah, pudendum is in splendid health. The pink of condition. That is really half the battle. It's just this little reaction of yours to stimulus. Come on, I'll just see if I can find the little fellow. Somewhere up here, isn't he?'

She nodded, looking down, eyes slitted and darkened with what he was sure were tears. His heart was thumping in his chest again. It was so delicious to do this, so delicious to tease and torment her, to know that there were weeks more to come, that he would examine her over and over again, bury his gloved fingers to the knuckles in her tight pussy over and over again. Gently probe for her clitoris. Pretend to have difficulty finding it, fumbling around it, so that when at last – 'Ah, here it is' – he pretended to find it, it would be in a worse state than ever. Swollen and erect, a little pleasure-thorn swollen on blood and shame.

'Oh dear, I see. I see. This is a very strong reaction to what were very mild stimuli. I can see why Dr

195

Tsemmfa was so concerned. And you say it has been happening for months?'

'Yes, Doctor. Six months.'

'Or perhaps a little more?'

She closed her eyes tight this time and, yes, her eyelashes were definitely darkened with tears. She sniffed, nodding.

'A little longer?'

She nodded again.

'Yes, Doctor.'

Almost whispered.

'How much longer? Seven months? Eight perhaps?'

'No.'

He could barely hear her voice.

'Then nine? Ten? A year?'

She shook her head again.

'It has –'

A sob broke in her chest and he licked his lips quickly, watching her hands bounce on her rising and falling breasts.

'It has always been like that, Doctor. For as long as I can remember.'

He waited a moment before replying, allowing incredulity to gather in his mouth.

'As long – as long as you can remember? But you told Dr Tsemmfa . . .'

She broke. The tears were flowing, dripping from her closed eyes on to her breast-clasping hands. He slipped his fingers out of her pussy and stepped up the couch, gently taking hold of her bare shoulders with his gloved hands, moistening them with her own spittle and pussy-juice.

'Oh, my dear. But you must not let it distress you so. It was very naughty of you not to tell Dr Tsemmfa the full truth, but I can quite understand why. You were ashamed, were you not?'

She nodded, splattering tears higher up her body, on her collarbones, and lower, on her upper stomach. His cock throbbed in his trousers as he read the tremor of her movement with his hands. He tightened his grip, shaking her a little as though to drive his words home. Very gently. Very considerately. Very compassionately.

'And that is quite natural in one so delicate and naturally tender as yourself. Quite natural –' slightly harder shake '– Quite understandable –' and again '– And honestly, now that I know the truth, I do not see that any harm has been done. In ninety-nine cases out of a hundred, treatment is unaffected by the length of time the patient has had the condition. Indeed, I am not sure if the longer-standing conditions do not respond more vigorously when they are finally treated. Come, come, my dear. You must not distress yourself so.'

She sniffed.

'You must not distress *me*, my dear. You know, it is really *not* a sign of confidence in me, is it? That you should weep like this? Come, let me have a little smile. You really are a most attractive young woman –' (*Careful now*) '– and to see you like this affects me profoundly in ways you can barely begin to guess. A smile for me? Please?'

Blinking, she tried to open her eyes and look up at him.

'For your brusque and brutal old doctor, who has distressed you so with his casual callousness but been punished twice over for it?'

She tried to smile, sniffing again, tears trickling down her cheeks now. His treacherous knee trembled again, and lurid fantasies drove themselves at him. She was sucking him, face still wet with tears, and he withdrew a second before orgasm to spurt copiously over her already glistening skin. He was taking her from behind, working at her breasts with stern fingers, massaging her own tears into her nipples.

'Thank you, my dear. What a pretty little smile you have. Really, you know, you are a very, very attractive young woman. One can almost believe that has played some role in your, ah, affliction. Has some jealous demon or elemental, perhaps, out of baffled rage at your purity and goodness, seen fit to visit you with suffering, that he might gloat over your tears? I really think it might be so. But in that case, relief will surely be yours one day. One day *soon*, perhaps. Do you not think?'

She sniffed and nodded.

'Come, my dear, let me wipe your tears away and see you smile again.'

He wiped at her face with his gloved hands, moistening the fingertips thoroughly, leaving little shining patches of spittle and pussy-juice on her skin where he had held her shoulders.

'A smile, for your concerned physician? Yes, that's better. Much better. Positive thinking is half the battle, you know. Or should I say, the *other* half of the battle, because, as I have already remarked, your pudendum is in splendid condition and that is the first half of the battle. Put them together and you have won. Eh?'

He gave her shoulders a final, affectionate, avuncular squeeze, careful not to wipe off too much of the tears, and walked back down the couch to continue his work on her pussy. Her legs had swung back together, folding the delicious slit back between the pale velvet facets of her thighs, and he put a fingertip to her knees and pushed them gently apart.

'My dear, if you could?'

She allowed him to swing her legs apart, to expose her pussy again. He pursed his lips for a moment, gazing greedily upon it. Its lips were more swollen still, folding back wider, glistening with pussy-juice, and the warm air between her thighs (he readied himself to inhale deeply and slowly through his nostrils when he had the chance) was charged with pussy-scent, rich and musky. Her own tears had excited her too. Which reminded him.

He put his hands back on her pussy, gently rubbing and stroking, working the tears he had wiped from her face into her. But there was scarcely any need: she was open and oozing, and he could have got three or four fingers into her now with ease. With a little effort he could have got his fist into her, maybe as high as the wrist, even the forearm. And how he longed to try it. Could he convince her it was some new treatment? Could he fist her as she lay on the couch, slim thighs apart, hands still shielding her breasts and those dainty little brown nipples as his clenched gloved hand worked back and forth in her unfolded pussy, slurping gently, slick with pussy-juice?

No, he decided sadly. No, he couldn't. Not today. But perhaps if he laid the ground carefully, perhaps at a later consultation, perhaps if he manipulated her carefully enough, convinced her well enough that her condition was more serious than he and Dr Tsemmfa had first thought, was even potentially life-threatening, perhaps he could indulge himself. And her, of course. Because he was sure she would come if he fisted her. That delicious little slot would tighten on his clenched hand, sealing around it like a mouth.

Mmmm. Delicious prospect. But for now he would have to confine himself to inserting only his fingers. He shook his head a little, realising that he had been rubbing and teasing her pussy-lips a little roughly as he surrendered to the delicious reverie of fisting and that she was more than ready for the internal examination to continue. He glanced up at her. She had stopped crying and tears were drying on her face, glistening saltily. He wanted to lick her cheek, taste the salt there and the subtler chemicals, but that, too, was impossible today. Next week, some week, who knew?

He slipped two fingers inside her pussy, and probed for the metal tube, almost missing it, so slick were her pussy-walls with juice, making his fingertips slide easily to and fro. But there it was. He tried to get hold of it and begin to tug it out, but the pussy-juice made his fingers slip. He'd have to get his fingers underneath and push it out rather than pull it. He pushed and probed, sliding his fingers deeper into her, trying to get them underneath the tube and push it up and out. She gasped a little and he glanced up at her again. Her eyes met his, still moist with tears, reddened and swollen, but for a moment a shock of surprise ran through him. Just for a moment her eyes widened on his, seeming to gleam not with unspilled tears but with secret knowledge, with secret complicity, as though she knew perfectly well what he was doing, as though *she* rather than he were in charge of the examination, as though she rather than he were the trickster, the manipulator, the puppet-master.

Just for a moment. But then her eyes slitted again with unhappiness and embarrassment and the fugitive gleam was extinguished as though it had never been there. And of course, it hadn't. The cornea was irrigated with an aqueous solution of sodium chloride secreted from the lacrymal glands in response to excitation of the limbic system. Of course they gleamed when the light struck them. He snorted a little to himself, finding it oddly hard to take his eyes off hers, almost having to pull them away, so that he could watch his hands as he worked on her pussy.

There. He had looked away from her, back between her thighs. He was watching his hands as they worked on her pussy, two fingers inserted deep into her, hooking beneath the metal tube, slowly and carefully sliding it up and out of her. But there was an odd sensation in his face. An odd crawling. Because she was still looking at him. He could feel her gaze on his face. He glanced up at her, but her eyes were lowered demurely, a chink of white enamel showing in her mouth as she bit into her moist lower lip, struggling to master the pleasure his fingers were causing her. She hadn't been looking at him. There had been no gleam of secret knowledge in her eyes. It was all his imagination.

He looked back at her pussy. Yes, there, gleaming dully between the juicy lips in the shadow of his fingers, was one end of the tube. He pushed harder from beneath, sliding it further up, as though he were delivering a silver dwarf. Because it was silver. A silver tube, inserted snugly into her pussy by Dr Tsemmfa, worked up and out now by him, Dr Liusvek. Another little push and – yes. It suddenly slid upwards slickly and easily, almost jumping into his waiting hands. He lifted it, letting it lie flat across both palms almost as though it were a dwarf-baby or an egg, an odd silver egg. It was gleaming silver, about an inch long, maybe half-an-inch across, with rounded ends so that it could slide in and out of a pussy harmlessly, and there was a very thin, almost invisible seam running around the middle, as though it could be screwed apart, then screwed back together again. As, of course, it could.

'I will just be a moment, my dear.'

He walked from behind the screen, back to his desk, his vision misting a little, ears roaring in confusion, gloved right hand glistening with pussy-juice as it shook, unzipping him with caution, and slide his cock out, gloved left hand clenching hard on the little silver tube he had slid from her cunt. When his cock was out his right hand flew at it, clasped the head, slid back the foreskin and began to rub her pussy-juice into his glans, polishing it, making it gleam rich, oiled purple. He lifted his left hand and slid the tube into his mouth, licking at it greedily. His cock pulsed within his sliding right hand. The taste of her. The taste of her at last. Musky, fishy, salty, sweet, rich and arousing on the smooth silver of the tube. And he could feel the warmth of her pussy in the silver, almost a feverish warmth, as though her pussy had been boiling between her slim thighs, as though when his fingers had first cracked the tightly pressed pussy-lips they should have released, with a hiss, a long white jet of musk-scented steam.

He looked at the clock. Five minutes. He couldn't take longer than five minutes or she might start to get suspicious. But five minutes would be more than enough, far more than he needed. His gloved right hand started to cycle on the head of his cock as he stumbled around his desk and slid open a drawer with his other hand, leaving smears of pussy-juice on the handle and wood. It didn't matter. She wouldn't see from the other side of the desk. Inside, carefully prepared the previous day, there were pages cut from a journal of tropical venereology. He worked quickly with his left hand as his right hand galloped on his cock, lifting the pages from the drawer and laying them on the surface of his desk, slightly overlapping in a square. He greedily absorbed the descriptions and diagrams of exotic genital disfigurations, the extravagant blisters and buboes on sweat-moist female pudenda. Nine pages in all – three by three – sitting on the top of his desk like proofs from a compendium of venereal disease, an *Encyclopaedia Venerea*.

He laid the last page into place, and just in time, because his balls were tightening, his teeth clenching, the muscles of his jaw and throat locking, and he was coming, spraying seed in long spurts on to the pages in a kind of liquid applause or oblation, as though he was sacrificing part of himself to a goddess of venereal disease, smothering her sacred symbols, the blistered and buboed vulvas, in a rich milk as he sucked on a silver egg plucked from the hot moist pussy of one of her priestesses. He managed not to groan, not to snort, coming in complete silence but for the faint splatter of his spunk falling on to paper. The last spurt fell, blood loud in his ears, and for a moment he thought he heard a faint sound from behind the screen – a sigh or gasp, almost a moan – as though she had seen and was dismayed by the sight of his perversion, the frenzied masturbation, the shameless ejaculation on to images of diseased vulvas. Just for a moment. But he hadn't heard that. No. He stared at the screen, blinking, trying to focus properly. No, nothing had moved. She hadn't been watching him, peeping from behind it. No, she had been lying meekly and quietly behind it all the time, legs swung back together, sealing her sweet, seething little pussy in slender thigh-flesh, waiting patiently for him to return.

He breathed out slowly and quietly, then breathed in, looking at the clock again. Kluishti, he had reached orgasm in less than a minute, but no wonder. He had thought he was going to come as soon as he slipped the tube into his mouth and tasted her, and that would have been disastrous, because his seed would have sprayed wildly all over his desk before he had a chance to lay down the pages torn from the venereological journal. He would never have been able to clean it away before he had to return behind the screen and complete the examination. No, there would have been damp patches when she came out. He would have had to send her straight to the door, without being able to sit her down in the chair and give her a few final words of advice, to prepare her for the next consultation.

So it was lucky he hadn't come as soon as he had put the tube into his mouth and tasted her, but he almost wished that he had. He sucked lovingly at the tube as he began to lift the spunk-splattered pages off the desk and back into the drawer, being careful not to let any of the spunk spill as he did so. Yes, he almost wished he had. Almost wished he had come as soon as he tasted her, almost wished he *had* sprayed the room with spunk so that she *had* seen it when she came out from behind the screen. And had smelled it. Had sat down in it on the chair, soaking her dress so that it seeped through to her knickers.

He lifted the last page inside and slowly slid the drawer shut, careful now not to make too *little* noise, then put his face close to the surface of the desk, scanning it for stray splatters of spunk. It was clean. He sat down, folding his softening cock back into his trousers, but tucking it up behind his belt again, ready for it to re-erect when he went to complete the examination. Thinking ahead. That was the thing. Thinking ahead, preparing, plotting. Spinning his webs for his juicy little fly and her juicy little pussy. Keeping in control. His cock twitched, nearly ready to begin hardening again.

He zipped up slowly, silently, then spat the tube out of his mouth into his hands. It was hard to hold onto it. His gloved fingers were still slippery with a musky, salty mixture of pussy-juice, spittle and tears, but the mixture was starting to dry and get a little sticky too, so that helped, and he managed to hold the tube steady and tried to unscrew it. Come on. Unscrew. Unscrew, you fucking thing. He looked up at the clock. He would have to go back to her soon. Soon. And the fucking thing *wasn't* unscrewing. Was he doing it the right way? Yes. There was a tiny arrow next to the line that ran around the middle of it. Unscrew that way. Or was it screw that way? No, screwing shut was easy; it was unscrewing open that was hard. The arrow had to be for that. Unless Tsemmfa had prepared it as a trap. Unscrew, you little fucker.

He was starting to sweat with effort and anxiety. His face would be shiny with it, revealing that he had been doing something *energetic* while he had been away from her. She might think – ah, Kluishti, thank God. It was unscrewing, suddenly slipping apart in his hands, and he could slip out the folded sheet of rice paper inside. He unfolded it, hampered a little by his sticky fingers, and spread it out flat on his desk. Tsemmfa had begun the first line of the poem in his graceful script, like a distant flight of swallows, wings black against white cloud. He closed his eyes, put his fists to his temples and bowed forwards slightly over the paper, thinking furiously. He had prepared many lines and half-lines, trying to guess what Tsemmfa would open with, sifting their conversations for clues, wondering which apparent hint had really been a bluff, which apparent bluff really a hint. This was not too bad, worse than he had hoped, better than he had feared. That. Yes, that one might do. With a little change there – yes, yes.

He repeated Tsemmfa's line silently to himself, then his own. Yes. He nodded, eyes coming open, absorbing Tsemmfa's line again. Yes. That would do. He slid open another drawer and picked up his brush where it had been waiting, already moistened. He dipped it into the ink that had been waiting beside it, and added his line, feeling it slide oddly out of his head through his hand on to the paper. His ink was red and his words hung beneath Tsemmfa's opening line like a distorted reflection in sun-reddened water. There. Finished.

He dusted his line quickly from the pot in the open drawer, blowing at it, and looked up at the clock again. He should wait a minute more for it to dry but he wanted to get back to her. He folded the rice paper up again carefully. Perhaps his line would smudge, but perhaps that would add a subtle ambiguity, cause Tsemmfa to frown and puzzle out what he had written, disturbed at the prospect of facing something truly brilliant, truly dazzling. Yes. He hoped it had smudged. He even paused for a moment, wondering whether he should make sure, open the paper again and check, even rub at his still damp writing with a fingertip here and there.

But no. Serendipity was best. He slipped the folded paper back into one half of the silver tube, put the two halves together and screwed them tight, ready to slide them up her pussy again, to be carried back to Tsemmfa and retrieved. Done. Now, back to work. And good, his cock was stiffening again. He pushed the chair back and stood up, glancing down to check that it was still tucked discreetly up behind his belt. Yes. He strode back to the screen.

'I'm sor–' he started to say, but stopped. Her pale body was archipelagoed with pink, patches of flank and thigh, back and belly darkened faintly to it, almost as though she had come behind the screen, fingering herself to orgasm while he was ejaculating on his desk. He remembered the sound he had heard as he came, the faint sound like a gasp or moan. Had it been her? Timing her own orgasm to his? But how had she known? And look, her eyes met his blinking and guileless, slender eyebrows lifted in wonder.

'I'm sorry, my dear. I was just refilling your pessary with a slightly stronger dose of the preparation Dr Tsemmfa has already been using with you. I feel that we ought to give it a week more, perhaps, before we try something more, ah, *experimental*, shall I say? Oh, but my dear, do not look so frightened. I promise you, I would never allow anything to go up that very sweet little, ah, orifice of yours that presented the slightest danger of anything more than a mild and transient allergic reaction. Please rest assured of that. So, if you would just . . .'

He had got over his worries about her as he was speaking, watching her fright at the mention of an experimental (ha!) treatment, the anxious, unconscious gnawing of her lip that gradually slowed and stopped as he reassured her. She was not acting. She couldn't be. And remember how she had blushed at the beginning of the consultation. No actor, however skilled, can call up a blush at will. Hadn't he read that, somewhere? Hadn't Darwin written on it in *Expression of the Emotions*? He somehow thought he had.

'Thank you, my dear.'

She had swung her legs open for him as soon as he rested a fingertip on her knee. He looked away from her, down between her legs, and his stomach rolled, his anxieties coming back in a sudden rush. Her inner thighs were wet with pussy-juice. She was sitting in a little patch of it, he now saw, the paper covering of the examination couch stained beneath her buttocks. Could she have leaked so much in the time he had been examining her? Or had she really been masturbating behind the screen, while he masturbated on to his desk? He looked at her again. She was looking anxious.

'Doctor?' she said.

'Yes, my dear?'

'You look worried about something. Is there something wrong? Something you haven't told me? My –'

She swallowed and the blush was back again. Something no actor can counterfeit. Surely. But this was no actor; this was an actress. Could a woman counterfeit a blush?

'My secret-shuns are not usually this heavy.'

'Secretions, my dear. It's pronounced se-cre-tions.'

'Yes, Doctor. My secretions are not usually this heavy.'

Surely she was not acting. She couldn't be.

'They *are* a little heavy,' he said judiciously, 'and I think I'm right in saying –' he leaned forward a little, peering between her thighs, gloved hands probing gently '– yes, your little soldier is standing to attention again. But I think that may be half the trouble. A new doctor, you see. Emotional disturbance. Anxiety can have strange effects on these conditions. In some ways, you know, there is reason to believe they are psychosomatic in origin, in part.'

'Syko – Sykosomatic, Doctor? In part?'

'Governed partly by the mind, my dear. A change in the body governed by the mind. Like that truly delightful blush of yours.'

She lowered her eyes, her truly delightful blush returning to her cheeks. Her eyes came back up timidly to meet his.

'Yes, Doctor? You mean . . . my pussy is partly under the control of my mind?'

'Your subconscious mind, my dear. When you are upset or excited, well, it can worsen your condition. That is why I think, if your secretions are a little heavier today, if your little soldier is a little more

208

inclined to stand to attention, it's really nothing to worry about. Once you are used to me, things will go back to normal. In fact, if the slightly stronger dose of Dr Tsemmfa's usual preparation has the effect I am hoping for – indeed, that I will be praying for, my dear – you will be secretion-free. Your pus–'

Damn! He had started to say 'pussy'. But it was OK, that was what she had called it. He smiled, snorting a little at his own slip.

'Your pudendum, my dear, will be dry and no more than a little scented, as is normal in a girl of your age taking moderate amounts of exercise. As you do, my dear, I hope? *Mens sana in corpore sano*? A healthy mind in a –'

But she was saying it with him.

'In a healthy body, Doctor. Yes. I take exercise. And if, as you suggest, it is partly syko –' she stumbled on the word again '– sykosomatic, a healthy body bringing about a healthy mind will bring about an even healthier body, won't it?'

'Uh, yes. I think it will, my dear. I think you understand the situation very well.'

'I think so too, Doctor.'

'Then good. I'll, uh, I'll just put the pessary back and have a quick look at your breasts. And remember, as I'm sure Dr Tsemmfa has already told you, you mustn't take the pessary out for more than a few minutes, even when you are bathing or in bed. Do you understand?'

'Yes, Doctor.'

'Good.'

He looked away from her, back down between her legs.

'One blessing of your heavier secretions is, of course, that it will be easier to insert the little fellow than it was to get him out.'

'Yes, Doctor.'

He moistened the tube on her inner thighs, rubbing it down one, up the other, rolling it almost like a piece of pastry being coated with a special glaze before being popped into the oven. Her pussy would be the oven. Lying there between her thighs, lips oozing, gaping a little. And swollen? Were they more swollen now? And the scent of her pussy-juice? Was it heavier? He swallowed, conscious of her eyes on him again, and put the tube to her pussy-lips.

'Ready?' he asked.

But when he looked at her, her eyes were lowered. She hadn't been watching him. Or was she just adept at reading the microscopic flicker of his eyes that told her with half-a-second to spare that he was about to look away from her pussy and back at her face? Her eyes lifted to his. She nodded.

'Yes, Doctor.'

Huskily. Almost seductively. With a timid undercurrent of excitement at the thought of a handsome middle-aged doctor sliding a silver pessary back into her private parts.

'Good.'

He pushed, sliding the tube into her pussy. Tsemmfa had warned her about opening it, hadn't he? He must have done. Repeatedly. But it wouldn't hurt to repeat it again.

'And of course, Dr Tsemmfa has warned you about opening the pessary?'

He had pushed it nearly as deep as it would go now, his gloved finger buried deep into her.

'Yes, Doctor.'

'It would really ruin the whole treatment and in fact now, with this slightly stronger dosage of the preparation, might even be dangerous. If you got any of the preparation directly on your skin. No, my dear,

210

please don't be frightened. I said *directly* on your skin. Filtered through the pessary it is perfectly safe, apart from the very slight risk of an allergic reaction. Come now, surely you trust me? Yes? Then let's have a little smile. A little smile for your brutal old doctor, who could kick himself for being so clumsy again and not choosing his words more carefully. Ah. Thank you. Thank you, my dear.'

He slid his finger slowly out of her and lifted it free.

'I always watch that bit, Doctor.'

'My dear?'

'At the end of the examination, after Dr Tsemmfa has reinserted the pessary. I always watch to see how far it stretches before it breaks.'

'My dear? I don't understand.'

'My pussy-juice, Doctor.'

'Yes? I'm afraid I still don't –'

'I always watch to see how far it stretches from my pussy to Dr Tsemmfa's fingers, after he's reinserted the pessary. How far it stretches till it breaks. Sometimes it stretches a long way, but not as long as it did just then, with you.'

Was she teasing him? Pussy-juice? Had she called it pussy-juice? And did she really watch it stretching between her pussy and Tsemmfa's fingers, after Tsemmfa had reinserted the pessary?

'Uh, yes, my dear. I see. As I said, I think it's simply concomitant with heightened emotions and psychosomatic disturbance that naturally accompanies, uh, that naturally accompany a change of physician. When you see Dr Tsemmfa, later in the week, things will be back to normal.'

'Less pussy-juice, Doctor?'

He swallowed, annoyed with himself that he had to.

'If you want to put it that way, my dear. But now, really, we must be getting on. If I could just examine your breasts, and then have a few final words before we arrange the next consultation?'

'Yes, Doctor. Would you like me to lick my fingers clean first? Dr Tsemmfa always lets me do that. I like the taste. It's almost as nice as . . .'

She had lowered her voice and he leaned forwards involuntarily, suddenly, horrifyingly sure that she was going to say 'spunk'. Or come. Or semen.

'As nice as – well, I don't know, Doctor. What does p.j. taste like? Could you describe it for me?'

'P.j., my dear?'

Christ. He was almost stuttering. His cock was solid in his trousers, arrowing upwards behind his belt. He watched her lips, suddenly fascinated. They pouted, slowly forming the first syllable of her answer.

'Pussy-juice, Doctor. I always call it p.j., for short. After the first few times I've used the phrase, I mean. It saves time.'

'I see, my dear. Most convenient. But time is getting on and –'

'Yes, Doctor. You would like to examine my breasts. But what about your hands? You'll leave p.j. all over my breasts. My titties, Doctor.'

Her hands suddenly folded away from her breasts and he stared, swallowing, feeling his cock pulse in her trousers. The nipples were erect, swollen up and out from the areolea like slim brown fingertips, as though there were another woman inside her body, just beginning to slide her hands out through the small breasts, to open her like a door and step out. But the woman inside would have nipples too and when they were erect it would seem as though there were a third woman, a woman inside the woman who had been inside the woman. Like a Russian doll.

'Don't you think, Doctor?'

212

He jerked a little. He had been staring at her breasts, musing, maybe even mumbling aloud, throat tight with titty-lust.

'Don't you think that's a better word for them, Doctor? Titties? For a girl like me, I mean. I have a pussy and titties. Not a cunt and tits.'

He swallowed.

'Yes.'

'Good. Thank you, Doctor. You can touch them now, if you like. I like them smeared with p.j. too. When you're finished, if you like, you can . . .'

Her voice was lowering again and he leaned forwards, eyes fixed on her small breasts again. He looked up at her.

'Yes, my dear?'

'You can – you can wash them. If you like. Dr Tsemmfa sometimes does it.'

'He does?'

'Yes, Doctor. With warm water.'

'I see. It's, uh, it's a new technique.'

'Yes, Doctor?'

Was there a whisper of mockery in her voice? But when he looked at her he couldn't believe it. So innocent. So demure.

'Yes, my dear. But if I could –'

'Of course, Doctor. I'm sorry. Please examine my breasts. My titties. At your leisure. And then, if you like, you can wash them.'

He moved towards her, reaching out for her breasts.

'My dear, I assure you, it isn't a case of what I *like* –' but his cock in his trousers belied every word '– it's a case of what is best for the patient. For you, my dear.'

He couldn't restrain a slight gasp of excitement as his gloved hands closed on her breasts, but a delicate

213

shudder ran through her at the same instant, distracting her. She wouldn't have noticed.

'Yes, Doctor.'

He examined her breasts, squeezing them gently, hefting them, pressing them together, pulling them apart, rotating his thumbs over the erect nipples, twiddling them. She gasped a little too.

'What's wrong, my dear?'

'When you do that, Doctor, it – it makes my pussy move.'

He glanced down between her legs. She was leaking freely again, remoistening the damp patch on the couch beneath and between her thighs.

'Yes, my dear. I see. Well, if the increased dose works, next time it won't be so bad. Your pussy will stop being so excitable, will stop responding so nastily to stimulation.'

'Oh, I hope so, Doctor. I do hope so.'

'As do I, my dear. As do I.'

He let go of her breasts, leaving them glistening with the moisture on his gloves. Glistening with pussy-juice. With p.j.

'Are they all right, Doctor?'

'My dear?'

'My titties, Doctor? Are they all right?'

'Yes, my dear. Perfectly all right.'

He turned away from her, walking to the sink to take the gloves off and wash his hands again.

'Are you going to wash them, Doctor?'

'Of c–' he started to say, then realised what she meant. He swallowed.

'No. No, my dear. That won't be necessary today.'

He reached the sink and started to tug the gloves off.

'Then can – can I lick them clean myself?'

He almost turned his head to look at her.

214

'Doctor?'

'If you like, my dear. Does Dr Tsemmfa allow you to do it?'

'Yes, Doctor.'

Her voice was muffled, distorted, as though she had already started to lick at her own breasts, cupping them upwards for her tongue. He longed to look back but forced himself not to, forced himself to concentrate on taking the gloves off, left hand, right hand. Then he could look at her. They came off with little pops and sucking noises and he dropped them into the bin beside the sink. He could hear her now. Hear her licking at her own breasts, cleaning them with her tongue. Soft moist slurps and sucks. His cock arrowed upwards in his trousers.

He turned on the tap and washed his hands, then dried them, then picked up the cloth, then finally, finally, turned back towards the couch. Oh God. There she was. Licking at her own tits with a slender pink tongue, cupping them upwards for herself with her small hands, working at the stiff nipples.

'My dear, here you go.'

She stopped licking for a moment as he dropped the cloth on to the couch beside her.

'Thank you, Doctor.'

'When you're cleaned up and dressed, come and join me.'

'Yes, Doctor. But about the specimen, Doctor?'

'Sp–'

Christ, he'd forgotten. The urine specimen.

'Oh, yes, the specimen. Did I say I would need it today?'

'Yes, Doctor.'

'I think perhaps you misunderstood me. Next time will be fine. So we can see how the new treatment is coming on.'

'The increased dosage, Doctor?'

'Yes. Yes. As you say, the increased dosage.'

'No, Doctor. As *you* say.'

He opened his mouth to reply but stopped. Her face had tilted back to her breasts and she started licking at them again.

'Wh– when you're finished, when you're dressed, please come and join me again for a few moments.'

She didn't reply, just nodded, making little slurping and sucking noises as she licked her breasts.

'Good. Very good.'

He walked out from behind the screen and back to his desk. He longed to stay and watch her finish her breasts, then mop herself up with the cloth, but it wouldn't do. He sat down at his desk, longing to take his cock out and start wanking again, but there would be plenty of time for that when she had gone and he could retrieve the cloth. Hold it over his face while he wanked, flooding his sinuses with the scent of her, then bury his cock in it as he was about to come and spurt into it, flooding her pussy-juice with his dick-juice. Yes. He shifted in his seat at the thought of it. That's what he would do after she'd gone, after he'd given her the little pep-talk he had in mind. Preparing her for the next session, maybe laying the foundation for the suggestion that he would make, two or three weeks away, that he might have to consider a radical new treatment. A physical treatment, not simply a pharmacological one. Physical, not simply pharmacological. Fisting. Fisting her tight pussy with his gloved hand. He shifted in his chair again, glancing at the screen, then up at the clock.

Stroke VI

It's the first week of the summer term at Spunkwell Towers finishing school. Early morning sunlight is streaming through the window of Callypydge dormitory, shining on the two rows of beds and on the pink blankets, shining too on the clean hair fanning out around sleeping heads on the white pillows. In the bed nearest the window a blonde eighteen-year-old is just waking up. It was her first night in the dormitory – in fact, her first night at boarding school, and perhaps that is why she frowns and suddenly begins to cry, tears streaming down her face. After a few moments a redheaded girl three beds down the row wakes up too, blinking up at the ceiling for a moment or two. She sits up in bed, looking towards the new girl.

'What's wrong, dear?'

The new girl stops sobbing and turns her head.

'Who's that?' she asks timidly.

'Me. Marjorie. Dormitory monitor.'

'Oh. It's – it's my bottom.'

'What's wrong with it?'

'It's – it's all wet and sticky and it ... it –' she starts to sob again '– it *hurts*.'

Marjorie's pretty face creases into a frown. She opens her mouth, drawing in breath for a moment, and shouts, 'Dormitory!'

The other girls start to wake up, some of them blinking up at the ceiling and yawning, others sitting up at once. A black-haired girl at the far end of the room picks her watch off her bedside table, looks at it, then scowls at Marjorie.

'For heaven's sake, Marj, it's *minutes* to rising bell. What on earth's happened?'

'It's the new girl. He's been back again.'

'What?'

There is a babble of excited voices. Marjorie throws back her bedclothes and gets out of bed. She's wearing short flowery pyjamas, her long legs bare and lightly tanned, lightly sprinkled with coppery hairs that glitter in the sunlight as she strides down the dormitory towards the new girl's bed, firm young breasts bouncing under her pyjama top. Eyes narrow with longing as she passes between the two rows of beds and one dark-haired girl, fat and pale and rather spotty, groans a little with lust. Other girls are getting out of bed too, trotting down the dormitory after Marjorie, more pairs of firm young breasts bouncing under pyjama tops. The new girl looks a little frightened and draws her bedclothes up to her chin, looking around her with wide eyes. Marjorie sits down on the edge of her bed and smiles at her.

'Don't worry, dear, we know what's wrong and it's nothing to worry about.'

'But what *is* wrong?' asks one of the other girls, a tall, big-breasted blonde wearing even shorter (and tighter) pyjamas than Marjorie. The black-haired girl snorts contemptuously, her breasts quivering under her red pyjama-top.

'Where have you *been*, Katherine?'

Marjorie turns her head and frowns at the black-haired girl.

'Don't be so catty, Alicia. Kate was in san' for most of last term, remember?'

Alicia's pretty mouth pouts.

'Sorry, Kate. I forgot,' she says insincerely.

'But what is going on?' Katherine asks.

'Yes, I was in san' too,' says another black-haired girl.

'And I never got the full story,' adds a brunette.

Everyone is crowding around the new girl's bed now, except for the fat and rather spotty girl, who is still climbing clumsily out of bed. Marjorie puts on her stern 'Dormitory Monitor' face and holds her hand up for silence.

'Very well, then I'll fill you all in. But first everyone move back a little and give her some air, the poor little thing.'

She turns back to the new girl and smiles.

'I'll fill you in too, dear.'

The new girl smiles back timidly, her face still wet with tears. Marjorie tuts and shakes her head.

'But come on, first let's dry your face. Has anyone got a handkerchief?'

'I have, Marjorie,' says a rather squeaky voice. It's the fat girl, out of bed at last. She's scrabbling eagerly in a pocket of her baggy and not very clean-looking green pyjamas.

'Yuck,' Alicia says. 'Don't use hers, Marj. Heaven knows where it's been.'

'I don't know about heaven,' says one of the other girls, 'but I do know I saw her squeezing her spots into it. Last night, before lights-out.'

There are mutters of 'filthy little beast' and 'typical Bessie'. The fat girl's face falls. Marjorie shakes her head.

'I'm afraid not, Bessie. When all is said and done, you *are* a filthy little beast and I can well believe that story about your spots. Has anyone else got one?'

'I have, Marjorie.'

219

It's a sweet-voiced brunette in rather fetching pale blue pyjamas.

'Thanks, Rosemary.'

She takes the clean handkerchief and carefully wipes the new girl's face dry.

'There, that's better, isn't it? Thanks awfully, Ro. What's your name again, dear?'

The new girl seems to have a lump in her throat. She swallows.

'Gwendolyn,' she says, almost in a whisper. 'Gwen to my friends.'

'Oh, yes, I remember now. Gwendolyn is such a pretty name. But I do hope I can call you Gwen?'

'If – if you like.'

'OK, then Gwen it is. Well, Gwen and Kate and Jean and anyone else who doesn't know properly what went on last term, here's the story. Miss Parkington specially asked us to keep it quiet, because she was worried about panic in some of the downstairs dorms. You know what that dizzy lot in Tongueteat and Wettcleft are like, to name but two.'

Alicia sniffs.

'I'm surprised it wasn't all over the school within a couple of days, with Fatso in the dorm. But she was probably hoping he'd come back for her too.'

There are sniggers.

'Fat chance of that,' someone else says.

Alicia laughs nastily.

'Yes, fat chance. That's exactly why she was so hopeful.'

Other girls laugh now too. Marjorie frowns, looking around at them all. Only Alicia withstands her gaze for long, though she too looks away in the end, biting her lip.

'That's enough of that,' Marjorie says. 'Bessie kept just as quiet as everyone else and she's to be commended for that. As for you, Alicia, Miss Parkington warned me that if anyone was going to give anything away, it would be *you*, so there. Yes, that's caught you at home, hasn't it? Now, if I can carry on *without* interruption? Thank you.'

She turns back to the new girl.

'Don't mind them, dear. I can keep them under control, as they well know. Now, the story. You see, last term we had rather an unpleasant plague in the upper dorms. At night, some horrid man was creeping around and, well, *molesting* girls in their sleep. And in an especially sensitive part, too.'

The blonde's mouth falls open.

'You mean? Their bot–'

She chokes with emotion. Marjorie shakes her head sadly.

'Yes, I'm afraid so. Bee yu gee gee ee arr wy.'

'And is – is that –?'

'Is that what's happened to you? I'm afraid it seems very much like it, dear. Oh! Stop that! Come on, stop it! Come on, be a brave girl. It's all over. No one's going to hurt you now.'

The blonde has dissolved into fresh tears, mouth quivering. Marjorie reaches under the bedclothes and pulls out one of the blonde's hands, squeezing it tight, shaking it.

'Come on now, Gwen. You're a big girl now. There's no need to react like this.'

'But – but it's so horrible. My poor bottom. Sticky – and – and – and I can feel it all soaking into my pyjamas and it's – it's just – horrible.'

'Ro,' Marjorie says. 'Hanky again, please. Thanks. Come on, Gwen, wipe your eyes. Come on. That's a good girl. Yes. And big blow. Big blow. That's right. Good girl. I know it must be a shock but it's all over now and you're safe.'

'Ooh,' says a voice from behind her. 'If I could just get my hands on the bloody brute who's responsible for this.'

Marjorie tuts.

'Language, Jean. Though I can think we all agree with your sentiments. Don't worry, we will get him, sooner or later. Hopefully sooner. Thanks, Ro. Sorry to make a clean hanky so damp so early in the morning.'

'That's all right, Marj. All in a good cause.'

'Yes, a very good cause. Now, Gwen. Feeling better now? Good girl. Well, as I was saying, last term we had this outbreak of, well, bee yu gee gee ee arr wy in the upper dorms. Some beastly man was creeping about in the wee hours and molesting girls as they slept. And the thing was, they were always blondes, like you, dear.'

'So Fatso never had a hope anyway,' says Alicia's voice from behind her.

'One more word out of you, Alicia,' Marjorie says without turning her head, 'and I will throw the floor open to suggestions for a suitable punishment. Bessie included. Right?'

Alicia's mouth sets in a thin line. She scowls, saying nothing. Marjorie caught her out like that the last term but one, and she isn't falling for it again.

'Good. Just keep quiet and listen. So, Gwen, as I was saying, it was always blondes, pretty little blondes, just like you. This beastly man was molesting them while they slept and the first thing they knew about it was when they woke up the falling morning and found they had, well, sore, sticky bottoms, just the way you've done. That's right, isn't it, Mary?'

A blonde girl sitting on the other side of Gwen's bed nods, blushing a little as the eyes of the dorm fix on her.

'Yes, Marj. That's right.'

'You see, Gwen? It happened to Mary too, in this very dorm. And worse than that. Show Gwen your scar, Mary.'

The blonde girl suppresses a smile. She's been waiting for this. She stands up and unties the cord of her pyjamas. She drops her pyjama bottoms and starts to peel her knickers down from her firm, pearly buttocks.

'Over the bed, dear,' Marjorie says.

'I didn't know she had a scar, Marj,' the brunette who lent the handkerchief says.

'Oh, yes. The brute didn't just molest her, he bit her too. There were great big tooth-marks all up her left cheek. Miss Parkington insisted on photographing them for the police. See, look.'

The blonde has pulled her knickers fully down. She leans forwards over the bed, settling forwards over Gwen's legs. Gwen can feel her firm little breasts flattening against her knees.

'Lift her jacket, Helen,' Marjorie says.

A petite black-haired girl lifts Mary's pyjama jacket, exposing her buttocks fully. The girls all lean forwards, peering, eyes shining, their mouths opening a little. Bessie, the fat and rather spotty girl, looks especially excited, but Alicia has a secret and rather cruel smile on her face. What can she be thinking of as she stares at the firm white buttocks stretched out on the bed?

'See?' Marjorie says. She puts her hand palm up just over Mary's left buttock, letting her fingernails rest lightly on the skin. She runs them down the cheek, tickling the skin gently, and Mary's bottom shivers and jumps. 'You can still see the scars quite clearly.'

The girls peer more closely still, the ones at the back having to stand on tip-toe and crane their necks.

The skin of the buttock is creamy smooth and seemingly unmarked. Girls exchange glances, eyebrows raised, mouths silently moving, heads shaking faintly in reply. *Can you? No. But better not say anything.*

'Do you see them, Gwen?'

Gwen has been peering too at Mary's bottom, craning her neck to see the left buttock. She looks at Marjorie, moistening her lips nervously, then looks at the circle of faces around her bed, then looks back at the bottom stretched out in front of her.

'I – I think so, Marjorie.'

'Yes, well that's the kind of brute we're dealing with. He doesn't just bee yu gee gee ee arr, he bites too. Hang on, are you sure he hasn't bitten you?'

'I don't think so. All I can feel is –'

She jumps with surprise. A bell has started ringing outside the window. There are groans and someone mutters, just out of Gwen's hearing, 'Damn. Just when it was getting interesting, too.'

The bell stops ringing and in the sudden silence they can hear movement in the rooms on either side. It's Knobworthy and Dicktickle dormitories getting out of bed.

'Sorry, girls,' Marjorie says. 'It's early school. Mary, off the bed and get washed and dressed. Jean, just trot along and get Miss Parkington, will you? Bessie and Ruth, you can get Dr Foster. The rest of you, get washed and dressed. I'll tell you how it went this evening. Gwen will probably have to go to san', so say goodbye, because you won't see her again for a few days.'

There are groans and scowls but Mary slips off the bed and stands up and everybody starts walking back to their beds to fetch their scrubbing brushes and towels. Everybody but Alicia, that is.

'You too, Alicia,' Marjorie.

'No, why do *you* always get all the fun? This is dorm business and the whole dorm has a right to –'

Marjorie jumps to her feet, scowling furiously.

'Right, Alicia, that's it. I've had it up to here with your disobedience. Dormitory!'

The girls turn to look and Alicia spins to face them.

'Get her,' Marjorie says.

Katherine and Ruth advance on Alicia, who snarls and rushes at them, arms flailing. They catch her wrists and almost everyone else joins in, taking Alicia by an arm or leg or by her hair. Alicia swears and spits. The fat girl Bessie stands back, watching hungrily.

'Shut up,' Marjorie says. 'You were warned, Alicia. Right, then. Strip her, then Bessie can suggest what we do with her.'

Alicia tries to break free but too many hands have fastened on to her. Ruth unbuttons her pyjama top and they quickly peel it off her. As if to prolong the stripping, she's wearing a tight white bra, her breasts almost bursting out of it as she pants with anger and humiliation.

'Let Bessie unclip her bra,' Marjorie says.

Bessie smiles cruelly and pushes forwards to unclip Alicia's bra. Noses wrinkle. Bessie has never been famous for personal hygiene. She unclips the bra, her fat fingers trembling with excitement, and eager hands tug it off, baring Alicia's firm breasts. Alicia snarls with anger, but her nipples have started to stiffen. Bessie turns to look at Marjorie, eyes shining. Marjorie's lips quirk. For once Bessie looks almost attractive.

'Can I pull her pyjama bottoms down too, Marjorie?' Bessie asks. 'And her knickers?'

Marjorie pauses a moment, seeming to consider the idea.

'Please?' Bessie pleads.

Marjorie shrugs a little, then nods. Bessie almost yelps with excitement as she turns back to Alicia, hooking her thumbs into the taller girl's pyjama bottoms, taking a deep breath, then tugging them down, all the way to her ankles. Alicia is wearing white knickers too. Bessie straightens and hooks her thumbs into these too. Alicia is struggling furiously, her breasts bouncing up and down, left and right, starting to shine a little with sweat. The other girls have started to sweat, too, with the effort of holding her in place. Bessie sighs happily, an expression of bliss on her face, and tugs Alicia's knickers down. As she stoops, pushing the knickers to Alicia's ankles, her face hovers near Alicia's buttocks and Alicia, twisting her head to watch her, suddenly releases a sharp fart. Bessie snorts and jumps back. Noses are wrinkling again. Alicia is smiling.

'You dirty cow,' Katherine tells Alicia.

Alicia's smile broadens.

'Just freshening the air after a dose of Lardarse.'

'Well, Ali, Lardarse is about to supply a few suggestions for what we can do to you,' Marjorie says. 'Aren't you, Lardarse?'

Bessie nods, her small, red-rimmed eyes slitted with rage.

'Well, Bessie?' Marjorie says.

Bessie's nostrils flare.

'She can drink piss out of my chamber pot.'

'Girls?' Marjorie says. But heads are shaking.

'No,' Ruth says. 'That's going too far. Out of someone else's chamber pot, maybe, if she'd done something really bad, but not out of Bessie's.'

'I agree,' Marjorie says. 'Try again, Bessie.'

Bessie's face fell when her first suggestion was rejected; now it brightens again.

'She can eat the new girl's snot out of Rosemary's handkerchief. After I've squeezed some spots into it.'

226

'Girls?' Marjorie says.

Three or four heads are definitely shaking, but others girls look more doubtful. Ruth is chewing her lower lip, frowning with concentration.

'Well, Ruth?' Marjorie says.

'Not sure. The snot bit is all right, but I think the spot-squeezing is going a bit far. If it was anyone else's spots, OK, that might be acceptable, but not Bessie's.'

There are nods at that. The new girl is decidedly attractive and the idea of being forced to eat her snot isn't so bad, but not if Bessie has squeezed her spots into the hanky too. Yuck.

'Well, OK then,' Marjorie says. 'She can eat the new girl's snot out of Ro's hanky, but spot-squeezing is out.'

Bessie almost stamps with frustration.

'Just one, Marjorie?' she pleads. 'Just a little one?'

Alicia makes a sudden jerk and almost breaks free of the hands that are still holding her. She twists her head to look at Marjorie.

'Don't you dare let her squeeze her spots into that hanky, Marjorie, or you'll regret it.'

Marjorie regards her coolly, then smiles, closing her eyes for a long moment.

'As a matter of fact, Ali, I wasn't going to let her. But seeing as you've decided to make threats, I've changed my mind. Bessie, you can squeeze one spot into Ro's hanky before Ali eats the contents. A medium-sized one, I think, though, if Ali makes any further threats I can always review that. Ro, let's have your hanky.'

Rosemary takes her handkerchief out again and unfolds it. The new girl deposited a wad of clear yellow snot in it when she was blowing her nose. Bessie's face is shining again.

'Let's have a look at your face, Bessie,' Marjorie says.

Bessie walks over to her and Marjorie sniffs.

'Dear me, Ali was almost right. A fart is almost refreshing after your B.O.'

Bessie absorbs the comment without blinking. She doesn't care: she's going to squeeze a spot into snot Alicia will have to eat.

'Head back,' Marjorie says. 'Face into the light.'

Bessie puts her head back and Marjorie peers at her face, searching for a suitable spot, not too big, not too small.

'That one, I think,' she says, pointing. 'Girls, do you agree? Turn around and let them see, Bessie. Point at it. There it is, near your lip.'

Bessie turns, pointing at the spot Marjorie has chosen. The other girls peer at her, narrowing their eyes to see the spot, and Alicia makes another attempt to break free, but they're ready for her this time.

'Looks OK,' Ruth says. Other girls echo her.

'Right then, Bessie, get it squeezed. We've not got all day, and poor Gwen still needs to be seen by Miss Parkington and Dr Foster. Ro, hold the hanky up for her.'

Bessie rubs at the spot Marjorie has chosen, carefully fixing its position and size, then closes her thumb and index finger on it and leans forwards over the handkerchief Rosemary is holding up for her. When her face is positioned right, she squeezes and everyone hears a tiny but distinct *split* and a tiny yellow blob flies into the snot lying on the handkerchief. There are noises of disgust but Bessie is beaming.

'Right,' Marjorie says. 'Grub's up, Ali.'

Alicia is struggling furiously again, and even though a dozen or more hands are fastened on her she is almost managing to break free.

'Force her down on to her knees,' Marjorie says, 'then hold her by her ears so she can't get her head down. Bessie, you can do that.'

They force her on to her knees and Bessie stands behind her and takes hold of her ears.

'Don't tug too hard, Bessie, or you can eat the snot instead, after Ali's dipped it in her chamberpot. Good girl. Ro, feed it to her, then.'

Rosemary carries the open handkerchief to Alicia, but Alicia's mouth is firmly shut.

'Pinch her nostrils shut, someone,' Marjorie says.

A pair of fingers close over Alicia's nostrils and pinch them firmly shut.

'Ro, as soon as she opens her mouth for air, push the snot inside and, Ruth, you push her chin up so she can't spit it out. OK?'

'OK, Marj,' Rosemary and Ruth say.

'Get ready then.'

Alicia's face is slowly reddening as she struggles to make use of the last traces of air in her lungs. Her breasts are quivering, nipples scratching at the air like slim pink fingertips. Suddenly a shudder runs through her and her mouth comes open, gasping. Rosemary is ready: she quickly scrapes the snot into Alicia's open mouth and Ruth pushes Alicia's chin up. Alicia's eyes bulge with anger and disgust.

'Swallow it, Ali,' Marjorie says. 'Then it's all over. Ro, squeeze her nips until she swallows it.'

Rosemary puts her hands over Alicia's breasts and carefully closes her thumbs and index fingers on her nipples almost the way Bessie closed her thumb and index finger on her spot. She begins to squeeze, softly at first, then gradually harder. Ruth is holding Alicia's chin up, sealing her mouth on the new girl's snot, and Bessie is holding Alicia's ears. Rosemary is squeezing Alicia's nipples very hard now, her slender wrists quivering a little with the strain. Alicia's eyes suddenly roll up in their sockets and a look of intense disgust passes over her face. Her throat bulges and smoothes.

'She's swallowed it, Marjorie,' Ruth says.

'OK, let her go then. Let her go, everyone. Bessie, you too.'

Ruth releases Alicia's chin and Alicia's mouth opens.

'Bitches!' she snarls. 'I'll get you all for this.'

Bessie lets go of her ears and everyone else is letting go of her arms and legs and stepping away from her. She falls forwards, retching and spitting, muttering and swearing.

'Ignore her, everyone,' Marjorie says. 'Get washed and dressed. But Jean, you get Miss Parkington first, and Ruth and Bessie, you get Dr Foster. Chop-chop!'

The girls scurry to obey. Alicia is picking herself up off the floor, eyes red and moist with tears of rage, still muttering. Marjorie turns back to Gwen, the new girl with blonde hair, and sits on the edge of her bed again.

'Sorry about that, dear. We've been neglecting you, haven't we? You'll get used to all this very quickly. Alicia has to have something unpleasant forced down her throat or up her fanny or bottom nearly every week. It's getting to be something of a dorm tradition. And –' she lowers her voice to a stage whisper, knowing Alicia is listening to every word '– she likes it really.'

Alicia glares at her, scowling worse than ever. Marjorie looks at her coolly.

'Yes? Can't a girl have a quiet conversation without your ugly face intruding? Go on, go and get washed and dressed. Put your pyjamas back on first, though, in case Miss Parkington sees you.'

Alicia's eyes narrow balefully for a moment but she obeys, pulling her knickers and pyjama bottoms up, then stooping to pick up her discarded bra and pyjama top. Marjorie watches her thoughtfully, then puts her mouth to Gwen's ear.

'You keep close to me for a few days, Gwen dear,' she whispers. Gwen shivers pleasurably at the hot breath tickling her ear. 'I don't like the look of young Alicia's face and she might be looking for a chance to get her own back. OK?'

Gwen nods, liking the way the movement makes her ear brush Marjorie's lips.

'Good girl,' Marjorie whispers. She kisses Gwen's ear and puts her head back.

The dormitory is almost empty now: all the girls have gone to the washroom to wash. Suddenly running feet sound on the corridor outside and Jean's head pops around the door.

'Miss Parkington is on her way, Marjorie. She's looking pretty angry too.'

'OK. Thanks, Jean.'

Jean nods and disappears, scurrying off to the washroom. How she longs to stay and watch the rest, but although she might almost think of disobeying Marjorie, she wouldn't even dream of disobeying Miss Parkington and her sharp ears have already caught Miss Parkington's familiar heavy footsteps coming up the stairs. Marjorie hears the footsteps too.

'Here she comes, Gwennie. Don't be frightened of her: her bark is much worse than her bite, honestly.'

Miss Parkington's footsteps are coming down the corridor outside now. Suddenly they stop and a voice booms out.

'Alicia Tresoyle, get tha friggin' skates on. If tha's not dressed and downstairs within five minutes tha'll be seein' me after school. Is that clear?'

Marjorie and Gwen can't hear Alicia's reply, but Marjorie smiles.

'Poor old Ali,' she says. 'She does make it difficult for herself.'

The heavy footsteps start up again and suddenly Miss Parkington is striding through the door into the dormitory. Marjorie surreptitiously reaches under the bedclothes and finds one of Gwen's hands. She squeezes it reassuringly, then lets go. Old Parky *is* a bit of a sight in the early morning. She's a tall, strongly built but decidedly flat-chested woman in her late thirties or early forties with a premature sprinkling of grey in her short dark hair. Smoke trails behind her from a three-quarters-smoked cigarette in one large, reddened hand and her feet, in square black shoes, are large, too, and sound heavily on the bare wooden floor of the dormitory. Marjorie can feel the bed shaking as she walks down the room and stops at the foot of the new girl's bed.

Miss Parkington lifts the cigarette to her thick lips and draws on it. Twin jets of smoke spurt from her large and rather hairy nostrils. The side of her face nearer the window is brightly lit and Marjorie, as ever, is struck by the coarseness of her skin. Why doesn't the old brute use a moisturiser? There's a small cut on her chin too with a blood-soaked scrap of tissue paper plastered over it, and under her left ear there seems to be a small triangle of dried foam. The jets of smoke streaming from her nostrils die out, the smoke spreading on the air so that her face is veiled for a moment.

'Now then,' she says, then breaks off, doubling up over her fist and coughing hard, with rich, bubbling hacks and splutters. Her face reddens and thick veins stand out in her forehead and down the sides of her neck. Marjorie glances at Gwen. She looks rather puzzled and a little bit frightened. Miss Parkington straightens and opens her mouth again.

'Now then,' she says, and breaks off yet again to double up over her fist. She coughs even longer this time, and when she straightens she hawks noisily, looks down at the floor and spits. A wad of something heavy and moist lands on the floor with a small slap. Miss Parkington eyes it with satisfaction.

'Aye, Ah thought that were t' problem,' she says.

Gwen's poor little face is struggling to conceal her disgust now. Miss Parkington beats on her chest with her cigarette hand, weaving quick trails of smoke and sending a fine rain of ash on to the foot of Gwen's bed. She hawks experimentally, then takes another drag on her cigarette, jets smoke from her nostrils again, hawks experimentally again, then nods.

'Aye, that's better,' she says. She stiffens for a moment, a wondering, almost mystical look on her face, and breaks wind loudly. Marjorie glances at Gwen, who looks horrified.

'Better out 'n in,' Miss Parkington says. 'Now then, lasses, what seems to be t' problem?'

Marjorie clears her throat.

'It's the new girl, Miss Parkington. During the night, she was bee yu gec gee ee arr ee deed again.'

'Aye?'

'Ay– uh, yes, Miss Parkington.'

'Again?'

'Well, I mean *a* girl has been bee yu gee gee ee arr ee deed in the night again, and this is the girl.'

'Reet, I see. What's tha name, lass?'

Gwen doesn't say anything and Marjorie realises she hasn't understood. She nudges her in the ribs, hissing, 'Your name, dear. What's your name?'

'Oh,' Gwen says. 'It's Gwendolyn.'

'Miss Parkington,' Marjorie hisses.

'M– Miss Parkington. G– Gwen, for short.'

'Aye, reet then, lickle Gwen, pleased to mek tha acquaintance. Tha's been buggered, 'ast tha? In t' neet?'

'Have you been buggered?' Marjorie hisses. 'In the night?'

'Uh, yes. Yes, I have, Miss Parkington.'

'Stuck it reet up tha back passage, did 'e?'

Gwen looks bewildered again.

'Did he stick it right up your back passage?' Marjorie hisses. Gwen still looks bewildered.

'Your bottom,' Marjorie hisses. 'Did he stick it right up your bottom?'

'Oh, yes, Miss Parkington. He did.'

'Poor lickle lass. An' come, did 'e, in t' end? Deposited 'is wad reet at t' far end o' tha back passage?'

'Poor thing. And did he come, in the end? Did he deposit his, ah, wad right at the far end of your back passage?'

Gwen frowns, starts to open her mouth, closes it.

'Did he ejaculate, Miss Parkington means,' Marjorie hisses.

'Oh. Yes, Miss Parkington. He did. My bottom feels all sticky and wet.'

'Aye?'

Miss Parkington draws on her cigarette again and jets smoke leisurely from her nostrils.

'Yes?' Marjorie hisses, adding, 'But I think it's a rhetorical question.'

Miss Parkington hacks, draws more phlegm into her mouth, seems about to spit it on to the floor, has second thoughts and swallows it. Shuffling feet are sounding outside along the corridor, slowly getting nearer.

'An' sore, is it, tha bottom?' Miss Parkington asks.

'And sore –' Marjorie starts to translate, but Gwen glances at her with a crooked smile.

'No,' she whispers, 'I understood that one. Isn't she a disgusting old brute?'

She turns back to Miss Parkington, her smile broadening.

'Yes, Miss Parkington. It's very sore.'

'Poor lickle lass. Ah, 'ere's t' doctor. 'E'll soon 'ave thee back on tha feet.'

A short, potbellied, elderly man has appeared in the door of the dormitory. His face is narrow, with red cheeks and broken red veins in his rather swollen nose, and he has dense, badly trimmed white whiskers, stained yellow with nicotine around his lips and nose. He's wearing a crumpled black suit, shiny and almost green with age, and in one grey-haired and far from clean hand he's clutching a three-quarters-smoked cigarette too; in the other, he's clutching a battered black bag.

'Mornin', Doctor!' Miss Parkington booms, then, turning back to the girls: ''E's rather deaf, tha knows.'

'Eh?' the doctor says in a quavering voice.

Miss Parkington draws on her cigarette again. She jets smoke, then draws a deep breath. It seems on the verge of triggering another coughing fit, but she recovers and booms, 'Ah said, good mornin' to ye!'

'Oh,' says the doctor. He struggles to pull on a watch-chain sitting snug against the taut round belly of his waistcoat. He gives up.

'About half past seven, I think. All the girls are going down to breakfast.'

'Ye daft old bugger,' Miss Parkington booms. 'Ah didn't ask what time it were, Ah jus' said good mornin' to ye.'

'Yes,' says the doctor. 'Very attractive, some of them. There's a couple of little minxes in the upper sixth whose temperatures I would take any day.'

He shuffles down the dormitory towards Gwen's bed.

'Oh, for fuck's sake,' Miss Parkington mutters. She hawks phlegm into her mouth again and does spit it out this time. It lands on the floor with another small slap.

The doctor reaches the foot of Gwen's bed and peers at her with eyes that, despite his age, are bright and curiously alert.

'Now, what seems to be the trouble with this very attractive young lady?'

'Buggered!' Miss Parkington booms. 'She's bin buggered in t' neet! Like a load of 'em were last term, do ye remember?'

'Eh?'

'Buggered!' Miss Parkington booms even more loudly. Gwen jerks with surprise and embarrassment. An upper window of the dorm is open and a few moments before she could hear the happy chatter of girls on their way to the dining hall for breakfast. Now there's no chatter, just muffled giggles. The quad must be full of girls queuing for breakfast, straining their ears to listen to what was going on in the dorm. Gwen starts to blush.

'Eh?'

Miss Parkington draws another deep breath, masters the onset of another coughing fit, and opens her mouth wide.

'BUGGERED!' she screams. Her face darkens through red to scarlet, through scarlet to crimson, and veins bulge out in her forehead and neck. 'SHE'S BIN BUGGERED IN T' NEET. LIKE A LOAD OF 'EM WERE LAST TERM!'

'Eh?'

Miss Parkington is opening her mouth to shout again, but Marjorie coughs discreetly.

'Miss Parkington, if I might?'

Miss Parkington looks towards her.

'Eh?' she grunts.

'Write it down in the doctor's notebook, Miss Parkington. I think it would save us all a lot of time.'

'Oh, aye. That's a reet sensible suggestion, young Miriam.'

'Marjorie, Miss Parkington.'

'Aye, Marjorie. That were what ah said, weren't it?'

She turns to the doctor.

'DOCTOR! CAN AH 'AVE YOUR NOTEBOOK?'

The doctor, who has been staring at Gwen again with a senile but rather peculiar smile, glances at her mildly.

'Eh?'

Miss Parkington is about to shout the question again when Marjorie coughs.

'If I might?'

She stands up, walks to the doctor and slides a notebook out of a pocket in his jacket. It has a little pencil tucked down the spine. She slides the pencil out, opens the notebook and offers it to Miss Parkington.

'Thank you, m'dear.'

Miss Parkington takes the notebook and writes in it slowly and carefully, breathing heavily. The doctor is staring at Gwen again with his senile smile. Spittle is leaking at one corner and slowly dribbling down his chin. It drips and a moment later lands on the floor with a tiny *split*. Gwen looks frightened and disgusted. Miss Parkington finishes writing and holds the notebook out to the doctor. The doctor doesn't notice, so engrossed is he in Gwen. Miss Parkington prods him with the notebook.

'Eh? Oh, I see.'

The doctor puts his bag on the foot of Gwen's bed and takes the notebook. He reads what is written in it, a look of unctuous concern slowly filling his face. He looks up.

'Oh, my dear young Miss! Buggered in the nee– in the night, were you?'

Gwen nods slowly, swallowing.

'Then, Miss Parkington, I must examine her at once. From the look of her I feel her temperature is elevated and must be taken without delay.'

'Aye,' Miss Parkington says. 'Ah thought ye would say that. Ye've got a thing about tekking temperatures, 'aven't ye, Doctor?'

'Eh?'

Miss Parkington takes a deep breath.

'Ah said – oh, for fuck's sake. Forget it.'

'Eh?'

'Forget it. Examine 'er arse. Ah said, EXAMINE 'ER ARSE! EXAMINE 'ER FUCKIN' ARSE! 'Ere, give us that notebook. Ah said, GIVE US THAT FUCKIN' NOTEBOOK!'

Marjorie coughs again.

'It might just be easier, Miss Parkington, if Gwen just gets ready?'

'Eh? Oh, aye, sensible suggestion, young Madelaine.'

'Marjorie, Miss Parkington.'

'Aye, Marjorie. That were what ah said, weren't it? Jenny, get ready for t' doctor to examine thee.'

'Gwen,' Marjorie says.

Miss Parkington looks at her.

'Eh?'

'It's Gwen, Miss Parkington. Not Jenny.'

'Aye, well, Gwen, Jenny, makes no odds. Out o' bed, lass, an' let t' doctor 'ave a look at tha arse.'

Marjorie looks at Gwen, ready to translate, but Gwen seems to have understood. Looking worried, she pushes the bedclothes back and slowly starts to slide out of bed, wincing as her bottom moves against the mattress.

'No need to get off t' bed, lass,' Miss Parkington says. 'Just kneel on t' top on all fours wi' tha pyjama bottoms an' knickers down. T' doctor can examine thee *in situ*, as it were. If t' daft bugger can work out what's goin' on, that is.'

But Dr Foster seems well aware of what is going on. He has dropped his cigarette on the floor, slowly ground it out with his shoe, then slipped the notebook back into his pocket and shuffled nearer to the bed, trying to rub his hands together. Gwen crawls a little down the bed and turns her bottom doubtfully towards him, reaching back behind herself to tug her pyjama bottoms down.

'My hands may be a little cold, my dear,' Dr Foster tells her. 'I'll just warm them for you.'

Marjorie helps her to get her pyjama bottoms down. Her knickers are pink and there's a big damp patch in them just where Marjorie thinks her bottomhole is. Marjorie helps her slide her knickers down too.

'I'll take over now, my dear,' Dr Foster says.

Gwen stiffens with apprehension. Marjorie moves aside and Dr Foster moves close to Gwen, reaching out with trembling hands to slide her knickers fully down. Marjorie moves a little further back. The doctor smells of stale tobacco and sweat, with an undertone of mildew.

'Ah!' he says happily.

Gwen's knickers are fully down and her bottom is exposed. It's apple-curved, the skin smooth and creamy, the arsehole hidden between firm cheeks that glisten with moisture about halfway down. Dr Foster puts his hands flat to the cheeks and thumbs them apart at the glistening patch.

239

'Oh, my dear!' he breathes happily. 'You poor little thing.'

Her arsehole has been exposed between her cheeks, sitting snug above the shell-halves of her blonde-fringed pussy. It's red and swollen and gaping slightly, moist with fluids that have trickled down her inner thighs. Dr Foster lowers his head towards her buttock-cleft and sniffs.

'Spunk?' Miss Parkington booms.

'Eh?'

Dr Foster peers back at her, smiling stupidly.

'IS IT SPUNK?'

'Oh, yes. Very nice. A beautiful little bottom. And she's definitely been buggered.'

He turns back to Gwen's bottom, lowers his head and sniffs. He peers back at Miss Parkington.

'You see, the smell is unmistakable. Salty and wet. The poor little thing has been buggered most thoroughly. Her ringpiece is in a most distressing state. Look at it.'

He moves a little to one side, thumbing Gwen's buttocks further apart. Marjorie notices Gwen wince with pain. Miss Parkington bends further a little, staring between Gwen's splayed buttocks at her glistening arsehole.

'Aye, terrible!' Miss Parkington booms.

'Eh?'

'Ah said, it looks terrible!'

'Eh?'

Miss Parkington is opening her mouth to shout again, but Marjorie holds up her hand.

'I'll do it, Miss Parkington.'

She slips the notebook out of Dr Foster's pocket.

'The pencil, Miss Parkington?'

'Eh?'

'You've still got the pencil, Miss Parkington.'

'Oh, aye. 'Ere tha goes.'

She tosses it to Marjorie. Marjorie catches it and writes quickly in the notebook. Dr Foster is peering happily between Gwen's buttocks again. She waves the notebook in front of his face.

'Eh? Oh.'

He lets go of Gwen's buttocks (Marjorie hears Gwen sigh with relief) and takes the notebook.

'Ah. Yes,' he says, reading what Marjorie has written. 'Yes. You noticed it too, Parkington. Her poor ringpiece *is* in a terrible state.'

'Daft old bugger,' Miss Parkington mutters. 'Ask 'im what we should do nex', Maisie.'

'Marjorie, Miss Parkington.'

'Aye, whatever. Go on, ask 'im. Though ah 'ave a funny feelin' ah know exac'ly what 'e's goin' to say.'

Marjorie takes the notebook back from Dr Foster and writes in it quickly again. She hands it back. Dr Foster reads what she has written, then looks back at Miss Parkington.

'What shall we do next, Parkington? Why, take her temperature, of course.'

'Aye, it's as ah thought,' Miss Parkington mutters. 'Eh?'

Miss Parkington waves her hand dismissively.

'Forget it. Tek 'er bloody temperature.'

'Eh?'

Miss Parkington jabs a blunt finger at Gwen's bottom, then, her cigarette stub still tucked between her index and ring fingers, makes an 'O' with her right hand and mimes sliding a thermometer into it.

'Oh, I see,' says Dr Foster. 'Yes, certainly. Right away.'

He slips his notebook into his jacket pocket and turns back to Gwen, patting her reassuringly on the bottom.

241

'I'll just take your temperature, my dear.'

Marjorie waits for him to shuffle to the foot of the bed and open his black bag. Instead, he scratches his nose for a moment, then reaches down and carefully unzips his fly. He reaches through the slit and rummages in his trousers, then slowly lifts out a long but only half-erect cock. It seems to have blue ink marks on it. No, tattooing. Short lines and numbers that are oddly distorted by the cock's semi-flaccidity. It's tattooed like a ruler or, yes, a thermometer. He fumbles at the head and starts wanking at it, trying to erect it fully. There's a muffled rasping sound. Marjorie looks up and sees that Miss Parkington has lifted a hand up her own skirt and is scratching her crotch. Dr Foster stops wanking at his cock.

'Parkington,' he says. 'I think I'll need some assistance.'

'Aye? Oh, I see. Molly, jus' suck t' doctor's cock for 'im, will tha?'

Gwen turns her head to see what's going on behind and gasps with horror when she sees Dr Foster's cock and realises what is in store for her. She reaches behind herself to pull up her knickers and pyjama bottoms.

'Glenda!'

Miss Parkington's voice lashes out at her. She has stopped scratching at her crotch.

'Tha canst jus' leave tha arse alone. Dr Foster is tekking tha temperature, dost tha 'ear me?'

Gwen swallows, her eyes starting to glint with tears.

'I – I'm not sure I understand, Miss Parkington.'

'Miss Parkington says you're to leave your bottom alone,' Marjorie says. 'Dr Foster has to take your temperature.'

Gwen swallows again.

'But he's – he's going to use his cock.'

'Is tha sayin' tha knows better than Dr Foster, young lady? Wi' a fine medical degree an' ower thirty years o' service at t' school?'

Marjorie translates.

'Well?' Miss Parkington says, scratching at her crotch again.

'No, Miss Parkington,' Gwen says, beginning to cry.

'Good girl. Now, Maureen, get t' doctor's cock sucked. Doctor!'

'Eh?'

'She's goin' to suck tha cock, Doctor. I SAID, SHE'S GOIN' TO SUCK THA COCK. Oh, for fuck's sake. Just do it, lass. Just do it.'

More muffled giggles have sounded through the open upper window. Miss Parkington removes her hand from under her skirt and strides to the windows. She opens one of the lower ones. Behind her, Marjorie is kneeling on the floor in front of Dr Foster, reluctantly opening her mouth to accept his cock. Miss Parkington looks out of the window, taking a puff on her cigarette. She jets smoke through her nostrils.

'Eh!' she shouts. 'What are you girls doin' in t' quad at this hour?'

Marjorie can't hear the reply: her ears are buzzing with disgust and shame as she accepts Dr Foster's cock into her mouth.

'Well, there i'n't no friggin' queue now,' Miss Parkington says. 'Get in to breakfast this minute, d'ye 'ear me? 'Ang on, is that Sally 'Ardthwaite there?'

Another inaudible reply. Marjorie is sucking hard at Dr Foster's cock, feeling it swell on her tongue. Gwen sniffs behind her. Tears are falling from her eyes on to her pillow.

'Aye, Susan 'Ebblewhite. That were what ah just said, weren't it? Well, t' rest o' you get in to breakfast an' tha, Sophie, get theesel up 'ere on t' double.'

Marjorie feels Dr Foster's hands trembling as it strokes her hair.

'Lovely, my dear,' he says. 'Just what I need. In my younger days, I don't mind telling you, I wouldn't have needed this assistance. The sight of a fine, freshly buggered arse like that would have had me up and ready to take a temperature in a twinkling. As it is, your assistance is most welcome. I'm nearly there, am I not?'

Marjorie nods, mumbling around his cock. It is surprisingly clean, the head hardly tasting of urine at all as it swells into her mouth. She sucks at it hard and realises she will be sorry to let it go. Her ears have cleared now and she can hear light footsteps running down the corridor outside the dorm. She opens her eyes, which she's closed as she sucks Dr Foster, and watches sideways as a slim brunette runs panting into the dormitory, almost falling over as one of her feet slips on the wooden floor. Susan Hebblethwaite, from Dicktickle dorm. She is rumoured to be in line for a highly prestigious scholarship in Applied Fellatio to Magdalene College, Cambridge.

'Less 'aste, more speed,' Miss Parkington tells Susan as she reaches Gwen's bed.

Susan nods without answering, her firm breasts rising and falling quickly under her dark blue cardigan.

'Well?' Miss Parkington says.

'Y– yes, Miss Parkington,' Susan answers, beginning to catch her breath.

'Good. Ah 'ope tha doesn't rush at a cock like that.'

Susan shakes her head.

'No, Miss Parkington. I don't, honestly.'

Miss Parkington takes another puff on her cigarette and smiles, revealing stained yellow teeth.

'Nay, lass, ah know tha doesn't. Ah were only teasin'. Tha's ower blue-eyed girl, aren't tha? Ower scholarship candidate for t' dreaming spires. Ower best 'ope o' success. Success, eh? Dost tha get it, eh?'

'Yes, Miss Parkington. I'll certainly try my best, Miss Parkington.'

'Ah know tha will, lass. Ah know tha will. But a lickle practice won't come amiss, will it, lass? That's why ah asked thee up 'ere.'

Susan glances at Dr Foster and the kneeling Marjorie. She sniffs disdainfully.

'To suck Dr Foster, Miss Parkington? I'm already doing that twice a week. He says I'm a very promising pupil: one of the best he's had in nearly thirty years.'

'Aye, lass, ah can well believe it, but nay, it's not to suck Dr Foster that ah've asked thee up 'ere this morning. As tha canst see, young Maggie's got that job well in, ah, mouth.'

'Mmm-mmm-mmm,' Marjorie mumbles.

Dr Foster sighs with pleasure.

'Nay, lass, ah've asked thee up to taste t' spunk in young Gracie's arse. That's 'er there, young lass on t' bed with 'er arse in t' air.'

Susan looks at Gwen's bottom and nods.

'To see if I can identify it, Miss Parkington?'

'Aye, lass. That's it. To see if tha canst identify t' spunker, if tha follows mah drift. Because tha'st sucked off all t' men an' boys at t' school, i'n't that reet?'

'Oh, yes, Miss Parkington. I have. Right the way up from the boot-blacks to Dr Foster and Sir Henry the bursar. But I haven't had much experience with the outdoor staff yet.'

'T' gardeners, tha means?'

'Yes, Miss Parkington.'

'Well, then, if tha fails to identify t' spunk deefini-tively, we'll 'ave t' gardeners up 'ere fust an' tha canst suck 'em off too an' see if tha recognises t' spunker amongst 'em, alreet?'

Susan nods and is about to reply when Dr Foster interrupts. He has decided that Marjorie's mouth has erected him enough to take Gwen's temperature.

'Parkington, I'm ready to take the young girl's temperature now, I feel, though to be honest I could stand here all day and be sucked by this delightful young girl. Her technique is somewhat naïve and unrefined, but really you know, it makes a most refreshing change from young Hebble–'

But at this point he notices Susan, who is pouting unhappily.

'Oh, my dear, speak of the Devil,' Dr Foster says. 'Not that I was, of course. You're looking particular-ly attractive this morning and your lips *really* are most enticing.'

Marjorie mumbles on his cock, making a slight slurping noise. He swallows, losing his thread.

'Really most enticing, my dear. Now, where – oh, yes.'

He pats Marjorie's slowly bobbing head.

'Thank you, my dear, but that really is enough. It has been most pleasurable. Thank you.'

Reluctantly, Marjorie slides her mouth off his cock, leaving it glistening and fully erect. The numbers tattooed along it can be read clearly now, going up in 5 degree jumps from $-10°$ right under the head to $60°$ near the base, though perhaps it reaches $70°$ or even $80°$ under the greying pubic hair that spills through his trouser slit. Susan's pout deepens as she sees his cock. Dr Foster looks down at it guiltily.

'Come, come, my dear, you can't blame me for enjoying a change now and then. You really are a most excellent little fellatrix – in the top three, as I have repeatedly told you, of those I have enjoyed in the thirty years of my service at Spunkwell Towers – and I look forward *most* happily to our next little lesson, on Sunday, but really, a change is as good as a rest and I am sure I will respond even more enthusiastically to your attentions than usual, after this. So can an old man not have a smile, from his own little scholarship girl? Well?'

Susan is softening. She tries to keep her pout, but it's fading.

'Come on, lass,' Miss Parkington tells her. 'Tha knows tha 'as a special place in Dr Foster's affections but tha can't expect 'im not to enjoy a nice fresh young mouth, every now an' then, canst tha now?'

Susan shakes her head reluctantly.

'Good lass. An' look, t' Doctor's John Thomas has been softening even as we speak –' Marjorie looks but can't see any signs of it '– an' 'e i'n't even tekken young Gloria's temperature yet. Gi' it a quick suck, to show tha's forgiven 'im, an' show young Moira what tha's really med of, eh? Eh?'

'OK, Miss Parkington,' Susan murmurs.

She walks forwards and kneels elegantly in front of Dr Foster, looking up at him reproachfully before taking hold of his cock in one slim hand and opening her mouth wide. She moves her open mouth over Dr Foster's cock, still looking up at him reproachfully. His cock hasn't touched her mouth or lips yet.

'Good lass,' Miss Parkington says.

Marjorie watches with interest. It's the first time she's seen Susan in action in over a term, and she wonders whether she will spot any new techniques. Dr Foster gasps with pleasure. Susan has closed her mouth on his cock and begun sucking.

'Lovely, my dear,' Dr Foster says. 'Absolutely lovely. Oh my, I'm up again already. I really am. Oooooh.'

Susan's head has started to rock back and forth gently, the shaft of Dr Foster's cock sliding in and out of her mouth. Dr Foster's eyes close and he shudders.

'Sarah 'Igginbotham,' says Miss Parkington sternly, 'tha art not to mek t' doctor come, dost tha 'ear me? Tha 'ast to keep tha mouth fresh for tasting t' spunk in young Joan's arse. Well? Dost tha 'ear me? Tek that cock out o' tha mouth this instant, young lady.'

Susan's eyes rise to Dr Foster's ecstatic face again. Marjorie suppresses a smile. Susan's eyes are twinkling with mischief.

'Ah said, dost tha 'ear me?'

Susan slides her mouth off Dr Foster's cock, licking her lips.

'Yes, Miss Parkington,' she says quietly.

'Good. Now, 'elp t' doctor tek young Guineviere's temperature. Tha too, young Muriel. After that, tha canst suck some o' t' spunk out o' young Jessica's arse through a glass tube an' if tha fails to identify it we'll 'ave the gardeners up to see if tha canst identify t' spunker 'mongst 'em instead. Alreet?'

'Yes, Miss Parkington.'

'Good. Then get on wi' it. An' mek sure t' daft old bugger doesn't come while 'e's up young Joanne's arse. That'll completely ruin t' chances o' tha gettin' a good clean taste o' t' spunk that's already in there, dost tha see?'

'Yes, Miss Parkington.'

'Reet, get on wi' it, then. I'll 'elp 'old t' young lass down if needs be.'

Gwen has been listening hard, sniffing as she tries to understand what instructions Miss Parkington is giving. Her pillow is quite damp with tears. Susan stands up and goes around the other side of the bed to help Marjorie position her for Dr Foster.

248

'Thank you, Susan,' Dr Foster says. 'Now, my dear young lady, I'll just take your temperature.'

He unbuttons his trousers, lets them drop around his ankles, pulls his underpants down, then slowly and shakily kneels on the bed behind Gwen, who moans a little as she feels the bed shake under his weight. Marjorie and Susan have taken hold of her, adjusting her bottom to meet Dr Foster's cock, making sure she does not struggle and try to break free.

'That's reet, girls,' Miss Parkington says. 'Keep a good 'old on 'er. She's not goin' to like this one lickle bit, but it's all f'r 'er own good.'

Dr Foster closes up behind Gwen, muttering to himself as he takes hold of his cock and guides it to the mouth of her arsehole.

'Now my dear,' he says. 'This *will* hurt a bit but it will soon be over.'

He pushes his cock forwards, and it touches the rim of Gwen's arsehole. Gwen gasps and tries to pull forwards.

'Now then, young Joan, none o' that, dost tha 'ear me?' Miss Parkington says. 'Tha's to let Dr Foster slide 'is cock up tha arse wi'out complaint, alreet?'

Marjorie puts her mouth to Gwen's ear.

'Stay still, darling,' she whispers. 'It will be over in a few minutes.'

Gwen stops struggling, as tears begin to fall freely from her eyes again.

'Good lass,' Miss Parkington tells her.

Dr Foster slowly begins to press forwards.

'Oh!' Gwen says. 'Ooh! Ooh!'

Spittle from Dr Foster's chin drips on to her bare buttocks as he leans forwards over her.

'One good thrust, my dear,' he says. 'One good thrust. If I can just . . .'

He reaches up her body, taking hold of her breasts beneath her pyjama jacket. Gwen stiffens, then begins to tremble. Dr Foster's hands are surprisingly strong, gripping her breasts hard.

'On the count of three,' Dr Foster says. 'One.'

Miss Parkington, Marjorie and Susan join in. Gwen gasps as Dr Foster's hands tighten on her breasts.

'Two, *three*.'

Gwen screams as Dr Foster's cock spears at her poor abused bottom. She tries to pull away from the pain and Marjorie and Susan have to tighten their grip.

'Ah! Ahhh!'

Dr Foster grunts and suddenly his hips jerk forwards. Gwen shrieks loudly and Marjorie feels her body relax under her hands, slumping towards the bed. Has she fainted? Yes. She's fainted. Dr Foster is grinning. He tries to look back over his shoulder at Miss Parkington.

'I'm up her, Parkington.'

'Aye, well, tek 'er temperature then.'

'Eh?'

'Temperature! Tek 'er fuckin' temperature!'

'Very well, Parkington, but I'll just take her temperature first. Oh, she's hot, Parkington. Very hot.'

'Are ye sure?'

Marjorie hears Gwen moan and feels her muscles tremble and then harden. Gwen has come out of her faint. She shakes her head, trying to work out what is going on, then realises that she has a large cock up her bottom. She moans.

'But I can't be *perfectly* sure, to be honest,' Dr Foster says. 'And perhaps she isn't so hot deeper inside. I'll try and get an average.'

He grunts again, his voice almost drowned by another cry of pain from Gwen. Dr Foster has started to push at her, working his cock deeper inside. Gwen's face is screwed up with pain.

'Ooh!' she says as Dr Foster begins to thrust at her. 'Ooh! Ah! Oooh! Ooh!'

The bedsprings begin to squeak rhythmically, sounding more clearly as Dr Foster's grunts fade. Then he starts to make a curious grinding noise. Marjorie notices that his eyes have begun to bulge and turn glassy. She points it out to Miss Parkington.

'Eh?' Miss Parkington says. 'Don't let t' bugger come up there. Doctor, ye've not got to come, d'ye 'ear me?'

Dr Foster is rocking happily at Gwen's bottom, his balls swinging between his thighs. Miss Parkington peers at them, taking a quick puff on her cigarette.

''Is balls are tightenin', girls. Get t' bugger off 'er or 'e'll ruin t' taste-test.'

Marjorie and Susan try to push Dr Foster off Gwen, but he grips her breasts harder and continues to bugger her.

'Foster!' Miss Parkington booms. 'Get off 'er, ye greedy sod! Ye can bugger a lass any day o' t' week but ye've got to leave this one unspunked. D'ye 'ear me?'

Dr Foster is gasping, a few seconds away from orgasm. Miss Parkington puts the stub of her cigarette in her mouth and kneels on the foot of the bed, pushing Dr Foster's black bag out of the way and puffing hard. She reaches up between Dr Foster's thighs and grips his balls.

'Get off 'er, ye greedy sod, or ah'll pull your balls off.'

She tightens her grip. Dr Foster grunts. His eyes lose their glassy look and his thrusts at Gwen's bottom stutter and begin to slow.

251

'D'ye 'ear me, ye greedy sod? Get off 'er!'

Miss Parkington tugs at his balls and Dr Foster grunts again. His eyes are clear now and he's barely thrusting at Gwen's bottom at all. His tries to look over his shoulder at Miss Parkington.

'If you want me to stop, Parkington, just say so. No need to drag my testicles out by their roots.'

Miss Parkington lets go of his balls and he slides his cock out of Gwen's bottom. It comes free with a wet pop and another gasp from Gwen. Miss Parkington takes the cigarette stub out of her mouth with the tips of her index and ring fingers. It's nearly smoked. She gets off the bed, taking another puff on it. Dr Foster climbs off the bed, his cock wet and glistening.

'Was she 'ot, Doctor?' Miss Parkington asks.

'Eh?'

''Ot? Was she 'ot?'

Miss Parkington jabs a blunt finger at Gwen's bottom, then at Dr Foster's cock.

'Ah,' Dr Foster says. 'I see, Parkington. Yes, I've taken a thorough sample at every accessible depth of her most delightful bottom, and I can conclude that she is definitely hot.'

'Reet. Well, that's a not unexpected result, i'n't it? Sandra, get tastin' Gayle's arse. There's a glass tube in Dr Foster's black bag, if ah'm not mistekken. Marjorie, get it out for 'er, will tha?'

'Marjorie,' says Marjorie mechanically. Poor Gwen. Poor little thing.

'Aye, that were what ah just said, weren't it? Get t' tube out, then.'

Marjorie walks down the bed to Dr Foster's black bag. She opens it. There's nothing inside but a hollow glass tube, about as thick as a finger.

''Ang on,' Miss Parkington says. 'Ah've jus' thought. There's plenty o' t' spunker's spunk on Dr

Foster's cock reet now. Samantha can lick it off while tha's inserting t' tube in Gwen's arse, Myrtle. Didst tha 'ear me, Sindy, lass? Lick Dr Foster's cock. After that, tha canst suck spunk out o' t' young lass's arse through t' tube, then lick 'er arse'ole thoroughly. That way, tha'll get a reet good taste o' t' spunker's spunk. Alreet?'

'Yes, Miss Parkington,' Susan says.

She comes back around the bed. Dr Foster is pulling his underpants and trousers back up.

'Foster, leave 'em alone. Young Susan's got to lick your cock fust.'

'Eh?'

'Oh, for fuck's sake. Lick 'im, Susan. Actions speak louder'n words.'

'Oh, my dear,' Dr Foster says as Susan kneels in front of him again. 'You want to lick me clean? How very kind. Her bottom was rather congested with the previous occupier's semen. It must have been a very heavy discharge, to judge by appearances. Not that I blame the fellow. Not that I blame him in the slightest.'

Susan takes hold of his cock and guides it towards her mouth.

'Keep away from t' 'ead, young Susan,' Miss Parkington tells her. 'T' daft old bugger's almost certainly started to leak pre-ejaculatory fluid an' tha'll get a contaminated sample. Melanie, 'ast tha done, lass?'

'Nearly, Miss Parkington,' Marjorie says.

She is bending over Gwen's bottom, murmuring reassuringly as she slides the glass tube from Dr Foster's black bag up it. Gwen is giving little cries of pain. Poor thing. Her arsehole is gaping and inflamed, rawer than ever from the second buggering it has received, sensitive to the slightest touch.

'There, Miss Parkington.'

Marjorie steps back. The tube is inserted deep into Gwen's bottom.

'Good lass.'

Susan has not inserted Dr Foster's cock into her mouth. Instead, she is licking her way up and down the shaft, frowning a little as she concentrates on the taste of the semen.

''Ast tha got a good taste, lass?' Miss Parkington asks her.

She nods.

'Dost tha recognise it?'

She pauses and then shakes her head slowly.

'I don't think so, Miss Parkington.'

'Reet then, get a suck on t' tube.'

'Yes, Miss Parkington.'

Susan kisses the head of Dr Foster's cock, then gets back to her feet and walks to the bed. She bends forwards, puts her mouth to the end of the glass tube sticking from Gwen's red-rimmed arsehole and sucks hard.

'Move it in an' out as tha sucks, lass. There'll be plenty clingin' t' walls, still, despite Dr Foster's temperature-tekkin'.'

Susan takes hold of the tube, still sucking on it, and nudges it forwards and back, trying to get more semen. Gwen moans and shudders.

'Is there much in there, lass?'

Susan takes her mouth off the tube.

'Not much, Miss Parkington. It would probably have been better to try this before Dr Foster put his cock up her.'

'Aye, well, it's easy to say that wi' 'indsight. Tek t' tube out, then, and lick 'er arse'ole. An' there looks to be a goodly lot on 'er perineum an' inner thighs, where it's leaked from 'er arse'ole. Morwenna, you can run an' get t' gardeners.'

'Yes, Miss Parkington,' Marjorie says. 'But Miss Parkington?'

'Yes, lass?'

'Will all this take long?'

'T' rest o' t' mornin', at least, lass. Tha canst stay an' 'elp Susan wi' gardeners' cocks, if tha likes.'

'Oh, yes, Miss Parkington. But it means we'll miss all our morning classes.'

'Aye, it does, but don't worry theesel. Ah'll give ye both notes to tek to your form mistresses.'

'Thank you, Miss Parkington.'

Susan is now sliding the glass tube from Gwen's arsehole, watched with interest by Dr Foster, who is idly strumming at his half-erect cock. Marjorie walks quickly from the dormitory. Behind her, the tube slips free and Susan puts her mouth to Gwen's arsehole, beginning to lick it, thoroughly familiarising herself with the taste of the semen ejaculated into Gwen's poor bottom during the night. Gwen wriggles but she doesn't cry out this time. Susan's tongue is soothing on her abused sphincter, slipping inside, swirling for the last traces of semen. It feels so nice. She moans with disappointment as the tongue leaves her bottom, licking down over her perineum for the semen that has trickled over it. Susan licks thoroughly, conscientiously, moving her tongue along Gwen's perineum, then lower still, over her inner thighs, making Gwen shiver with pleasure.

'Well, lass?' Miss Parkington asks Susan when she moves her head back, licking her lips. ''Ast tha got a good taste?'

She nods.

'Yes, Miss Parkington. A very good taste.'

'An' dost tha recognise it?'

'No, Miss Parkington, but it's quite a tricky business, semen identification. More of an art than a science. I may have to suck every man and boy in the school to orgasm again before I can say for absolute sure.'

'Ah'm reet glad to 'ear that, lass. Ye can start this mornin', wi' t' gardeners. Grace, tha canst get along wi' Dr Foster to t' sanatorium. Pull tha knickers an' pyjamas up. Now, this'll be fun. Doctor! Doctor Foster!'

Dr Foster, who is still staring at Gwen's bottom and gaping, red-rimmed arsehole, turns around, blinking mildly. Gwen hasn't moved and Susan is whispering a translation of Miss Parkington's words into her ear.

'Eh?'

'Oh, for fuck's sake,' Miss Parkington says. 'Where's 'is bloody notebook?'

'In his pocket, Miss Parkington,' Susan says, moving her head back from Gwen's ear. 'But I think Marjorie took the pencil away with her.'

'Christ.'

Miss Parkington takes a final drag on her cigarette and drops it on the floor.

'Gladys, dost tha know where t' fucking sanatorium is?'

Gwen is still pulling her pyjama bottoms up, wincing with pain.

'Gwen!' Susan says. 'Miss Parkington wants to know if you know where the sanatorium is.'

'Um, yes, I think so,' Gwen says. 'Near the library, isn't it?'

'Aye, that's reet. Tek t' daft old bugger there, will tha? Then find another pencil an' ask 'im to treat tha arse'ole. Alreet?'

Susan translates. Gwen swallows.

'B– but what if he wants to take my temperature again, Miss Parkington?'

''E won't, lass. Trust me. 'E's tekkin' a class in advanced fellatio this afternoon school an' 'e'll not want to spill any semen. At 'is age, tekkin' a young girl's temperature is far too drainin' for 'im to over-indulge in it.'

Susan translates again. Gwen nods.

'OK, Miss Parkington,' she says.

'Good lass. Get on tha way, then. Dr Foster!'

'Eh? Oh, Parkington, I've been thinking, perhaps I'd better get this young lady over to the sanatorium and treat her bottom. I think Dr Williams would definitely like to have a look at it too.'

'Aye, ye do that, Doctor.'

'Eh?'

'Tek 'im to t' sanatorium, Gwen. Get t' daft old bugger out o' mah sight before ah do summat ah regret.'

Susan translates.

'Who's this Dr Williams?' Gwen whispers as she gets carefully off the bed, wincing when she moves too quickly.

'A dreamboat,' Susan says. 'Seven inches of sheer sucking delight.'

'And does he like taking temperatures too?'

'Not that I know of. I've never tasted anything on his cock that would suggest it, but he *is* very fastidious. Perhaps he washes it off.'

'Good girl,' says Dr Foster, holding out his arm for her. 'Now, just come along with me and I'll get Dr Williams to have a good look at that poor bottom of yours.'

Gwen looks doubtful, but takes Dr Foster's arm and begins to walk slowly with him down the dormitory.

'Does he like taking temperatures, Dr Foster?' she asks.

'Eh?'

Miss Parkington rolls her eyes at Susan.

'Daft old bugger. Now, where's that young Melissa an' t' gardeners?'

As though on cue, boots sound on the corridor outside the dormitory. Dr Foster and Gwen have reached the door, Gwen still trying to find out if Dr Williams likes taking temperatures. The boots rumble along the corridor and six men in soiled outdoor clothing, wearing heavy boots and dirty caps, are led into the room by Marjorie.

'Here you are, Miss Parkington,' she says. 'All the gardeners except for old, uh, 'Arry, who's off sick today.'

'Good lass. Line up, you lot, an' tek your caps off in t' presence o' ladies,' Miss Parkington tells them. Then, turning to Susan: 'T'weren't old 'Arry's spunk in Gayle's arse, were it?'

Susan shakes her head.

'No,' she says. 'I don't think so. If I remember right, his is much more smoky, with a much more pronounced aftertaste.'

'Aye, but all t' same, if nothin' turns up this mornin', tha canst tek theesel along to 'is cottage after lunch an' give 'im a suck jus' to mek sure, alreet?'

'Yes, Miss Parkington. I think he'll enjoy that.'

'Aye, 'e will lass, 'e will. Reet, you lot.' Miss Parkington turns to the gardeners, who have lined up along in the middle of the dormitory aisle, twisting their caps nervously in their hands. 'We've 'ad an 'ayneeous crime committed 'ere, in this very room jus' last neet. A young girl by t' name o' Greta was grievously buggered in 'er very own bed. Young Celeste 'ere, 'oo ah'm sure all o' you 'ave 'ad the pleasure o' meetin' at one time or another, 'as tasted t' spunk left in young Gwen's arse an' is confident she can identify t' spunker, that is to say, t' perpetrator

258

o' t' buggery, by suckin' 'is cock. That's why ye're all 'ere, now. Young Stella's goin' to suck ye all off.'

The gardeners murmur and shuffle. They're all ages from a fresh-faced youth of seventeen or eighteen to a stooped grandfather of seventy or eighty, but Marjorie notices that they've all got bulges in their trousers. The youngest glances shyly at Susan but blushes and looks away hastily when she smiles at him happily.

'Aye, ah thought ye'd like to 'ear that,' Miss Parkington continues. ''Oggish, pleasure-loving swine that ye are, but ah want ye to know, if young Celia identifies t' spunker it's goin' to go very 'ard wi' 'im. So if 'e's 'ere now or anyone 'as any clue as to 'is identity, 'e's got one last chance to give 'imsel or t' spunker up.'

The gardeners look at each other, frowning. For a moment Marjorie thinks they're trying to see looks of guilt on each other's faces. Then she realises they're threatening each other. They don't want the guilty man to give himself up, if he's one of them. They want to be sucked by Susan. Susan herself is watching anxiously.

'Well?' Miss Parkington says. 'Gaffer?'

A thick-set middle-aged man with a broken nose shakes his head.

'No, Miss Parkington,' he says. 'We haven't the foggiest notion who might have committed this appalling crime.'

The others nod.

'None at all?' Miss Parkington asks.

'None at all, Miss Parkington. And though the procedure you are suggesting violates some of our deepest held principles, we are prepared to endure it for the good of the school and for the welfare of the young ladies whom it has always been our very great pleasure to serve.'

The others nod again. One of them murmurs, 'Well said.'

'Aye?' Miss Parkington says. 'An' what principles are those?'

The middle-aged man with the broken nose looks at his feet.

'Chaps?' he mutters. The oldest gardener coughs.

'Er, habeas corpus?' he suggests.

The others nod.

''Abeas corpus?' Miss Parkington says. ''Abeas fuckin' corpus? A young girl is brutally buggered, another young girl is prepared to interrupt 'er valu-able education to assist in t' investigations, an' you can stand there an' calmly tell me 'abeas fuckin' corpus?'

There's an uncomfortable moment of silence.

'Er, well,' the middle-aged gardener with the broken nose says, 'now that you put it like that, Miss Parkington, perhaps it wasn't the happiest of suggestions. In fact, I think I can safely say, on behalf of all of us, myself included that, er, well, we're quite happy to submit to the procedure you propose.'

'Aye. Well, ah think ah can see that for mesel,' Miss Parkington says nastily.

The gardeners shuffle, trying to cover their bulging groins with their caps.

Miss Parkington snorts.

'Mona, unzip 'em an' tek their cocks out. Ah doubt tha'll 'ave much difficulty findin' 'em. Alreet?'

'All right, Miss Parkington,' Marjorie says.

'An' now, no doubt, ye're all expectin' me to tell young Saffron to suck ye all off, is that it?'

The gardeners nod happily. Susan smiles and tries to catch the eye of the youngest gardener again. Bags him first, she thinks. Marjorie is kneeling in front of the first gardener, unzipping his trousers and reaching inside for his cock.

'Well, ah've a good mind not to. Ah've a good mind to tell ye all to wank off instead an' 'ave 'er taste your spunk that way.'

The gardeners look anxious, especially the two whose cocks are out, and Susan stops smiling. Marjorie is unzipping the trousers of a third and reaching inside for his cock.

'But thankfully for you, ah won't. Young Cilla's up for a scholarship an' she'll be up against some pretty damn stiff competition this year, so she needs all t' practice she can get.'

The gardeners relax and Susan starts smiling again. Marjorie is on her fourth gardener, unzipping his trousers, reaching inside for his cock. The three gardeners she has already prepared stand with their knees trembling slightly, cocks jutting out ahead of them. Susan eyes them hungrily. The youngest gardener's isn't quite as long as she remembered it, but it is quite as thick.

'Well, Sadie, tha 'adst best get on wi' it, then.'

'Yes, Miss Parkington. Can I choose who I start with?'

'Aye, if tha wants to, lass. Do tha best, an' if any o' them buggers don't enjoy it, they'll 'ave me to answer to.'

As Marjorie unzips the fifth gardener's trousers and reaches inside for his cock, Susan walks forwards and kneels in front of the youngest gardener.

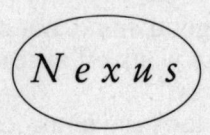

NEXUS BACKLIST

This information is correct at time of printing. For up-to-date information, please visit our website at www.nexus-books.co.uk

All books are priced at £5.99 unless another price is given.

Nexus books with a contemporary setting

ACCIDENTS WILL HAPPEN	Lucy Golden ISBN 0 352 33596 3	☐
ANGEL	Lindsay Gordon ISBN 0 352 33590 4	☐
BARE BEHIND £6.99	Penny Birch ISBN 0 352 33721 4	☐
BEAST	Wendy Swanscombe ISBN 0 352 33649 8	☐
THE BLACK FLAME	Lisette Ashton ISBN 0 352 33668 4	☐
BROUGHT TO HEEL	Arabella Knight ISBN 0 352 33508 4	☐
CAGED!	Yolanda Celbridge ISBN 0 352 33650 1	☐
CANDY IN CAPTIVITY	Arabella Knight ISBN 0 352 33495 9	☐
CAPTIVES OF THE PRIVATE HOUSE	Esme Ombreux ISBN 0 352 33619 6	☐
CHERI CHASTISED £6.99	Yolanda Celbridge ISBN 0 352 33707 9	☐
DANCE OF SUBMISSION	Lisette Ashton ISBN 0 352 33450 9	☐
DIRTY LAUNDRY £6.99	Penny Birch ISBN 0 352 33680 3	☐
DISCIPLINED SKIN	Wendy Swanscombe ISBN 0 352 33541 6	☐

DISPLAYS OF EXPERIENCE	Lucy Golden	☐
	ISBN 0 352 33505 X	
DISPLAYS OF PENITENTS £6.99	Lucy Golden	☐
	ISBN 0 352 33646 3	
DRAWN TO DISCIPLINE	Tara Black	☐
	ISBN 0 352 33626 9	
EDEN UNVEILED	Maria del Rey	☐
	ISBN 0 352 32542 4	
AN EDUCATION IN THE PRIVATE HOUSE	Esme Ombreux	☐
	ISBN 0 352 33525 4	
EMMA'S SECRET DOMINATION	Hilary James	☐
	ISBN 0 352 33226 3	
GISELLE	Jean Aveline	☐
	ISBN 0 352 33440 1	
GROOMING LUCY	Yvonne Marshall	☐
	ISBN 0 352 33529 7	
HEART OF DESIRE	Maria del Rey	☐
	ISBN 0 352 32900 9	
HIS MISTRESS'S VOICE	G. C. Scott	☐
	ISBN 0 352 33425 8	
IN FOR A PENNY	Penny Birch	☐
	ISBN 0 352 33449 5	
INTIMATE INSTRUCTION	Arabella Knight	☐
	ISBN 0 352 33618 8	
THE LAST STRAW	Christina Shelly	☐
	ISBN 0 352 33643 9	
NURSES ENSLAVED	Yolanda Celbridge	☐
	ISBN 0 352 33601 3	
THE ORDER	Nadine Somers	☐
	ISBN 0 352 33460 6	
THE PALACE OF EROS £4.99	Delver Maddingley	☐
	ISBN 0 352 32921 1	
PALE PLEASURES £6.99	Wendy Swanscombe	☐
	ISBN 0 352 33702 8	
PEACHES AND CREAM £6.99	Aishling Morgan	☐
	ISBN 0 352 33672 2	

PEEPING AT PAMELA	Yolanda Celbridge ISBN 0 352 33538 6	☐
PENNY PIECES	Penny Birch ISBN 0 352 33631 5	☐
PET TRAINING IN THE PRIVATE HOUSE	Esme Ombreux ISBN 0 352 33655 2	☐
REGIME £6.99	Penny Birch ISBN 0 352 33666 8	☐
RITUAL STRIPES £6.99	Tara Black ISBN 0 352 33701 X	☐
SEE-THROUGH	Lindsay Gordon ISBN 0 352 33656 0	☐
SILKEN SLAVERY	Christina Shelly ISBN 0 352 33708 7	☐
SKIN SLAVE	Yolanda Celbridge ISBN 0 352 33507 6	☐
SLAVE ACTS £6.99	Jennifer Jane Pope ISBN 0 352 33665 X	☐
THE SLAVE AUCTION	Lisette Ashton ISBN 0 352 33481 9	☐
SLAVE GENESIS	Jennifer Jane Pope ISBN 0 352 33503 3	☐
SLAVE REVELATIONS	Jennifer Jane Pope ISBN 0 352 33627 7	☐
SLAVE SENTENCE	Lisette Ashton ISBN 0 352 33494 0	☐
SOLDIER GIRLS	Yolanda Celbridge ISBN 0 352 33586 6	☐
THE SUBMISSION GALLERY	Lindsay Gordon ISBN 0 352 33370 7	☐
SURRENDER	Laura Bowen ISBN 0 352 33524 6	☐
THE TAMING OF TRUDI £6.99	Yolanda Celbridge ISBN 0 352 33673 0	☐
TEASING CHARLOTTE £6.99	Yvonne Marshall ISBN 0 352 33681 1	☐
TEMPER TANTRUMS	Penny Birch ISBN 0 352 33647 1	☐

THE TORTURE CHAMBER	Lisette Ashton	☐
	ISBN 0 352 33530 0	
UNIFORM DOLL	Penny Birch	☐
£6.99	ISBN 0 352 33698 6	
WHIP HAND	G. C. Scott	☐
£6.99	ISBN 0 352 33694 3	
THE YOUNG WIFE	Stephanie Calvin	☐
	ISBN 0 352 33502 5	

Nexus books with Ancient and Fantasy settings

CAPTIVE	Aishling Morgan	☐
	ISBN 0 352 33585 8	
DEEP BLUE	Aishling Morgan	☐
	ISBN 0 352 33600 5	
DUNGEONS OF LIDIR	Aran Ashe	☐
	ISBN 0 352 33506 8	
INNOCENT	Aishling Morgan	☐
£6.99	ISBN 0 352 33699 4	
MAIDEN	Aishling Morgan	☐
	ISBN 0 352 33466 5	
NYMPHS OF DIONYSUS	Susan Tinoff	☐
£4.99	ISBN 0 352 33150 X	
PLEASURE TOY	Aishling Morgan	☐
	ISBN 0 352 33634 X	
SLAVE MINES OF TORMUNIL	Aran Ashe	☐
£6.99	ISBN 0 352 33695 1	
THE SLAVE OF LIDIR	Aran Ashe	☐
	ISBN 0 352 33504 1	
TIGER, TIGER	Aishling Morgan	☐
	ISBN 0 352 33455 X	

Period

CONFESSION OF AN ENGLISH SLAVE	Yolanda Celbridge	☐
	ISBN 0 352 33433 9	
THE MASTER OF CASTLELEIGH	Jacqueline Bellevois	☐
	ISBN 0 352 32644 7	
PURITY	Aishling Morgan	☐
	ISBN 0 352 33510 6	
VELVET SKIN	Aishling Morgan	☐
	ISBN 0 352 33660 9	

------ ✂ --

Please send me the books I have ticked above.

Name ....

Address ....

....

....

.... Post code....................

Send to: **Cash Sales, Nexus Books, Thames Wharf Studios, Rainville Road, London W6 9HA**

US customers: for prices and details of how to order books for delivery by mail, call 1-800-343-4499.

Please enclose a cheque or postal order, made payable to **Nexus Books Ltd**, to the value of the books you have ordered plus postage and packing costs as follows:
UK and BFPO – £1.00 for the first book, 50p for each subsequent book.
Overseas (including Republic of Ireland) – £2.00 for the first book, £1.00 for each subsequent book.

If you would prefer to pay by VISA, ACCESS/MASTERCARD, AMEX, DINERS CLUB or SWITCH, please write your card number and expiry date here:

....

Please allow up to 28 days for delivery.

Signature ....

Our privacy policy.

We will not disclose information you supply us to any other parties. We will not disclose any information which identifies you personally to any person without your express consent.

From time to time we may send out information about Nexus books and special offers. Please tick here if you do *not* wish to receive Nexus information.   ☐

------ ✂ --